GREAT ELEPHANT

BOOKS BY
ALAN SCHOLEFIELD

A View of Vultures
Great Elephant

Great Elephant

Alan Scholefield

HERON BOOKS
COLLECTORS EDITION

Published by
Heron Books
18 St Ann's Crescent
London, SW18

By arrangement with
William Heinemann Ltd

For my wife

ANTHEA

Printed in Great Britain by
Clarke, Doble & Brendon Ltd,
Cattedown, Plymouth

AUTHOR'S NOTE

Chaka became King of the Zulus in 1816 and lived for most of his reign at the great royal kraal of Bulawayo in northern Natal. Correctly, this should be written Kwa Bulawayo (at the Place of the Killing) but for simplicity I have chosen the more familiar form of most Zulu words. Chaka's headquarters are not to be confused with the present-day Bulawayo in Rhodesia, although there is a link. One of Chaka's favourites, a young war-chief named Mzilikazi, who fell out with the King, fled from Zululand with his own regiment and cut a bloody swathe through what is now the Transvaal before coming to a halt north of the Limpopo River. There he founded the Matabele nation. He named his 'Great Place' Bulawayo after the original kraal in Zululand.

Following are some of the source books consulted in the preparation of this novel which may be of interest to anyone wishing to read further about the period: Bird, J. *The Annals of Natal* (P. Davis & Sons, Pietermaritzburg, 1888); Bryant, Rev. A. T. *Olden Times in Zululand and Natal* (Longmans, 1929); Casalis, Rev. E. *The Basutos* (London, 1861); Ellenberger, D. F. *History of the Basuto* (London, 1912); Fynn, H. F. *The Diary* (Shuter & Shooter, Pietermaritzburg); Gardiner, Capt. Allen. *Narrative of a Journey to the Zoolu Country* (London, 1836); Gibson, J. Y. *The Story of the Zulus* (Longmans, 1911); Isaacs, Nathaniel. *Travels and Adventures in Eastern Africa* (Van Riebeeck Soc., Cape Town, 1936); Krige, Dr E. J. *The Social System of the Zulus* (Longmans, 1936); Mackeurtan, G. *The Cradle Days of Natal* (Shuter & Shooter, 1948); Owen, Capt. W. F. W. *Narrative of Voyages to Explore the shores of Africa etc.* (London, 1833); Owen, Rev. Francis. *The Diary* (Van Riebeeck Soc., Cape Town, 1926); Ritter, E. A. *Shaka Zulu* (Longmans, 1955); Walker, E. A. *A History of South Africa* (Longmans, 1928).

NARRATOR'S FOREWORD

Since I was only a youth when I fled the carnage that surrounded the assassination of Chaka, King of the Zulus, I have had to rely for the reconstruction of some of the events on my Father's Journal, the material published by Nathaniel Isaacs Esq., in the *South African Commercial Advertiser* between June and October, 1832, and the Diary kindly lent me by H. F. Fynn Esq.,—but above all on my own memory of childhood in Zululand.

ROBERT FRASER BLACK

'Paradise'
Cape of Good Hope
1841

Book One

The Place of the Elephant

It has been remarked by an ancient historian that in peace children bury their parents, and in war parents bury their children; it appeared otherwise in the dominions of Chaka; there, Death reigned without a rival ...

> *Travels and Adventures in Eastern Africa,*
> by NATHANIEL ISAACS.

A*

My FIRST FRIEND was a Zulu; my first enemy was a Zulu, and the first home I can recall was a Zulu dwelling built high on a hill above an ocean of tawny grass that stretched into the rolling downs as far as the eye could see. We seemed very close to the sky on the top of our hill, especially at night when the stars pressed down and the Southern Cross wheeled slowly towards the black horizon. Had I ever mentioned this feeling of closeness to a Zulu he would not have been at all surprised since the very word 'zulu' means Heaven. If Zululand was Heaven, God save all sinners.

Yet that is not strictly fair. Like any other place it was part Heaven part Hell, and like any other race the Zulus were part Man part Beast. I loved them, I hated them. I admired them, I despised them. I feared them and respected them and on occasions I could laugh at them and with them. There was only one state of mind that never existed: indifference.

I was still a small boy when we first came to Zululand in our wagons and it may be worth mentioning right here at the beginning that I don't know whether or not we were the first white people King Chaka had ever seen. All I know is that we were living there when Mr Fynn came, but I have a feeling that the Portuguese ivory hunter Velho Pereira might already have been known to Chaka. It was not the King's policy ever to make statements of fact even if he knew them. He liked to be surrounded by doubts and controversy in the midst of which he could give the *appearance* of knowledge. This was one of the ways he ruled: there were many others not quite so pleasant.

Zululand, which was ruled by King Chaka all the time we were there, lies more than 100 miles north of what we used to call Port Natal and which was renamed Durban only six years ago. It is, as I have said, a land of rolling hills where the long grass blushed green in the heavy summer rains. It was bordered on the

3

east by the hot, humid air of the coastal strip and in the west by the austere spurs of the Dragon Mountains where the frost strikes chill in winter and the snow lies deep on the peaks. It is a kingdom as remote from civilisation as Monomatapa. A thousand bush-covered miles to the south the British ruled the Cape Colony; three hundred miles to the north were the Portuguese. It was a place of much beauty and we had come to it at the end of a great journey.

In my experience people go into a wilderness for two reasons: to escape from life or to escape from death. My father's was a mixture of the two: James Fraser Black was escaping from the living-death of imprisonment. Transported from his native Scottish Highlands for attacking a school-fellow—there had been great provocation—he fled the convict ship that was to have borne him to exile in New South Wales when at anchor in Simon's Bay. Since then he had lived beyond the law, travelling ever ahead of it as it crept slowly behind him. He had found time, in his wanderings, to marry my mother, Lisé de Blaize, a frontiersman's daughter, only to watch her die with an arrowhead in her side. I cannot remember my mother, nor did I ever miss her. My stepmother gave me all the love I ever needed. It was there, inside her like a bottomless pool; no matter how much was drawn off it never emptied. Even when my half-brother Donald was born it made no difference between us at all.

My stepmother's name was Frances and my first memories are of golden hair and serious eyes and strong, competent hands that held me tight as the home-made soap got into my eyes and ears. I have never cared much for being washed.

There is one other person I should mention: the Bushman, Stone-Axe. He was my father's man, part-servant, part-comrade. My father had once saved his life and he, in turn, had saved my father. They were so close, mentally and physically—Stone-Axe would never let my father out of his sight—that in my early memories they seem to merge and become one: the big, bearded Scotsman with the steel hook worn on the stump of his left wrist, and the yellow-skinned Bushman with the sad slanted eyes and almond face. He was never without a short springy bow in his hand and a quiver of poison arrows down his back.

There was no menace or malice in Stone-Axe. His love for my father was as pure as springwater and as innocent. But let anyone menace my father and the gentle little hunter gave place to

4

a professional killer. I have seen him put two arrows into a sailing kestrel before my father's rifle cleared the scabbard; that is how quick and accurate he was.

I think he looked on my father as a helpless child—and in many ways, compared to a Bushman, he was—and for this reason Stone-Axe had, in the Zulu phrase, taken him under his armpit. With the possible exception of Mgobozi-of-the-Hill, Stone-Axe was the best dark-skinned man who ever lived.

This then, with the addition of two Hottentot servants, was the group that one spring day drove their wagons out of the high mountains into the hill country of King Chaka. Had we known whose land it was we might have turned back. As it was, our introduction could hardly have been more spectacular or favourable.

We had started the day early, breakfasting as usual in the predawn hush when the air was soft, and cool grey mist hung in the kloofs. Stone-Axe had shot a reedbuck the day before and my mother—I have always called her that and I see no need to change now—fried the heart, liver and kidneys in a little mutton fat. This we ate with flat maize cakes baked in a mud oven and mugs of scalding black sugarless tea.

Breakfast was always a restless time. While my mother cooked, the rest packed the wagons for the long day's haul ahead and even I was called in to help. When the last ropes were tied we gathered round the fires, the Hottentots and Stone-Axe at the rear wagon, ourselves at the front. My father always ate on his feet, as though anxious to be off. With his hook he loosely held the mare's reins and with his good hand he shovelled the food absent-mindedly into his mouth.

We were too sleepy to talk and the sounds I remember best were those little crooning noises my mother made as she gave Donald the breast.

After breakfast we inspanned the bullocks, twelve to a span, and one of the Hottentots, either Izak or Cupido, would come forward with the long wagon-whips and my father would swing himself onto Violin and say: 'Let's be moving,' and the driver would shout 'Huk-yeah!' and the lash would crackle in the air above the bullocks' rumps and there would be the sound of strains and creaks and slowly the wagon would rumble forward.

There is something strangely tense and portentous about these starting moments when you are trekking. A day lies ahead and

5

no one knows what it will bring. Hopes tend to be negative: you hope that a fellie in one of the wheels won't break; you hope that an ox won't die of snakebite; that the rivers will be easy; the road not too steep. There is nothing positive to hope for because you cannot know what it is. You hope above all to reach water and shade at three o'clock in the afternoon with half a score or more miles behind you. This is achievement. And for good measure you hope that at the end of the day there will be five or six guinea fowl or a buck ready for the pot. This is success.

We always travelled in the same way. I sat on the front seat of the leading wagon with my mother, and Donald slept in the tent. My father rode about a hundred yards ahead of us and Stone-Axe, when he wasn't quartering the bush like a hound, held onto the stirrup-iron and ran softly at his side. Sometimes I would stare down at the grass flowing slowly under the *disselboom* and the hours and miles would merge into a dreamy time of insubstantial fancies. I was never bored while we were trekking.

But these reveries were a luxury, for even at that early age my education was under way. My father, being Scottish, had a great respect for learning and I often heard him regret the abrupt end to his own schooling. This was the only thing I ever heard him regret until much later. My mother had received her schooling at the Cape and later in England. I could not have wished for a better teacher. She had brought with us her Uncle's library, two chests full of books that had been in the wagons when Dr Goodsir died of fever in the Bachapin country, so there was no lack of material. Perhaps they were not the sort of books one might normally have chosen for a child's learning and I cannot remember whether we showed any real eclecticism. Naturally the books were all lost in the end but I can remember some of them still. There was Linnaeus with his fierce Latin, and translations of Thunberg and Sparrman which my mother read to me, her voice becoming thick with nostalgia as she repeated the descriptions of the Cape of Good Hope. There were books on minerology and zoology, natural philosophy, medicine and even one on marine navigation which seemed a long way from any point of utility. There was a Portuguese dictionary and a Dutch dictionary and Dr Goodsir's Journal. This my mother treated with great reverence, reading it aloud to me so I was able to gain some insight into the past of my father and mother and, of course, my own.

She also taught me counting, using the oxen as a living abacus

6

and I was able to do sums like: if Vaalman and Bles were taken out of the left yoke and placed on the right, what would be the total number of legs on the left-hand side and how many on the right? When I had given the correct answer she would make me subtract the legs and horns of the left side from those on the right, or multiply the number of legs by the number of horns or count the number of spokes in all the wheels and divide it by the *juk-skeis* that dropped into the yoke on either side of the bullocks' heads. In this way she made it interesting, if a trifle bucolic.

I remember one day she said: 'Now, Robbie, if you took Swartland, Vaalman and Bles out of the span how many horns would you have left?'

I thought for a moment and said: 'Nineteen.'

'Nineteen?'

My father had drawn up with us at that time and was listening. I saw him do a rapid calculation and then frown.

'Yes,' I said. 'Nineteen.'

You could see my mother wasn't too pleased at this. I suppose she wanted to show my father how good her teaching was.

'Come now,' she said. 'You can do better than that.'

I was smiling inside as I repeated: 'It's nineteen, mother.'

'Nineteen be hanged,' said my father, shaking his head. 'I think we'll sell the boy, Fran. That's if anyone wants a lad with a head full of nothing. Try again.'

'It's nineteen, father!'

'Well, I'd be glad to hear how you account for that.'

'Because Big Tom has three,' I shouted gleefully, and jumped down from the fore-tree and showed him the vestigial horn that sprouted from the great hind-ox's forehead between the natural horns.

'I'll be damned,' my father said. 'I'd never noticed that.'

'Don't swear in front of the boy, Jamie,' my mother said with mock severity, but you could see how pleased she was.

Of course I hadn't found that freakish hornlet all by myself. Stone-Axe had shown it to me in the shy-secret way he had of showing things he knew. He was my other teacher.

I don't suppose there was anything in the world that Stone-Axe didn't know; I mean that was *worth* knowing, and yet if you looked at him you might not have thought so. He was just under five feet tall and he wore a buckskin kaross over his shoulders and a jackal skin around his middle. On his head was a greasy

7

leather cap ornamented with glass beads and there were strings of beads and bracelets of iron and copper round his wrists. From his left arm hung a small leather bag in which he kept his food, reed pipe and tobacco. His face always wore the same soft expression and his eyes were so far apart it gave him a childlike look. You might have thought he looked a bit simple; you would have been extremely wrong.

All round Zululand in those days kingdoms had vanished. It was as though a great plague had struck the country. Villages were empty, crops unsown, cattle dead or missing. Sometimes the only living things were small bands of people existing on roots and tubers, hiding in secret caves and all of them—except those who had turned cannibal—starved to the very edge of death.

It would be easy enough to blame the devastation on King Chaka but it was not wholly so. When he fell upon a neighbouring tribe to incorporate it into his new and growing nation, its fleeing army would fall like wolves upon *its* neighbour and that army on the next and so on, the stronger on the weaker. Thus were the Great Migrations started.

No one will ever know the numbers who died, but my memory is of a million bones whitening in the African sun. Never have the vultures and the hyenas seen such feasting.

It was through this wasteland that Stone-Axe kept us alive. He would spend all day hunting for food and we grew quite used to, and indeed thankful for, the offerings of wild iris bulbs, tubers, garlic, the core of aloes, acacia gum, Hottentot figs, berries and wild fruit which he gathered. I cannot remember whether we ate lizards and locusts but I'm certain we tasted the grub of the white ant and I know he used to make a sort of flour out of grass seeds and the powdered pips of melons.

Now, as we approached the borders of the Zulu country the land was sleeker and food was not so great a problem.

We had been travelling for about six hours on this particular day when we heard the elephant. There are certain sounds that come suddenly in the bush and freeze the blood. The scream of an enraged elephant is one of them. We had been moving through wooded glades of acacia and wattle surrounded only by the rustling and chirruping of birds, when suddenly we heard the scream and there was the animal about forty yards away to our left. Violin snorted, nearly throwing my father, and the bullocks veered away to the right, breaking into a shambling trot that set the wagons rocking and groaning. Donald woke up and began to cry, my mother was shouting to Cupido to get round to the leading bullocks' heads, my father was trying to check Violin's sudden fright, everything was loud with noise and confusion. If a wheel had struck a boulder or a stump just then we might all have landed up under the feet of the following span.

By the time Cupido and Izak had checked the oxen and brought the wagons to a halt we must have been half a mile from the place where the elephant had screamed.

'Claw!' Stone-Axe was shouting to my father. 'Claw! There is a man.'

My father turned Violin and cantered warily back the way we had come. Stone-Axe ran swiftly at his side.

In the glade they came upon a terrible sight. The bush looked as though it had been struck by a whirlwind. Branches were scattered everywhere, small trees uprooted, great clumps of grass torn out of the ground leaving naked brown scars. At one side of the glade was the elephant, blood streaming down its flanks from a heavy assegai that still protruded from its shoulder. On either side of its jaw were gaping holes where the tusks had been hacked out.

Other rivulets of blood flowed down its chest and legs from wounds in its neck. But worst of all was a great gout up near the spine, as though a cannon ball had struck. The bull was down by its rump and was slowly pulling itself forward with its front legs. Its trunk was stretched out as far as it could reach. It screamed again with pain and rage, and my father and Stone-Axe were able to see what it was reaching for. Only inches from the tip of the questing trunk was a tribesman. He was covered so completely in blood it was difficult to tell exactly what colour he was underneath. He had been flung into the lower branches of a thorn tree and now the elephant was using its last remaining strength to try and finish him off. Slowly, almost as an act of will, it dragged along its paralysed legs. In a matter of seconds the painful journey would be over as the trunk curled around the wounded man.

My father, as he was afterwards to write, sat Violin as if in a dream, watching the elephant's titanic struggle to reach up into the tree. Had the man's life depended on him he would have been crushed to death. As it was, Stone-Axe, without saying anything

9

at all, whipped my father's rifle from his saddle, raced straight to the rear of the elephant and, like a monkey, ran up its broad back. He placed the muzzle of the rifle directly over the brain and pulled the trigger. The bull collapsed like a building, sending up a cloud of dust, but Stone-Axe had already leapt nimbly to the ground and was standing there as though he did this sort of thing before breakfast every morning.

'Hau!' he shouted, dancing first on one leg and then on the other. 'Hau, the Great One is dead! Hau! Axe of Stone . . .'

'Hold your tongue, you little fiend,' my father said, recovering from the suddenness of the Bushman's action.

Stone-Axe smiled up impudently. 'Where was the Great Bull Calf?' he said, waving the rifle mockingly at my father. 'Where was Iron Hand?'

'I'll give you Great Bull Calf with the toe of my boot if you can't be silent,' said my father, grinning. 'Here, help me with this laddie.'

They brought the body down from the tree as gently as they could. The black skin was ripped by thorns and the man's left arm stuck out at a peculiar angle. He was quite unconscious. As they carried him to the wagon my father said: 'I can't tell which is his blood and which is the elephant's. We'd best wash him down and find out.'

We all stood around staring at this new phenomenon which had suddenly materialised. He could hardly have been ignored. He was big, a shade over six foot, with a deep sloping chest, heavy shoulders and huge biceps and he was stark naked except for a prepuce-cover on his member. My mother had long since grown accustomed to nakedness and now she used Donald's bath, which was no more than a wooden bucket, and a clean rag from the wagon and gently sponged the blood and dust from his body. He looked even bigger when he was cleaned off. My mother probed his ribs and collar-bones and finally she looked up and said: 'There, I don't think there's anything seriously wrong except the arm.'

At that moment he opened his eyes, sat up, took one terrified look at the strange objects and people surrounding him, opened his mouth once or twice, hissed through his teeth like a spitting cobra, remembered his manners, said 'Sakubona,' and then fainted clean away again.

And that was how we came to meet Mgobozi-ovela-entabeni,

'Mgobozi-who-comes-up-over-the-Hill', but whom we were always to call Mgobozi-of-the-Hill.

The surprise was not all on one side and Cupido and Izak and even Stone-Axe took a step backward when they heard the deep voice, although Stone-Axe pretended he had stepped on a sharp stone and that it wasn't anything to do with Mgobozi's sudden revival of consciousness and equally sudden relapse.

The little Bushman leant over and pinched Mgobozi's great thigh muscle between his thumb and forefinger and shook his head in awe. Then, seeing that the huge Zulu did not stir, he flung himself down in an exactly similar position, straining his arm to get the effect he wanted, sat up, blinked, hissed, made a more than adequate imitation of Mgobozi's deep salutation and flopped down again on the grass chortling with laughter.

'I suppose,' said my father, nudging Stone-Axe to his feet with his boot, 'you'd have split your sides if the bull had trampled him. Here, give me a hand and let's see if we can get that arm back.'

The left arm was out at the shoulder and my father got Stone-Axe and one of the Hottentots to hold Mgobozi down while he tried to pull it back into the socket. But with only one good hand it was too much for him.

Each time he pulled and twisted his hand slipped and he fell away. 'He's sweating,' he said. 'Come on, we'll do it the other way round. Cupido lad, you and Izak take the arm and I'll try to hold him.'

My father got down on the ground half under Mgobozi and wrapped his arms around the great barrel of a chest. 'All right, now pull and twist. No! No! Not like that. You're not feeling a young girl. Take him properly.'

The Hottentots gripped the wrist and forearm and strained with all their strength but they only succeeded in pulling both my father and the recumbent Zulu along the grass.

At that moment Mgobozi awoke for the second time. If he had been somewhat put out earlier he was now plainly thunderstruck. He was being held around the chest by someone with a hook for a hand and was being pulled from the front by two yellow-skinned people he had never seen before.

What we didn't know at that time was that we were man-handling one of the greatest warriors that the Zulu kingdom had ever known, the Hammer of Chaka himself. If we had we might have been more delicate. As it was Mgobozi gave a loud cry,

11

flung Cupido and Izak into the nearest bush, crashed backwards onto my father, knocking the wind from his body and then leapt to his feet. If he'd had a war-club in his hand just then he would probably have brained the lot of us even *with* only one arm; instead he found himself facing the slight figure of Stone-Axe, who had an arrow tight against the bow string.

'Damnation!' my father said, dusting himself off. 'That's gratitude for you!'

Mgobozi stood perfectly still. He was aware that a Bushman arrowhead was steeped in poison. Stoically he waited.

'Now,' said my father, coming round in front of him. 'Let's try the whole thing again.' First he pointed to his own shoulder and then to Mgobozi's and then made motions of trying to get the arm back. Slowly the truth dawned on the Zulu and his face broke into a wide grin. It was a sort of sickle-shaped grin that drew all his features, including his eyes, into its orbit. It made one want to smile. He began to talk at a stupefying rate.

Of course none of us could speak Zulu at that time, though we were soon to be fluent in it, and my father looked about helplessly as the words washed over him.

'Izak,' he said. 'You can speak Xhosa, you try him.'

The two languages are similar in many respects and soon there was a faint understanding between the two of them.

'What's he saying?' asked my father.

'He's speaking about his arm.'

'What about it?'

'He knows how to mend it.'

'All right then, let's mend it. What do we do?'

'He says we must dig a hole,' the Hottentot said doubtfully.

'Are you sure? We're not proposing to bury him.'

'He says the hole is for his arm,' Izak said with even less assurance.

'Well,' said my father, scratching his head, 'if you're certain that's what he said, let's do it.'

My father sent Cupido for a spade and a pick and they began digging a hole on a flat piece of ground. Mgobozi, still smiling widely in spite of the pain of his arm, stood next to them making encouraging noises.

'Is that deep enough?' asked my father.

Izak translated as best he could and Mgobozi shook his head. The ground was hard and the two Hottentots were perspiring freely. The hole was only about a foot deep. It took them another half-hour of digging and shaping before Mgobozi was satisfied. The hole was now deeper than the length of his arm, and narrow. He lay down, put his arm in the hole and told Jacob to start packing the earth back around it just as one does with a fence post. Soon, all the earth was shovelled back into place and Stone-Axe, who had been watching with great interest, circling about like an agitated jackal without anything to do, stamped his feet down on the soil, binding it and making it firm.

So the position was this: Mgobozi lay full length on the ground with one arm quite out of sight as though he were grasping for something in a deep ant-bear hole. The rest of us stood about looking mystified.

'Ask him what we do next,' said my father.

After a consultation Izak said: 'We must take him by the legs and waist and lift.'

'Well,' said my father, 'on his own head be it.'

My mother, who had been watching with a worried frown, said: 'Be careful, Jamie, you could break the joint.'

'It's his funeral. We're only following instructions.'

Slowly Cupido and Izak began lifting the heavy body, using the shoulder as a fulcrum. Mgobozi's face lost its smile and his eyes clouded with pain. Sweat began to pour freely from his black skin. The two Hottentots were clearly unhappy about their task, as though they guessed who Mgobozi was and what their fate might be if something went wrong.

As they lifted, the huge muscles of his arms and chest bunched and stood out like boulders. My mother began to make small noises of concern and I could see my father, perhaps because of what had happened to his own arm, sharing the Zulu's pain.

'Let him down, let him down!' he cried.

Mgobozi had fainted again and we stood around him feeling weak with the shared pain and exhaustion, all except Stone-Axe, who had been captivated by the whole exhibition.

'That's enough,' my mother said, as though voicing all our thoughts.

'I'm sorry, Fran, but we'll have to try again. I've never seen it done this way but I don't see why it shouldn't work. Come on now, lads, we'll take him together. You, too, Stone-Axe. Grip him by the waist and when I give the word jerk and twist. All right. Now!'

13

They raised and twisted together and there was a sudden loud crack and the shoulder joint jumped as the arm slipped back into place. 'That's it!' my father said, wiping the sweat from his eyes. 'It's back.' Gently they pulled his arm from the hole and my father waggled it from side to side and then nodded his satisfaction. 'He'll do.'

They left him in the shade of the wagon and went about preparing a mid-day meal since we had stopped anyway, and I squatted down and looked at Mgobozi's hand, the one they had dug up. It was clenched in a fist and I wondered what he'd been holding in it. I tried to pry his fingers loose to find out but they were like steel strips and wouldn't budge. I supposed he must have clenched it like that because of the pain. Anyway, after a while I'd tried every finger and they just stayed shut so I sat there and waited.

Then I thought that if I tickled his wrist he might let go of whatever it was he was holding, so I got a piece of grass and began to scratch it over his skin and one by one the fingers loosened their hold. There, in the middle of his palm was a small piece of dolomite, perfectly smooth and round, and it was such a pleasant-looking stone I felt it must have given him comfort, and anyway it was iron and might have passed some of its strength on to him. I bent forward to take it and his hand shut like a trap. I whirled round and there he was smiling at me. 'Sakubona, umlunghu,' he said and put the stone into my hand.

He'd given me a terrible fright, but my father always said it didn't do to show these things to the savages so I said 'Sakubona' because there didn't seem anything else he would understand, not speaking English or anything, and you could see how delighted he was because he smiled even wider and stood up and stretched himself. Then he felt himself all over, which was just a waste of time because my mother had already done that. He looked down at himself in a sort of worried introspective way as though trying to work out where he was and what had happened and it all seemed to fall into place because he nodded, shook himself, stared around to get his bearings and then set off at a smart pace in the direction of the clearing.

I think he must have forgotten about me, because it wasn't a very mannerly thing to do, just leaving me there like that without a word. So I ran after him and said : 'You'd better see my father before going off. He won't be very pleased.'

14

Mgobozi stopped and it was quite apparent that he *had* forgotten about me for he scooped me up and put me on his shoulders and then began to run.

My father would probably have shot him if he had seen me being kidnapped like that and I'm just not sure what my mother would have done. But no one saw us and there I was, sitting astride this giant warrior, being kidnapped and taken into the dark regions where only the savages lived.

At least that's what I thought at the time, but we only went to the clearing where the elephant was and Stone-Axe was already there. He was cutting off one of the feet.

'Sit still, little Master,' Stone-Axe called, as he grabbed for his bow.

I knew he would try to shoot Mgobozi out from underneath me and just at that moment I saw two assegais and a shield and I was sure we'd only come there to collect them.

'It's all right,' I called. 'He's only come for his spears.'

Which was true because he found the assegais and the great cowhide shield that was pure white except for two black spots on the right-hand side and he also found his war-club. Strangely enough, even though he hadn't put on any more clothes, holding the spears and the shield and the club he no longer seemed naked and I think this must have been worrying him. All fitted out with his weapons again he looked just about the most magnificent person I'd ever seen.

When we got back to the wagons my father said we'd stay there for the night since we'd wasted so much time and Stone-Axe made Mgobozi's hole bigger and put glowing coals in it and then the elephant's foot and covered it in more coals and we let it roast there for the rest of the day and ate it in the evening. Even my mother said she had never tasted anything more delicious.

It seemed quite natural the next morning that Mgobozi came with us. Of course, though we didn't realise it at first, we were going with *him*. I remember that morning quite well because first my mother told me to stop following him everywhere and then my father said the same thing. I remember eating breakfast with him at the rear wagon and later on he let me carry one of his spears; the same spear that I knew later as Chest-biter because he used it to thrust. It was the first time any of us had seen the short stabbing spear which had been Chaka's own invention.

At first, when King Chaka had begun to forge his Zulu nation the army fought like its neighbours. Dressed in sandals and carrying a shield and two throwing spears, each warrior would take his place in the line of battle facing the enemy and after one or two champions had fought in single combat the warriors would throw their spears at the enemy and wait until the enemy had returned the fire. Then both sides would pick up the other's spears and throw them back. It was a sort of mutual co-operation as far as weapons were concerned.

Instinctively, Chaka knew this was wrong. First he went to the Mbonambi clan, the great armourers of the East-Nguni nations, of which the Zulus were one sub-division, and had them make him a short-shafted assegai with a long, heavy head. To show its efficacy, so the old stories go, he used it to overcome the Mad Giant and having proved its worth brought the armourers from their dank and dripping forests to live and work in Zululand.

The next thing he wanted was mobility so he caused the army to throw away its sandals. There were some old diehards among them who thought the young king was going too far and they began to grumble. So one day Chaka had the parade ground thickly strewn with thorns and ordered his regiments to stamp them out of sight. He told them he was making them do this because of his great love for them and because it would toughen up the soles of their feet wonderfully well. There was no more grumbling after that.

The next time the Zulus went to war, their enemies threw their spears and waited for the Zulu response, but something entirely new happened. The Zulus charged down on them and, using their own shields to hook sideways those of their enemies, were able to plunge their short stabbing assegais into the exposed left breast. Those who turned and ran were soon overtaken and slaughtered by the swift-footed Zulus now unencumbered by sandals.

I learnt all this from Mgobozi later on and he was not given to lying, except about his sexual power.

Anyway, that morning he showed me how he used Chest-biter. I was too little to hold the shield so he got Stone-Axe to act the enemy and with the lid of the cooking pot he hooked the shield

16

to one side and would have exposed just the right spot for Chest-biter except that Stone-Axe was small enough to disappear behind the great cowhide shield completely. He came up between Mgobozi's legs and with horny forefinger and thumb took hold of his testicles and gave them a tug and Mgobozi let out such a yell that my father came over and asked what was happening. When I told him he laughed and said I'd better come away because it wasn't the sort of thing my mother would like me to see.

Poor mother. It is sad to recall how innocent we all were then and how happy. I was to see so many things less pleasant that I should not have remembered Mgobozi's discomfiture if my father had not recorded it.

As we travelled along we were gradually able to piece together what had happened to Mgobozi. My father had told Izak to find out what he could about the land we were in and I suppose he thought the best way of doing it was to hear Mgobozi's story. By this time I had picked up a few words of Zulu so I helped.

We found out that he was not actually a Zulu at all but came from the Msane clan who lived north-east of Zululand across the Hluhluwe River. The strange thing about it was that the Msanes were non-violent and pastoral. They did not even own a weapon, unless wooden hoes can be called weapons. It must have come as a great surprise to them to have produced Mgobozi who, if he'd ever actually picked up a hoe in his life, would have used it to break someone's skull. He had been on his way back from a visit to his clan when he had nearly lost his life.

He told Izak he had been coming through thick bush when he'd met two strange men. He was not quite clear who or what they were. Both were dark-skinned though one, with a scarred face, appeared to have been made dark by the sun for his hair was long like ours and he wore it on his chin as well. The other was, like the Zulus, almost hairless and even his skull was shaven. The bearded man, whom Mgobozi took to be a European since most of the tribes in the area thought hirsuteness was a filthy habit, spoke a dialect akin to Zulu but said he came from many miles to the north, which placed him in Portuguese territory. This, anyway, was what my father surmised and he was afterwards proved right.

The other man was, by Mgobozi's description, an Arab, perhaps from Sofala or Zanzibar.

17

At first they seemed quite friendly and Mgobozi sat with them over a meal of boiled rice. The Portuguese told him they had come south in search of ivory and that very day had located a herd of forty elephants, many of them big tuskers. Mgobozi expressed mild amusement at the thought of two men nursing such optimism but they replied they had a plan which might work if he helped them. Nearby was a small kloof, the sides of which narrowed abruptly to a natural cul-de-sac. If they dug elephant pits where the kloof was at its narrowest and drove the herd over them they would be certain of killing most of the beasts before they could turn. When again Mgobozi expressed amusement that two men—or even three if he counted himself—would seriously set out to dig the huge pits needed to trap animals the size of elephants, they replied that shallow trenches were all that was needed since what they really had in mind was not trapping the animals but causing them to flounder and mill about in the same spot while they fired down from the sides of the kloof at point blank range. The trenches would confuse the animals and give the hunters time to reload the great ball muskets.

Mgobozi had heard of these fire-sticks from Chaka but had never actually seen one. No one knows how Chaka became familiar with guns but it is likely he was told about them by the great overlord Dingiswayo before his death. At any rate Chaka pretended to despise them. Later on my father gave an exhibition to the Zulu Army. He, Stone-Axe, Izak and Cupido fired a couple of volleys and all the Zulus fell down on their faces and made a hissing noise and waggled their fingers. Muskets were always known as 'issebums' after that but Chaka wasn't too pleased at the reaction.

Anyway, Mgobozi thought it was a good opportunity to see how a gun worked, so he asked the Portuguese to demonstrate. Now a musket used for shooting elephants was a fearsome weapon. It had a longer barrel and a larger bore than the standard military rifles and threw a single big bullet moulded from tin, or antimony, and lead. The Portuguese was happy enough to show Mgobozi, so after their meal he loaded one of the muskets and fired at a small tree.

Mgobozi maintained he didn't even flinch when the gun went off but I'm not sure I believe that. The ball smashed the trunk in half and sprayed splinters around the clearing. He decided right then that the gun would be a fine new weapon to take back with him. So for his services in helping them to trap the elephant herd, he demanded the gun.

Mgobozi always was an open-hearted, almost simple man, unused to subtlety or trickery, happier to be in the thick of battle rather than ensnared in argument or discussion. He said that the two men looked at each other with eyes half-hooded and then the Portuguese shrugged and told him the gun was his if they came well out of this thing.

I think even at that age I was astonished at Mgobozi's ingenuousness. I know my father was because he shook his head from side to side and a look of amused wonder spread over his face.

They spent three days cutting a system of trenches in the narrow throat of the kloof and covering them with reeds. On the fourth day they were ready. While they were working one was always on duty watching the herd. It had drifted slightly to the south-west but was still near enough to the kloof for easy driving. The wind was also in the hunters' favour. They worked around the back of the herd, allowing their scent to be carried on the breeze and soon the animals grew restless and began to move. The men made no noise but used only their own vague presence in the bush to promote a sense of unease among the elephants, so that when the beasts entered the mouth of the kloof they did so seemingly of their own volition.

Now the plan called for a change of tactics. If the fire power on the roiling herd was to be effective both guns would have to be used. This left Mgobozi at the mouth of the kloof. His job would be to stampede the herd towards the trenches and try to turn back any seeking a way out.

Mgobozi, who had not been unimpressed with the cunning and caution used by the two hunters, now watched with increasing admiration as they developed a method by which one man could control Mgobozi's area. They hollowed out a series of ant-heaps, poured black gunpowder into the centre, packed it tight with damp mud and laid a powder train from each one to act as a fuse. Some fuses interlocked so that by lighting one, three small explosions would occur. It says a great deal for Mgobozi's natural military intuition that although he had never used powder before he was able to follow their explanations.

By early afternoon the herd was well into the kloof. It was still showing signs of doubt but the bulls had taken defensive positions and the cows and calves were browsing. Soon the leaders would begin to move out of the kloof again in search of water; it had to be done now.

The Arab took the left side of the kloof, the Portuguese the right and Mgobozi watched them work their way up the sides until they were well above the herd. Then they moved laterally until they were poised above the trenches. In the distance Mgobozi saw the glint on the Portuguese's gun muzzle as he waved.

They had left Mgobozi with flint and steel and he struck a spark onto the first powder fuse. He found a powder fuse uncommonly interesting, he told us, and he stood watching the hissing fire-train eating its way to the charge. Almost too late he remembered that this was no pretty demonstration.

The first ant-heap went up with a roar, and the second and the third. By this time Mgobozi was running from one fuse to the next. Immediately one of the bulls began to trumpet and the herd swung down the kloof towards the mouth. But the ant-heaps were going up one after the other, blowing earth and small stones into the air. Once again the herd turned, this time going at full tilt, trunks outstretched, ears at right-angles to the forehead, smashing through thick undergrowth as though it was bracken.

In a matter of seconds they were out of sight and he could only hear their crashing progress as they bored deeper and deeper into the kloof. Then came the sound of firing and he knew they had reached the trenches.

He could picture the turbid mass of grey bodies, swirling and churning, unable to get their footing, slipping, stumbling, attempting to turn in the narrow cul-de-sac but trapped by their own numbers as others following pressed further and further along the walls trying to batter their way out the other side. But there was no way out. The boom of the muskets and the screaming of the elephants shattered the heavy silence of the bush.

So intense had been his concentration that he did not see or hear the big bull. He only became aware of it as a grey shape in the bush. It was standing quite still, about twenty yards away, regarding him with hot, angry eyes.

Mgobozi was an old hunter. He had accompanied Chaka on the royal hunts many times. He was well aware that in unbroken ground it was certain death to run from an elephant. Slowly he lowered his useless shield to the ground, transferred his throwing spear to his right hand and held the short, stabbing assegai in his left.

One part of his brain noted that the firing had stopped. He knew the hunters would come back down the kloof to finish off the wounded. He waited.

It seemed, he told us, describing the scene with great vividness, that they had been looking at each other for half a day, although it couldn't have been more than a matter of minutes, when a shot rang out. This time it was much closer and it acted like a goad on the elephant. The bull gave an angry trumpet and then came out at Mgobozi, its ears flapping out like big grey sails.

Mgobozi allowed it to cover half the distance between them before he acted. He began to run in a semi-circle towards the elephant, reducing the angle and causing the beast to turn crab-wise. This gave him a momentary opening and he flung the assegai with all his strength, hearing it thud into the bull's shoulder. It stuck there, flapping up and down with the animal's movement, as ineffectual as a bodkin.

For the next five minutes he played a tactical game with the bull, allowing it almost to reach him before he slipped away on one side or the other. Fast as the elephant was able to turn, Mgobozi was faster. And all the time he was leading the bull further and further up the kloof towards the guns.

He might have succeeded had his foot not come down in an ant-bear hole. He felt himself falling, but even before he had hit the ground the curling trunk had caught him around the midriff. With a great wrench his body was swung off the ground. He remembered feeling his left arm almost torn from its socket and then the elephant threw him.

But instead of throwing him forward, which is the usual practice with elephants, who then kneel of their victims, this bull flung him over its head so that he cartwheeled through the air and landed amid the branches of a tree. At that moment a musket went off almost in his ear and he heard the crunch of the stricken animal as it fell. Then he lost consciousness.

What happened next is mainly surmise on the part of Mgobozi and my father but with the evidence that was left to them they couldn't have been incorrect except on unimportant points. Either the Arab or the Portuguese must have put in the spinal shot just as the elephant threw Mgobozi. The bull then collapsed, the bullet causing both semi-paralysis and unconsciousness. The hunters

21

must have thought the animal dead because they hacked out the tusks and, without a backward glance at Mgobozi, went about their business.

Some time later, and Mgobozi was not even sure whether it was the same day or the next, the elephant had regained its senses and had been in the process of trying to reach him and finish the job it had started, when Stone-Axe killed it.

At this point in my father's Journal he has written : 'A strange incident. It is my opinion that the Zooloo, in spite of his wounds and injuries had good fortune to come out of it so well, in as much as the hunters would not have given up a muskett and he would have been obliged to use force on them and they would have killed him. I am oppressed by the thought of this conduct since it cannot help smooth the path, already stony, between Christian and Caffre in this Unknown Land.'

Looking back over the years these words are more prophetic than my father could have known.

We had gradually been moving away from the high mountains into rolling savannah country. Mgobozi had recovered completely from his injuries and now my father spent more and more time with he and Izak trying to learn something of the kingdom we were approaching. It is not difficult to understand my father's state of mind. He and my mother—and myself, for that matter—had been wandering for years in wild and little known places of southern Africa. Since my father would have been arrested and imprisoned had he set foot in the Cape Colony he had had to keep going north. Now he found himself in a land which by its very remoteness offered sanctuary. For the first time for years he could think about stopping in one place for more than a couple of weeks. But first he wished to know *where* he was going to stop, and with *whom*. He needed an ally—and the strongest ally was the best ally.

At this time Chaka was not the strongest ally we might have acquired. He was an upstart among the tribes of the East-Nguni nations, a military opportunist in the process of forging a nation out of a small and insignificant tribe with the remnants of the surrounding tribes which he was reducing by battle. He was certainly not as powerful as King Zwide of the Ndwandwes and if we had known this my father might have changed our direction to ally himself with the latter. It is as well he did not, for Chaka's star was in the ascendant, that of Zwide sinking to the horizon.

However, as it happened we only learnt of Zwide later for fate had sent Mgobozi to us and it is almost an understatement to say that for Mgobozi, Chaka, the Great Elephant, was both father and mother. Mgobozi was Chaka's man, which meant that the account of the King which we heard was not completely unbiased. But neither, taking things all in all, was it to prove basically inaccurate.

We came to Bulawayo, which means the Place of the Killing, at mid-morning on a hot early summer day. Since dawn we had been travelling through butter-rich pastureland amid endless herds of sleek cattle. My father turned to my mother and said : 'I've never seen grazing like this, Fran, not even in the Snowy Mountains.' Here and there a herdsman saluted Mgobozi but otherwise our progress seemed to cause little excitement.

My father was fascinated by the long-horned cattle. He called Izak and Mgobozi and began to fire questions at them. His youth and early manhood had been spent at Bitterfountain, a farm in the Snowy Mountains and it had bred in him a great knowledge of, and respect for, husbandry. If, basically, he was anything at all he was a stock-farmer and it seemed we were now gazing at a stock-farmer's paradise.

We came to learn in time that cattle to a Zulu were more than the sum of their parts : possession meant not only the wealth of the individual but the wealth of the nation. They were used as currency, in payment for brides, and as gifts. They were the nation's security as well as its honour and pride. My father, half listening to Izak and Mgobozi, absorbed the countryside as though in a trance.

And with reason. The herds were all matched. Here was a completely black herd, there a red-and-white, behind us black-and-white and then those with more white than black and again another herd more black than white. Most had been decorated in one way or another. Some had their ears cut into fantastic shapes, others wore slits in their dewlaps and had the skin tied up in tassels and buttons on their necks and heads. Even the horns were trained in different shapes. Some were made to hang down, or were cut so that they swung as the animal walked. By scraping one side of the horn and softening it in water the Zulus were able to curve them into outlandish shapes like the sides of a basin

23

or bring the ends around to meet. None of us had ever seen anything like it before. By comparison our own bullocks, plodding wearily through the herds, looked like impoverished and uncouth relatives.

'Look!' my father cried, pointing away to the left. 'Look at that!'

He had seen a small herd of faultlessly matched milk-white cows, each an exact replica of the other. This was Chaka's famous Pongolo herd, which he had bred from six pure white heifers. As though aware of their stature in the nation's heirarchy they did not even spare us a passing glance. We had been so intent on the cattle that we had failed to observe where we were and now as we looked up we saw for the first time the great para-military kraal of Bulawayo. It took our breath away.

It had been built on a gentle slope of parkland dotted with mimosa trees and resembled a huge plate tilted slightly so that, from across the valley, we could see its full face. The kraal was about a mile in diameter and completely surrounded by a palisade of tree trunks. Within the palisade were about one thousand five hundred beehive-shaped huts. Then came another wooden wall so that the huts formed a thick segment on the perimeter of the kraal. The centre was an open space used for cattle. The upper segment of the circle had its own wooden fence and there were two or three substantial buildings there which, we were told, housed Chaka, his staff and his 'sisters'. This euphemism for the seraglio brought out a smile on Mgobozi's face. I'm not sure whether Chaka, at the time of our arrival, was still going through his celibate phase but I know that later on, when the seraglio numbered more than one thousand two hundred 'sisters' he would often look uncommonly weary in the mornings.

A small stream ran down the centre of the valley floor and here we stopped to prepare ourselves. We washed in the clear running water and changed our clothes and then prepared our gifts. A small crowd had gathered to watch us, but they kept to one side, allowing us to get on with what we were doing. This impressed my father who remarked that in the land of the Bachapins we would have been overwhelmed by tribesmen and their wives importuning us for tobacco and snuff and fingering our clothes. It was quite true that here we were unmolested but not for any other reason than that our journey towards Bulawayo had long since been noted; and, of course, there was the presence of Mgobozi. We did not know it then but Chaka had issued a command that we were to be treated as chiefs from another land. I suppose we owed all this to the nimbleness of Stone-Axe.

When we had completed our ablutions one of Chaka's *indunas* came down to the river and indicated to Mgobozi that the Great Elephant was ready to receive us, so we lumbered forward across the shallow ford and up the swelling rise and left the wagons and servants at the great wild fig tree that shaded the entrance to the kraal.

It was, my father records, a moment of great tension for all of us. Here no other power ruled but the whim of Chaka. We were lost to our own kind and our existence had no more validity than that of a fly. We would have passed from this world to the next without the faintest trace of our going.

I know the servants were equally ill at ease. Cupido had once professed to being a Christian and now as we paused at the gate of the stockade I looked back and saw him clutching his musket for dear life, his lips moving in silent prayer. We passed through the gate and into another world.

There were perhaps fifty thousand people awaiting our arrival in the huge central arena of the kraal. Their total silence lent a quality of eeriness to the scene. They stood rank upon rank, lining the sides of the arena making three sides of a square. At the top, and facing us on a mound of red clay stood a man of heroic proportions, lent height by his artificial stance but big neverthe-less. At this distance we could not really make him out but it was obvious who he was.

Just then Mgobozi turned to my father, told him to mount Violin—the hornless cow, as he called the mare—and ride around the arena. As he began to canter a great shout went up from the multitude who pointed their spears and sticks at him and shuffled their feet, for they had never seen a horse before. The noise was deafening.

Throughout his life Chaka was to practise the philosophy of first impressions and on this occasion he almost outdid himself. He had brought from their barracks some miles away not one, but both the great fighting divisions, the Belebele and the Isi-Klebeni and their regiments were formed up in perfect parade order. Close by him, as was their right by tradition, was the 'Single Clash', the Old Guard as we came to know them, and the 'Fasimba', Chaka's Own. Then, down the sides of the square were the 'Look Out', the 'Shorn Rings' and the 'Wild Men'.

All this I was, of course, to learn later. At the time I was much more conscious of seeing my father cantering two, then three times around the arena. I was holding on to my mother's hand and wondering, as he passed out of our sight into the clouds of dust that were being thrown up into the air, whether we should ever see him again.

But at the end of his third circuit Mgobozi held up his hand and my father dismounted. Then we were all led forward through the settling dust to the Royal Mound. Again the eerie silence fell on the thousands of onlookers.

We were stopped ten paces from Chaka, and Mgobozi began to speak. In a voice which was used to command in battle he said: 'Bayete Baba, you who are as large as the world! Noble Elephant! You who are as high as Heaven! The bird who eats all other birds . . . !' Chaka raised one hand in acknowledgement and smiled at Mgobozi as the list of praise names rang out over the heads of the waiting populace.

I'm not sure exactly what Mgobozi said because we had no means of knowing at that time but later he told me he had been recalling the incident of the elephant.

I am bound to say now that if this is true it is the first time in my experience that a Zulu, especially one of Mgobozi's standing, ever told a story against himself, for loss of face was a serious blow to prestige. I am inclined to think that Mgobozi conveniently forgot certain aspects of his rescue. But whatever *was* said it seemed not only to boost his reputation but ours as well.

While his panegyric was in full flow we were able to observe Chaka. He had moved from his mound and was now seated in a massive chair which had been hewn from a single block of wood. Even sitting down he was an awesome sight. At that time he must have been in his late twenties and an almost perfect physical specimen. The Zulus are a tall well-made race but Chaka excelled any Zulu I ever met. He was over six feet with wide shoulders and a narrow waist. His muscles had that whipcord look about them that seemed to deny excesses; and this, in fact, was true. Chaka tried to live, as best he could, the life of an ascetic, not for reasons of morality, but because he wished to develop the greatest fighting machine in the world as he knew it. He asked of his men nothing he was not prepared to do himself.

Above the powerful column of his neck was a wide mouth with thick pink lips and eyes that were out of keeping with the

26

purely animal characteristics of the rest of his body. They seemed to look beyond us to some far-off place. There was sadness in them as well as a sort of remote bleakness. They were magnetic eyes and stared out from beneath brows which were constantly furrowed in thought.

On his head was an otter-skin turban, topped by a crane's feather. A dozen bunches of red wing-feathers from the green lory bird were attached to his hair with thorns from the mimosa tree. He wore discs of dried sugar-cane about an inch in diameter in the cut lobes of his ears, armlets of white ox-tails, and a kilt of monkey skins cut into hundreds of strips, each elaborately twisted. In one hand he held a short stabbing spear, the prototype of the new weapon. This he had named 'Ixwa' which, pronounced in the Zulu way, makes the sound of a blade being withdrawn after a deep body thrust. In his other hand he held the great milk-white shield with the black spot on the right-hand side. This was a mark of his kingship. I saw thousands of black-and-white shields during my stay in Zululand but never another with only one black spot, the size of a man's palm, on the right side.

During Mgobozi's speech the huge crowd had pressed forward to see and hear what was happening. Dust rose from the dung-and-earth covering and the heat was stupefying. My memory of that time is overburdened by a feeling of dizziness caused by these circumstances so I shall let my father's Journal recount what then happened.

'When Mgobozi had finished,' he wrote, 'he took his stance on the left side of Chaka among the members of the court. I then offered to Chaka the presents I had brought with me, consisting of twelve brass bangles, four dozen glass beads, a length of calico and a bottle of sweet oil. I had no sooner returned to my place than my ears were assailed by a voice addressing me in English. In my astonishment I could not at first make out where it was coming from and then I espied an elderly Caffre hunched upon the earth next to Chaka's chair.

'I learnt later that this was a man called Jacob Sumbiti, a member of a tribe who lived hundreds of miles to the south of Zululand. He had learnt his English in the prison at the Cape of Good Hope. But now he was asking, on behalf of his King, what was contained in the bottle. I replied that Chaka would be able to estimate the value of it when applied to bruises and swelled parts of the flesh.

27

'The King was immediately interested and I was again called forward to rub his leg with some of it, an honour to which none but his subjects of rank are admitted; and during my performance none of his people dared to advance to within twenty yards without danger of his displeasure.

'Elephant tusks were then brought forward and laid at our feet. Chaka raised his assegai and after he had struck with it right and left the whole mass broke from their positions and formed up into regiments. Portions of these rushed to the river and the surrounding hills, while the remainder, forming themselves into a circle, began dancing with Chaka in their midst.

'It was a most exciting scene, surprising to us, who could not imagine that a nation termed "savages" could be so disciplined and kept in order.

'The dance continued for about two hours and I would have asked the King's indulgence to allow my wife and child to be seated on the ground had I not wished to make a favourable impression upon him. But eventually he came towards us, the black torso shining with the evidence of his exertions, and through his interpreter told us not to be afraid of his people, who were now coming up to us in small divisions, each division driving cattle before it.

'The men were singing and dancing and whilst doing so, advancing and receding even as one sees the surf do on a seashore. The whole country, as far as our sight could reach, was covered with numbers of people and droves of cattle. These were the same matched herds as we had seen during our journey. After exhibiting them for a further hour the people drew into a circle, of which we were the centre, singing and dancing.

'At this time nearly two hundred of Chaka's "sisters" also entered the circle, each one naked of clothing except for a fringe that hung low down on her hips hiding her pudendum. These women, some of whom were no more than young girls, were oiled and glossy and extremely nubile. They danced in parties of eight, each arranged in fours. Some wore strings of beads which were crossed from the shoulders to the knees and each wore a headdress of black feathers and four brass collars fitting closely to the neck. Shortly the King too joined in their dance and the interpreter Jacob Sumbiti who had come to stand with us assured us that Chaka was the greatest king in existence, that his people were as numerous as the stars, and that his cattle were innumerable.

'It was late in the afternoon before the dancing stopped and the people dispersed. Chaka ordered an *induna* to lead us back to our wagons. He sent us a sheep, a basket of corn, an ox and three gallons of corn beer. We were so exhausted we hardly had the strength to eat. Each was made numb by the events of the day.

'But one thing is clear to me: we have been in the presence of majesty.'

Looking back now it is possible to pinpoint the moment of my father's conversion. That first day he had seen the might of the Zulu nation; on the next morning he was able to assess the power and intelligence of its ruler. Putting those two things together he knew he had reached a place which offered a natural sanctuary. It would mean serving an overlord—and a savage one—but this was a small price, in his opinion, to pay for the advantages.

We had made a late breakfast the next day when we were once more summoned to the Great Elephant's presence. This time everything was totally different. Chaka was having his morning bath. We discovered it was a daily ritual. Gone were the great crowds of people, gone were the cattle. The vast kraal had settled down, after its day of festivity, to the business of everyday life.

My mother, who had Donald to care for and steadfastly refused to leave him to Stone-Axe's tender mercies as she had the day before, begged to be excused from the audience; so it was only my father and I who wandered through the now almost empty arena in search of the King. We found him, surrounded by courtiers and chieftains from outlying kraals, washing himself in the shade of one of the big fig trees that grew near the door of his barn-like palace. My most vivid memories are of colour, the bright green of the grass and trees, the deep blue of the sky, the shining black bodies and then later the redness of the blood.

Most of the faces were unfamiliar to us and I looked around in vain for Mgobozi. Chaka acknowledged our presence with a nod and Jacob came over and bade us be seated. As he performed his toilet Chaka talked constantly to those around him. I was to see him at his morning ceremony many times after that and I was always taken with the assiduous way in which everything was performed. First he rubbed his magnificent body with a paste of bruised beef and ground corn, then three young boys approached

29

carrying gourds of water at arms' length—a most difficult feat because of their weight—and he scooped the water over his body, washing away the glutinous covering. Lastly, when the air had dried his skin he rubbed himself with the tail fat of a sheep, which gave his body a fine glossy appearance. Then he held up the bottle of sweet oil which we had given him and, smiling, nodded to my father again. Only after he had rubbed his legs and arms did Chaka seem satisfied.

He then opened the conversation with us by saying a very strange thing. He had come down from his bathing place and was standing before us, the sun glinting on his newly-anointed body.

'King George and I are brothers,' he announced through Jacob. At first we were so astonished we could not make out what he meant because he didn't actually say 'King George' but 'Umjoji' and it took us a moment to realise that he meant King George of England. Even then it presupposed a knowledge we did not know he possessed. This further strengthens my belief that the great overlord Dingiswayo, who had met and known the British, must have instructed Chaka on the white people before he died; and then, of course, there was Jacob himself who had spent years at the Cape.

'Has he many warriors?' Chaka asked.

'Many,' my father replied.

'It must be so. He has conquered all the whites and I have subdued all the blacks.' He said it with an air of satisfaction even though the statement, as far as he was concerned, was not true.

'Is King George as handsome as I?' he pursued.

My father, conscious that a few well-chosen words might go a long way to help us, said he thought not.

'How many wives has he taken?'

'Only one.'

Chaka nodded. 'It is better so. I do not indulge too much. Too much intercourse is bad. King George will reach a great old age.'

He paused for a moment, studying my father and me, and then he said : 'Why do you wear a hand of iron?'

My father replied that his left hand had been lost many years before and he wore the hook in its place.

'It is good for digging,' Chaka said contemptuously, 'but not for carrying a shield.' And with that he turned on his heel and walked back to his chair which had been set up in the midst of his

30

courtiers. There was a ripple of laughter from those nearby at his latest sally and I could see my father's lips tighten.

Chaka's face had, for no reason that we could discover, become congested with anger. This was something with which we were soon to become well acquainted. One minute he was almost bland, the next a tyrant.

My father, feeling dismissed, was about to rise to his feet and take his leave when Jacob held him firmly by the shoulder. 'The King will tell you when to go,' he whispered.

Meanwhile Chaka was going about the business of his nation and since we could not understand what was being said we sat on the hard ground under a blazing sun, uncomfortable and somewhat bewildered. Every now and then he looked scornfully in our direction but we had no way of knowing whether he was discussing us or not.

And then suddenly a dreadful thing happened. Chaka was in the middle of a rather lengthy speech when an old man, who was squatting on his haunches some yards away from the King, sneezed. For no particular reason my eyes had been focussed on that section of the court. The old man's head had started to fall back, his top lip had begun to retract and his nostrils to dilate; all the symptoms of a coming sneeze. But in his eyes there was only stark terror. He grabbed for his nose in an effort to smother the sneeze but the angle of his head already meant that he was looking up towards the sun, which is often enough to make one sneeze by itself. Then his body jerked and his hand flew away from his face and the sneeze blew out over the company.

Chaka stopped talking. There was an appalled silence. Then he nodded once in the direction of the old man. At once two huge Zulus, who had been squatting out of sight behind him, sprang forward. I can still remember the soft thud of their bare feet as they ran towards the old man—the only noise in that awful quiet.

As they reached him the old man made no move to escape. He simply squatted there, his black face now a slate-grey. Without out a word one of the slayers reached over from behind, locked his arm around the old man's neck. The second slayer came forward. In his hand he held a bundle of sharpened bamboo splinters and now, as the old man's body was turned upside down, he drove the long slivers up the anus and deep into the entrails. Then the neck was given a sudden jerk, snapping the bone like a twig.

'Take him away,' Chaka said. 'He makes me laugh.' I know

31

that is what he said for I heard it many times in the future. It was death to cough or sneeze in his presence.

I don't think I had actually taken in the enormity of what was happening. But as the slayers dragged the dead body out of the kraal where the vultures and hyenas were waiting, I could feel my father's hand on my arm and the tremors in his own body communicated themselves to me so that I began to shake with a nameless and indefinable horror.

Abruptly I heard myself screaming: 'Shoot him, father! Shoot him!' as I was trying to struggle to my feet. But my father held me down and covered my mouth with his hand. He made no move to reach for his gun.

Chaka had risen at my outburst and came down to tower over us. It was strange, but his face seemed to have lost its look of anger. 'He was an old man,' he said, looking more at me than at my father, 'and he can no longer fight. Must I feed useless mouths?' He did not wait for a reply but walked slowly through the press of courtiers towards the Royal Hut.

On the way back to the wagons my legs felt as weak as reeds that have been soaked in water. A ball of vomit lay at the bottom of my stomach. Just before we left the arena my father stopped and said: 'Remember, Robbie, they have different customs to us. I think it would be better if you didn't tell your mother. It might upset her.'

I looked up at him but his eyes slid away from me and I said nothing.

I couldn't sleep for a long time that night. My mother had decided I must be sickening for something and had put me under a kaross in the rear wagon. From where I lay I could hear them talking.

'You should have seen him,' my father was saying. 'Everything he does has dignity. Why, you can't imagine King George stripping off and bathing himself in the middle of London, can you?'

'That's quite true,' my mother said dryly. 'I can't. At the same time, I would not go five yards to watch King George or Chaka, or any other man for that matter, taking a bath.'

'Oh, that's not what I mean at all. It's the ritual. You know those boys who hold out the gourds of water, well, they have to do it at arms' length. They've got to keep their arms quite rigid. Imagine the training you need for *that* with a heavy gourd.'

'You've really made up your mind about this place, haven't you?'

'Yes, I think so, Fran. It's all we ever wanted. And you?'

'To tell you the truth, I don't know. I feel . . . I feel there's a savagery here that's—'

'But that's what they *are*. They're savages!'

'Yes, I know, but I've not had this feeling before. The Bachapins were so mild by comparison and some of the other tribes . . .'

'Oh God, the Bachapins! They were useless! Can you imagine what the Zulus would do to them?'

'Yes, Jamie, I can. Don't forget we came through a wasteland. I can well imagine what the Zulus would do to them. That's what I'm talking about.'

'There's no harm in strength,' my father said. 'No harm in being on the stronger side.'

'A year ago you wouldn't have said that.'

'Well, I'm saying it now. We've travelled more than a thousand miles looking for a place to settle. We can't go on travelling for the rest of our lives and we can't turn back. This is the end of the road. Surely you must have known that.' Then he added bitterly: 'Don't forget you chose to marry an escaped prisoner. This is how escaped prisoners have to live.'

'Jamie, Jamie. Have you ever heard me regret coming with you?'

'No, I haven't. Except for now. What is it, Fran?'

'The children.'

'Ah, I see.'

'Well, it's only natural,' my mother said defensively. 'When you have children your outlook changes. Before, I was happy just to *be* in Africa. To wander in wild places. But you can't bring children up that way.'

'Exactly what I'm saying! That's why we should settle here.'

'How do you know they'll even *let* us settle?'

'We saved Mgobozi's life. He owes us a favour.'

There was silence for a while and then my mother spoke again and her voice was tinged with sadness. 'You've changed, Jamie, but then, I suppose we both have.'

'Nonsense! You're the one who's changed. You want to go back to the Cape and live at Paradise and bring the boys up like little gentlemen and take tea with the Governor. Don't think I haven't heard you talking to Robbie and reading to him about the Cape!

Well, it's not possible, and that's that. Forbye, *I* don't want to return to a prison cell.'

'Very well, do what you want.' For the first time in my life I heard a faint trace of self-pity in my mother's tone. My father must have heard it too, for his voice immediately became softer, almost cajoling.

'I tell you, Fran, we'll live like royalty here. You've seen the cattle! The climate's good, the grass is fine. There are plenty of elephants to shoot for ivory. We'll grow rich here and eventually others will come and we'll trade. But we'll have been the *first* and that's what will matter.'

That's how it was left. At no time did I hear my father speak of the old man who was killed.

From the top of the hill we could see the whole of our world and there was no one in it but ourselves. It was not a very high hill—a small plateau really—nor could we see more than a few miles in any direction. But this did not matter: it was ours. Often, while we were building our house, and afterwards for that matter, I would lie out on the slopes of the hill with Stone-Axe and look out over the undulating country.

On one side the plateau sloped gently down into a wide valley dotted with mimosa trees, giving it the appearance of stately parkland, on the other it fell more abruptly to the banks of a sparkling stream that wound its way to the White Umfolosi River. Even though we had not been granted more than nine or ten thousand acres there was a great variety of landscape. In the space of a few hours one could meet a herd of giraffe browsing from tree to tree in the valley, and then traverse the side of the plateau and come down to the river where the weeping willows grew and sit on the bank and catch yellow-fish and chew the piercing sweet pulp of wild *imfé*.

Sometimes this variety confused the mind and one would be swimming in the iron-stone pools of the river and thinking about the long warm grass of the valley, or if one was in the valley the thought of lying under an acacia tree on the slopes of the hill and watching the great thunderheads pass slowly by would seem infinitely beguiling. The point is one could do all these things in a single day and every place seemed new and clean as though it had just been created that very morning.

We were high enough so that in winter the brown grass sparkled with frost in the early morning and the days were pale blue and the sunlight was yellow. And on these days Stone-Axe and I would go out hunting guinea fowl and partridge. He had made me a bow from tightly-bound split-cane and arrows of the thick stems of dried elephant grass tipped with bone. They were light but flew true and if we were hunting guinea fowl we would get up in the frosty darkness and go down to the wild fig trees and willows along the river. As the first streaks of dawn lighted the sky you could see the black shapes of the roosting guinea fowl like big finches' nests high up in the bare branches and sometimes we would bring down five or six before the rest would take fright and rush out of the trees with their strange clanking call.

But if we were hunting partridge there was no chance of using a bow and Stone-Axe would bring his throwing sticks and we would walk the birds up, letting fly as soon as they rose from beneath our feet. It sounds an impossible task to hit a flighting partridge but Stone-Axe was uncanny, and even I learnt the art after a long while.

And later, when my father made his plough and planted corn in the valley, we would sometimes hide in the winter fields all night so we would be there when the great spur-winged geese came hissing down in the early morning for a feed.

Sometimes we might kill nothing and then Stone-Axe would build bird traps. He knew several ways but the one I remember best was by balancing a big flat stone against a system of levers made of willow twigs. Under the stone which he poised almost vertically, he would scoop out the earth—this so the birds would not be crushed—and scatter seeds. The weight of a tiny veld sparrow or glass-eye on one of the horizontal twigs was enough to bring the stone down. When we'd caught a dozen or more, Stone-Axe would gut them with his finger-nail, burn off the feathers with a handful of blazing grass, and then cook them over the coals, holding them delicately on the point of a long white thorn.

In summer the skies turned a deeper blue and the green grass grew thigh deep and the orange noons trembled in the heat. Like animals we would seek the shade of the river trees. The stream flowed over dark rocks and in the shadow the water had a bluish tinge. Except in times of drought the pools were always full and you could tell where the sun had been because the top layers of

35

water were warm and the bottom cold. I spent so much time in the water that soon I could swim like an otter. Summer or winter Stone-Axe rubbed his body with sheep's fat and saw no reason for washing it off in cold water. So while I swam he would lie on the bank and make soft buckskin shoes for my father or mother or mend his arrows or make me another bow. Wherever he was his hands were never still.

Sometimes we would go all the way to the White Umfolosi and he would make traps out of reeds and withes and we would come home with a whole basket of eels. There wasn't much he couldn't do if he wanted to.

And then on summer afternoons we would watch the thunderheads build up until the sky became dark and the forked lightning flashed and the rain fell in solid sheets. But these storms disappeared almost as quickly as they came and within an hour or so you could go out into the wet veld and smell the earth and catch flying ants.

My father named the hill 'Ben Mhor', after one he had known in Scotland, and on the top he built our house, which he called 'Morile'.

I'd better explain that we, like the other white people who came after us, made a grave mistake about what we considered *our* land. It was now some months since we had first come to Zululand and it was really through Mgobozi that Chaka had been prevailed on to let us live there; that and his great respect for the might of King George. Ben Mhor lay some ten miles north of Bulawayo and between us and Chaka were the two great military barracks of the Isi-Klebeni and the Belebele divisions.

It seemed to us that Chaka had granted the land in perpetuity and of course this wasn't so at all, which was eventually made rudely clear. No one *owned* or *gave* or even *bartered* land after the European fashion. All the land belonged to Chaka, who kept it for his people; it was their inheritance and their heritage; it *was* the people. What he had done, in fact, was to allow us to live on a piece of *his* land for as long as *he* cared.

On the flat top of the hill where a grove of wattles bordered the basin of a natural spring, my father built the house. He built it partly in the Zulu fashion and partly to his own ideas. It was the first real house I had ever seen.

A Zulu hut is built by making a framework of interlaced saplings and covering roof and walls first with grass and then tightly

36

woven mats. This was altogether too flimsy for someone like my
father and he built Morile as he might have built a stone-and-
lime house in his native Highlands. The wagons were used to
draw stones from the river; grey mud we fetched from a marshy
area in the valley, dung was supplied to us by our bullocks and
there was any amount of thatching grass. These were the basic
ingredients of the house : the walls were of stone and mud, the
roof of thatch and the floors of dung. The latter might sound like
an unpleasant novelty but it was surprisingly effective. First a
covering of pulverised ant-heap and clay was laid. This was
beaten hard with stones until level and then two or three times
a week one of the servants would smooth it over with dung. Half-
an-hour of hard rubbing with a river stone and the floor shone
like dark-green marble.

The design was curious : part-European and part-Zulu. My
father built four stone round-houses of Zulu design and then
simply linked them by four oblong rooms. This made it appear
like the exterior battlements of a very small castle. The round-
houses were the four corners of the house and they, with their
linking rooms, formed a hollow square. I have described it as a
very small castle, but this is really overstating the case. The house
was rough-made and primitive and the design was dictated by
principles of defence. I had not realised this until I saw that the
exterior windows were mere firing slits. I now knew why we had
built at the top of the hill.

While my father and Izak laid stone after stone and the walls
grew higher than my head, Cupido, who had once worked with a
wheelwright in the Colony, began to make our furniture, if it
can be so called. Since there were no planks in Zululand he had
to make do by cutting branches or slender saplings and binding
them with strips of buckskin. For carpets we had zebra skins. It
was only when we had nearly finished the outside and were
already using the front rooms that my father ordered the second
wagon to be dismantled and the wood used. In this way Cupido
was able to make two good tables. During all this time Stone-Axe,
with my slender assistance, fed us.

Once the house was built we used the front rooms for living
and sleeping and the servants the back. The kitchen was on one
side. In the hollow square, which was later to be my mother's
garden, the Hottentots built a clay oven.

To a sophisticated city-dweller this may not sound much of a dwelling, but for Zululand it was a palace and castle made into one. Perhaps it was this early display of power, albeit defensive, that first made the Zulu people suspicious of our motives. For, of course, we had onlookers all the time the house was building.

Sometimes they would be lonely herdsmen moving their cattle to another part of the country, sometimes travellers journeying between Chaka's kraal and that of his half-brother to the north, at others it might be elements of the Belebele or Isi-Klebeni divisions out on manœuvres who would halt at the bottom of the hill and stare at the strange construction and then go racing away into the far mountains. Mgobozi came several times bringing presents of cattle. Every time Stone-Axe saw him he laughed and held up his thumb and forefinger and Mgobozi pretended to be annoyed and would rattle Chest-biter on his great shield.

Chaka never came at all and this was not surprising since it would have been undignified for him to have expressed any open curiosity about what we were doing. But I have not the slightest doubt that no single stone was laid without his knowledge.

Perhaps the most important of our visitors at that time was Ngwadi, Chaka's half-brother and ruler of a small principality to the north of us. He even had a small army of his own, which was quite unknown in Zululand and which is evidence of how much Chaka loved him. They both shared the same mother, the Female Elephant, Nandi.

It must have been six or seven months after we had arrived in Zululand when Ngwadi paid us his visit. I remember it was a still autumn day when the smoke of the cooking fires rose in an unbroken column and my father was putting the last of the thatch on the roof.

We watched them come up the slope of the hill and once again I was impressed at my father's choice of a site. The field of fire was entirely in our favour and we could have shot them down at will.

Like the others, I suppose that Ngwadi's curiosity had got the better of him. There were four of them in the party. Ngwadi himself carried only his spears and shield but his two wives brought food. One carried a basket of beef on her head, the other a calabash of beer. The fourth member of the party was a young boy a year or so older than I. He was Tanga, Ngwadi's son and was to become as close to me as a member of my family. But that was in the future. As the adults engaged in formal greetings we stared at each other pretending we were not too impressed with what we saw. My father had heard of Ngwadi and now went out of his way to entertain him and his family. It didn't do one any harm to be friendly with the King's half-brother.

Ngwadi's two wives seated themselves in the sun and modestly refused to come into the house so the rest of us trailed after my father who began showing off the uncompleted house like a country squire. I was watching Tanga. Like his father he tended to be on the lean side for a Zulu with long slender limbs and a thin intelligent face. By now we could all make ourselves understood in the Zulu language and my mother asked Tanga if he would like to see our books. These were our most treasured possessions and I was glad when Tanga simply looked confused.

'He doesn't even know what they *are*,' I said.

'Well, take him and show him. I had to show *you*.'

I didn't remember having been shown at all, but I shrugged and said : 'All right.'

We went into the front room and I got the books out of the wagon chests.

'You can't touch them,' I said. 'You can only look.'

Of course the printing didn't mean anything at all to Tanga and his face took on a sort of haughty, bored expression. After a while he said : 'Are they for eating ?'

I smiled scornfully, not even bothering to reply.

'Are they for war or for casting spells ?'

'They're for looking at, with your *eyes*.'

'Why ?'

This wasn't getting us anywhere so I pulled out Dr Goodsir's manuscript of his travels. He had drawn many of the animals and plants he'd encountered and now I heard the air in Tanga's lungs being expelled with a long hiss.

He put out a finger and touched the paper beneath the illustration of a *hartebeeste*.

I jerked the manuscript away. 'It's not for touching.'

'*Hartebeeste*,' he said, giving the Zulu name for the antelope.

I turned the page. The finger came out again, this time hovering in the air. '*Duiker*.' I turned again. 'Waterbuck . . . ironwood tree . . . wild fig . . . anteater . . . black widowbird . . .' At almost every drawing the finger shot out and hovered. His eyes were alight now and he was smiling.

'You don't know everything,' I said and skimmed some pages

39

until we reached the proteas and sugarbushes and the particular flora of the Cape of Good Hope. He inspected them for a few minutes and then, because they did not mean anything to him, his interest immediately waned and he began to look vaguely around the room.

It was only when I came back to the things he recognised that his interest returned. Now, of course, I can understand why: the Zulus had no written language nor any real graphic skills.

'Can I make it?' he said.

'Make what, a drawing?'

'Yes.'

'You don't know how.'

'Teach me.'

The trouble was I couldn't draw either but there was no point in mentioning that so I just said: 'You've certainly come to the right—'

'Teach what?' my mother said, coming into the room.

'I'm going to teach him to draw,' I said.

'That's very kind of you,' my mother said, smiling. 'Why don't I teach you both? It's about time you learnt, anyway.'

So that was how I became friendly with Tanga. At first he used to come over from his kraal, which was about five miles to the north of us, once a week.

One of the most precious commodities we owned was a small supply of paper and this we were not allowed to use until we had perfected a drawing. All the rough sketches were made with carbon on clay tiles and then when my mother thought we had practised enough she would bring out a sheet of paper, the quill, and the ink made from brown sugar and soot moistened with water, and allow us to transcribe the final sketch.

I was never much good at drawing but Tanga seemed to take to it naturally. I still remember one of his drawings of the house and although the perspectives were not too good it was quite recognisable. He was better on animals and trees and the things he knew instinctively.

But the point about these drawing lessons is that they led on to other things. Soon he began to come over twice a week and sometimes three times and my mother began to teach him to count and a few words of English. Just to show you how backward he was he didn't believe you were counting unless he saw your fingers moving. They had a strange system of counting by tens, a hundred being a 'great ten'. They couldn't imagine much more after a 'great ten'.

However, all the learning wasn't on one side. I began to return his visits. At first I used to go with Stone-Axe but after a while when I grew bigger I was allowed to go by myself. My mother was a bit worried at first but my father said I must learn to become a man and this was one of the ways. You could see he was pleased that I was friendly with a nephew of the King.

At first the Zulus at Ngwadi's kraal viewed me with suspicion but then when they saw that I played in the dust like any other Zulu child and that I was respectful to my elders and that I didn't transgress any of their customs, their suspicions abated and I was tolerated. I admit I was lucky because really I didn't know whether I was transgressing or not since I didn't know the customs. But I learnt. I learnt how to wash myself as a man washes—head, then arms, then body and legs. I learnt how to sit with my knees erect and not folded under me like a woman. I learnt that one didn't eat in front of one's elders but took what food one was given and ate it in some other place. I learnt how to make clay models of cattle and use the wide-spreading mimosa thorns as horns. I learnt how to skip with a grass rope, and play a sort of blind man's buff, and the stone game called *ngelitshe*, and another called *khobola* which was a sort of juggling game with stones. And I learnt about snakes.

Because Tanga was of the blood royal he didn't go out herding the cattle and goats like other boys of his age. Instead he took me out hunting snakes. I am sometimes appalled now when I look back on the chances we took.

Although there were fewer snakes where we were than on the bushy lowlands near the coast there were enough to make a definite impression on our lives. To the ordinary senses another was added; an unconscious care in all one's actions. You watched where you put your feet when walking, you looked into your bed before getting in, turned over your clothes in the morning before putting them on. We were always hearing of two kinds of victims: those who suffered snakebite and those who were taken by crocodiles in the Umfolosi.

There were night-adders and puff-adders, mole snakes and grass snakes, tree snakes and rock snakes, pythons, cobras, black and green mambas and snakes whose names I didn't know and didn't want to know. I remember a Zulu herdsman—this was

41

later on and he was one of ours—being brought in one day with a cobra bite on the inside of his thigh. He was already almost beyond speech and the leg was swollen and of one thickness all the way down to his calf. My father tried everything: he cut round the bite and sucked, he used the bezoar stone, he made the herdsman drink pail after pail of milk, he made him drink a dilute solution of ammonia, but nothing seemed to help. The next day the herdsman went blind and the day after he died. Of course if he'd been bitten by a mamba he would never even have reached the house. I never heard of anyone recovering from a mamba bite. It didn't help matters much when Mgobozi, in one of his more asinine moods, told me that the way to deal with a python was to let him swallow one of your feet and then, when his mouth was distended, put the blade of a knife into the corner and slit him all the way up. He thought it was a great joke until I caught a harmless mole snake and put it in his blankets when he was asleep. Because it was a cold night the snake cuddled up and when Mgobozi awoke it was lying across his shoulder with its head tucked into the hollow of his neck. A mole snake can look very like a black mamba in a poor light and he made a great fuss.

Anyway, Tanga and I didn't know too much about snakes at that time so we weren't afraid of them—at least *he* said he wasn't.

Puff-adders you could most always find lying out in the open somewhere, like a pathway, fast asleep in the sun. Cobras liked the warmth of rocks. Pythons would be hunting rats in the wild *imfé* along the river bank and tree snakes would be up in the branches. We never went hunting mambas.

I remember one day we were out in the valley and Tanga noticed a movement in the grass. It was the tip of a snake's tail disappearing down a hole. We ran forward but it had gone so we began to dig with a hoe and an iron-wood stick. The earth was soft after rain and within minutes we came on it, a writhing mess of greeny-yellow whorls in the broken ground. Tanga gave it a couple of smart cracks with one of his sticks and threw it out onto the ground. It was a spitting cobra with a dark brown band around its neck. The blows had injured its spine but it wasn't by any means dead and thrashed on the grass, alternately trying to wriggle away and raise its hood to spit at us. We began to play with it, allowing it to move away a few feet before we flicked it back with our sticks. We tossed pebbles at it. We caught it by

42

the tail and dragged it backwards. We tapped it on the head and let it bite the sticks, laughing as the tacky venom dripped down onto the ground. We must have been tormenting it for about five minutes when Tanga suddenly went rigid. His face was terrified. I glanced quickly over my shoulder and was gripped by the same fear. Another spitting cobra, the mate of the one in front of us, had emerged from the hole. Its head was about two feet from the ground and the hood was distended. Its mottled yellow skin gleamed in the sunshine, its hood swayed from side to side and its forked tongue flickered like a dark shadow around its lips.

It wasn't more than six feet from us and I knew in that instant that one of us would be blind before the day was out for a spitting cobra rarely misses the eyes of its victim. My own position, half crouched and staring at the snake over one shoulder was relatively safe; I had only to move my head a fraction. But Tanga seemed transfixed. He was squatting full face to the cobra and was unable to take his eyes from it.

At that moment the cobra's head moved back a fraction and then jerked forward. I have a fleeting impression of a viscous globule flicking through the air and then I launched myself at Tanga knocking him sideways onto the ground. The venom hit him just below the right ear.

After I'd killed both snakes and wiped the poison off his skin with a handful of leaves we went down to the stream. Both of us were shaken and we swam in silence and with little enjoyment. Afterwards as we lay in the half-shade of a willow, I said : 'I thought Zulus weren't afraid of snakes.'

It was a stupid thing to say but my stomach was still crawling with the reaction and I had to say something. When Tanga kept silent I gave a rather sick laugh and went on : 'You just sat there; that cobra could have eaten you alive.' Still he said nothing. 'The next time we go hunting snakes,' I said remorselessly, 'you'd better let me do the killing. Keep your hands over your eyes if they frighten you.'

I had been chewing a piece of *imfé* and now spat out the used pulp. I didn't mean it to hit Tanga, in fact I'd been trying to spit it in the river, but it didn't get that far and landed in a messy blob on his leg.

He looked down at it in disbelief for a second and just as I was about to open my mouth and say I hadn't meant it he gave a sort

43

of shriek and flung himself at me. You couldn't really call it a fight, not on my part anyway, because it was like trying to defend yourself against someone with about ten arms. I felt him hit me once or twice and then he had a grip on my leg and I was flying through the air. I fell half in and half out of the water and broke my collar-bone on a rock. I lay there looking up at him and thought he was going to kill me. His eyes had gone a sort of bright red. This was something I was to notice about the Zulus, this strange pigmentation of the eyes when they became aroused. It was as though a red film dropped down over the pupils.

But anyway he didn't kill me, he just stood there trembling and looking as though he was *going* to and then the redness disappeared and his face became normal. Oddly enough as he was helping me to my feet he began to cry and that set me off. It wasn't so much the pain of the broken bone because I didn't know it was broken then, nor can I remember any pain. It was just seeing him cry and the reaction, I suppose.

By the time I got home my shoulder was hurting badly and I told my mother I'd fallen from a tree. Anyway, it wasn't all that serious because I was young and the bone mended quickly. The strange thing about the incident is that the friendship between Tanga and me became something more than just friendship after that day. He even took me to his own secret cave a bit further upstream and brought me a pipe and taught me to smoke it there. That's how close we became.

Winter gave way to summer and summer changed back to winter, spring and autumn being hardly noticeable in these latitudes. It seemed that one day the thunderheads rolled through the sky bringing heat and humidity and the next they were gone and my mother was lighting a log fire in the big stone fireplace of the living-room.

The house was finished, the furniture made, the zebra skins felt soft underfoot and the kitchen walls were already taking on a blackened look from the fire-soot. And as the seasons changed so did our lives. We became more settled. The days were gone now when Stone-Axe and I wandered free as birds. We still went down and shot guinea fowl in the early mornings and we still went to trap eels in the Umfolosi River but these adventures became rarer. I was growing up and there were things to do.

44

We had become farmers. From the initial gifts of cattle by Chaka and Mgobozi my father increased his stock by barter until he had a herd of nearly sixty cows and a good stud bull which he had bought from Ngwadi. He also bought goats and for the house he kept a small flock of fat-tailed sheep which gave us meat, wool and fat for making soap. He and Izak built a wooden plough and soon the Home Farm, which is what he called that area of the valley nearest the house, was green with growing corn and caffre-corn. He built a press for the wild *imfé* and made sugar and a kind of rum that almost dissolved one's teeth—I know because I tried it. He dammed up the stream and drove irrigation channels down to the ploughed lands. And he also had time to ride out with Stone-Axe and look for elephant in the bush along the Umfolosi and I don't think he ever went out without bringing back at least two tusks. These he stored in the house.

Sometimes he would say to my mother : 'Come and count your money, Fran,' and they would go and look at the growing pile of yellow tusks.

We were like a small self-supporting island in the middle of a sea of grass. The sheep provided us with meat and wool, the caffre-corn was turned into bread, the corn was eaten either boiled or roasted or crushed, the cattle gave us milk, beef and leather, we grew pumpkins, wild beans and sweet potatoes in the kitchen garden, Stone-Axe brought honey from the *krantzes* above the stream and we did not have to go far to collect blackberries and wild figs, medlars and gooseberries and watermelons. My mother, who had been brought up at the Cape, had learnt Dutch and Malay cooking and so we lived well. We even grew wild tobacco for my father and the servants. We did not want for much. It seemed at that time that whatever my father turned his hand to increased.

I remember one day a horrible old woman came to the house and tried to sell him magic spells to make the corn grow better and to improve the stock and he just laughed at her and pointed out over the land and said : 'What need have I of spells and magic? I fertilise my fields and I use only the best breeding bulls for my stock. Sell your charms elsewhere.' Her eyes glittered with rage and she hissed like a cobra, but she could see he was right.

Setting it down like this I seem to be describing Arcadia. In many ways it was, but only because we were isolated from the mainstream of Zulu life. There were tensions and fears and suspicions just as there were in any other community. What we didn't know was that many of them centred upon us.

It had taken me a long time to get over my first impressions of Chaka's ruthlessness but, and I am saddened to say it, familiarity does breed, if not contempt, an unconscious dulling of one's sensibilities. And Chaka was never the same from one meeting to another and this in itself was diverting. Sometimes he would ignore us and we would leave Bulawayo at nightfall without having said a single word to him. At other times he would welcome my father like a brother and take us into his own hut and talk and talk. He was avid to learn about Europeans. He already knew that we were only the van of a flood of trekking Whites who would come to perch on his southern borders like waiting vultures.

I don't know how many days I spent with my father in one or other of Chaka's royal kraals and not unnaturally the visits have merged in my memory, but I remember one quite clearly and it may serve as a model for the others. It was the first time I had seen either Mbopa, who was the major-domo of the court, or Dingane, another of Chaka's half-brothers.

We had arrived early but already the great arena was restless with people. Just after sunrise Chaka emerged from the Great Council Hut, followed closely by Mbopa, and walked to his chair which had been placed beneath the fig tree. The councillors were already seated in a semi-circle around the throne. As Chaka approached, a hush fell over the assembly. He was dressed in his most extravagant best, the kilt of monkey tails swinging as he walked and his head haloed in lory feathers. He carried neither assegai nor shield but instead held in his hand a toy spear made of iron-wood. When he reached a point midway between his hut and the tree the crowd rose as though on a command and then in perfect unison raised their right hands and the roar 'Bayete!' exploded onto the morning air. Sometimes I have seen him nod good-humouredly to the greeting but this morning he looked neither left nor right. Once he was seated and the concourse had settled down he spied us standing on the outskirts and beckoned us to sit on one side of his councillors. As we threaded our way through the packed bodies I heard some angry mutters. This had

46

grown more obvious of late and it was something I could not fathom. Although we kept to ourselves and harmed no one we seemed to be growing less and less popular with the ordinary people.

'The Great Elephant who stamped his enemies flat, the Lion of Lions . . .' The Praiser had begun the daily ritual, his voice reaching out over the kraal. With a vicious movement of the hand Chaka cut him short and indicated to Mbopa to bring forward the first litigants. The Great Elephant appeared to be in a foul temper and I felt sorry for anyone who crossed him that day.

The first few cases concerned strays and damage caused by one kraal's cattle to the fields of another. They were of minor importance and Chaka dealt with them swiftly. I remember one was between two herdsmen who each claimed the other was transgressing his land. So Chaka asked each separately where he thought the other's boundary extended to. Like greedy fools they minimised the other's land and magnified their own. Chaka's judgement was swift and rough : he ordered them to swop areas and stick to the boundaries they had suggested. This meant there was a no-man's-land between the two and Chaka forbade them to go into it on pain of death. Bewildered and unable to account for what had happened to them they crept quietly from the court.

And then came the first death of the morning. A herdsman was led before Chaka to tell his story. He was one of two herdsmen, he said, guarding a royal herd many miles to the north. During the night a party of Ndwandwe scouts had surprised them and driven off half a dozen cattle, at the same time killing the other herdsman.

While he listened Chaka began to move angrily in his chair. 'And so you come running to me !' he cut in abruptly.

'*Yebo, Baba.*' The herdsman could barely stand, he was so afraid.

'How many Ndwandwes were there?'

'Many—many—'

'Perhaps six or seven?'

'Perhaps, Father.'

'Perhaps seven or eight?'

'Perhaps, Father.'

'What about five or six?'

'Five or six there may have been, Father.'

'Or three or four?'

47

The herdsman opened his mouth and then closed it again, shrugging his shoulders. There was an air of expectancy among the onlookers. Suddenly Chaka addressed them: 'Listen to this man, my children. Remember what he says. Out of the night the Ndwandwes plunder our cattle! Out of the night they come to kill our brothers! The reckoning is long overdue, soon they will eat earth!' There was a roar of approval from the crowd. 'Heaven thunders wisdom!' they shouted. 'But first,' Chaka continued, 'we must learn to be men. You, herdsman, know you not that one Zulu equals five Ndwandwes? So that even by your own count the odds were favouring you and yet you let them kill and steal. There is no place for such as you among men. Take him away! I have spoken!'

Before he knew what had happened the herdsman was caught up by two slayers, his neck twisted and his head battered in. One second he was alive and standing before Chaka, the next he was simply dead meat being carted to the bush outside the kraal where the carrion-eaters lived.

My father had grown used to such scenes and sat staring straight ahead as though his eyes were fixed on some far-off object, but I had not and looked away as they killed the man. I had looked away just at a moment when everyone's attention, including Chaka's, was fixed on the killing, and I saw something the significance of which I could not know then but which was to become plainer in later years.

Mbopa, the fat chief councillor, was in close conversation with someone I had never seen before but whom I came to know as Chaka's half-brother Dingane. He was dressed almost as gorgeously as the King himself, except that in place of the lory feathers he wore a head-dress of white egret plumage. But he was lacking in the majesty, barbaric though it was, that surrounded Chaka like an aura. His face was fleshy and his small eyes were close together. His lips were loose and he wore a petulant, self-indulgent expression. But this time I marked an addition: there was fear in his eyes. He seemed to be pleading in a rapid undertone with Mbopa but that wily old fox was simply shrugging his shoulders. Then Dingane caught him by the arm and drew him closer and whispered quickly into his ear. Mbopa seemed to consider for a moment and then he smiled and nodded his head and a look of relief spread over Dingane's features.

48

Meanwhile the herdsman had gone to join his ancestors and Chaka was turning around impatiently in his chair, waiting for Mbopa to bring on the next case. This he did immediately.

He walked with measured steps to the door of the Great Council Hut and issued a series of curt orders. We heard a slight scream and then a scuffle and a young girl was dragged out into the sunlight before Chaka. She was quite naked and could not have been more than fourteen. Her breasts were high and pointed and her thighs were like dark brown satin. In a few years those same dugs would hang almost to her naval and her buttocks would grow fat and gross. But on that morning she was perfect. She had a pretty oval face that became ugly with fear as we watched. She was one of Chaka's 'sisters'. Mbopa called out the charge against her which was that the monthly pudendal examination carried out that morning by Chaka's mother, Nandi, had revealed she was no longer a virgin. The crime of ravishing one of the seraglio was so heinous that a shiver of apprehension passed through the crowd.

Chaka, in keeping with the law relating to unmarried men, used a form of coition in which the orgasm occurred on the external genitalia of the girl, neither fertilising her nor breaking her hymen. What had now occurred amounted therefore to treason against the head of State as well as a transgression against the moral law, both of which carried the death penalty.

Of course, I wasn't aware of all these subtleties at the time nor would I have been interested. I was watching the girl and she, in turn, was watching Dingane. He had tried to efface himself behind Chaka but as he moved so her eyes moved with him. In them was a look of such hatred that even Dingane seemed to blench under his dark skin.

And then a strange thing happened. Instead of thrashing himself into a rage as everyone expected Chaka looked at the girl, nodded indifferently, and the slayers broke her neck. I saw a look of the utmost relief pass over Dingane's face.

The King turned to Mbopa. 'Who is the man?' he said casually, almost too casually.

The Major-Domo pointed to a young man sitting in the fourth row of the spectators. 'He is there, Great Elephant. The guilt is in his face.'

I don't think the young man knew what had happened. Like the herdsman and the girl he was alive one second and dead the

49

next. Only the loud crack of breaking bones marked his passing. Fortunately, death overtook him before he had time to be afraid.

It was now about mid-morning and the court was adjourned while Chaka had his bath. Later he asked my father and me to join him in his hut for breakfast. We ate boiled and grilled beef, spinach, corn porridge with honey and washed it all down with sour milk. The meal was served to us on wooden platters by several of Chaka's concubines. Having learnt already what had occurred that morning to one of their number they were that much more anxious to please, but since Chaka was lolling on a pile of rush mats covered in skins and the law was that no one should ever look down upon the King, the women were wriggling along on their knees and elbows, their naked bottoms looming everywhere. If Stone-Axe had been present there would have been a riot. In a way it was funny and I glanced across at my father to see if he was amused but there was a look on his face that I'd never seen before.

'You also, Claw,' Chaka said, noticing the expression. 'Would you die for one of the King's sisters?'

Chaka had said it as a joke, but as with all his jokes there was a sharp edge of danger about it.

My father, who had been taken off guard, quickly regained his composure. 'For one of the sisters, no. For the King, yes.'

Chaka nodded. 'It is well said, Claw. You always say what I wish to hear and there is nothing bad in that—if it is true.'

'It's true.'

'We shall see, an opportunity will doubtless come. But it is not dying that is so difficult. Every soldier expects to eat earth in battle and when it comes he is pleased. It is living that taxes a man.'

'Even when death comes to the wrong man?' I said. It was unpardonable of me to speak in front of my elders like that, especially before the King himself, but I was still deeply affected by the death of the young couple.

My father flushed and would have silenced me with blows if Chaka had not held up his hand. His eyes swung round and fastened themselves on mine and for the first time I was really able to feel his power. For a moment my body felt as if it were turning to water, and then he spoke. 'So, the little hunter is unhappy. You are not only foolish with cobras, it seems.' How he had heard of my exploit with Tanga I never knew but it was a measure of his intelligence service.

At that moment his mother, Nandi, entered the hut and shooed out the members of the seraglio, ordering them to their own enclosure. Chaka's face lit up at the sight of her.

'Welcome, Mamo,' he said. 'Come sit with us and eat.' He cut off a choice piece of grilled buttock meat and offered it to her.

She was an old grey-haired Zulu woman with a gnarled body and an irritable face. Now she shook her head abruptly. 'How many virgins will there be left if *I* sit and talk?' she said crossly, bustling the last of the sisters through the door. She paused and turned to us. 'At *my* age! Herding them like sheep when I *should* be holding a grandson in my arms and teaching him how to be a king.' She gave my father and me a look of great scorn and said severely to Chaka: 'Even the White people know the worth of marriage.' With that she stalked from the hut, a frustrated and angry old lady.

Chaka smiled fondly after her. 'She is rightly called the Female Elephant,' he said. 'There is a *mother*! No one has ever had such a mother. I was once an outcast and she fought for me. Now I am a king and I would only have to ask, and old as she is she would lead my armies. A *woman* that one!' Then he sighed. 'She's been wanting me to marry for years.'

'Why don't you?' my father asked.

'And beget sons?' He turned to me. 'Would you murder your father?'

I shook my head, horrified.

'If he were a king you might *answer* the same but it would have no meaning. Few kings ever die of old age. Why breed your own murderers when there are already those living who were born for it?'

Although he was putting it obliquely, which was the way he often spoke, I was certain that he knew.

He nibbled at the meat his mother had refused but after toying with it for a moment threw it onto the platter and pushed it away. There were only the three of us now in the hut and we watched him in silence. At length he said: 'You worry about death, so do I. My death. Do you know what would happen to the Zulu nation if I died? It would disappear. I built it up, I made it strong—and only strength will maintain it. These people of mine are children and like children they have to be disciplined and

51

led. Do you think I don't know that the young man was innocent of fornication? You must take me for a fool. He died because his death was needed just then—his alone. He died because he was a nobody. His death has already been forgotten. It will cause no dissension. But if I had decided to put the culprit to death— or even put no one to death—my people would have been dismayed. I do not want a dismayed people at this time.'

He paused for a moment and my father and I shifted our positions on the floor. We had been straining to follow his reasoning.

'To the north are the Ndwandwes,' he continued. 'Their king, that dried-up old foreskin Zwide, has sworn to make us eat earth. I am not ready for them yet. They are too powerful. But soon my army will go to do battle with them and a nation at war must be a united one lest everything crumble and become dust. Do you understand me, Claw?'

'Yes, I understand.'

But I knew my father only understood the obvious point. He had not seen what I had seen.

'And so,' Chaka said, smiling a smile that was at once beguiling and alarming, 'there are times when I need to be harsh and when my people need to *see* me being harsh. And there is another thing. Our unity must *last*. It is not only for the Ndwandwes, although this is the first thing, but after we have conquered them there will be other crises and we shall have to stand together. That is why I am glad we are friends, Claw, because it will be your people who will come next.'

'You need have no worry about my people, nor will they come for a long time.'

'Sooner than you think,' Chaka said. 'Already they are moving like locusts, slowly at first and then faster and faster, eating up what stands before them.'

'You need have no fear,' my father replied. 'You are too powerful.'

Chaka smiled again, this time more grimly. 'I have no fear, Claw, because you are here. You know their ways but are not of them. You prefer to live here rather than among them. Therefore you will guide me.'

'I will do anything I can,' my father said.

'*Every*thing you can,' Chaka corrected him. 'That is why I let you stay.'

52

'I see,' my father said, frowning.

Chaka raised his hand. 'And also because I love you.' My father looked relieved.

The King drank a mouthful of sour milk and wiped his lips with the back of his hand. He made himself more comfortable on the pallet of skins. 'I am told, Claw, that your cattle wax fat and your crops grow tall. Is that so?'

'Not too badly,' my father replied, with all the innate caution of a farmer unwilling to tempt fate.

Chaka nodded slowly. 'See that you do not do *too* well,' he said. 'Jealousy is a troublesome thing and I wish to avoid trouble at this time. And remember this, there are some things which even I have not the power to change.' He paused for a long moment. 'The hunters of wizards grow impatient. It is because I love you that I also tell you this.' He waved his hand and the audience was at an end.

We did not go directly home but first travelled a mile or so to the westward to pick up two hoe blades which my father had ordered. The smith had his forge in a grove of euphorbia trees well out of the wind. There were several others waiting for ornaments and implements and after my father had tethered Violin he greeted them pleasantly and so did I. There were a few muttered responses; some did not even bother to reply, which was unusual. The smith told us briefly that the blades were not ready yet and might not be that day. My father, who has an uncertain temper, replied equally briefly that we would wait, so we sat down in the shade and watched the apprentices heating the iron in sandstone crucibles. They used leather bellows with nozzles made of eland horns and brought the charcoal up to a white heat before the iron was soft enough to work between two heavy rocks.

It was late in the afternoon before work on our hoes was started and almost nightfall before they were ready. I could see that my father, though he hadn't said much, was furious at the delay. It had been quite apparent that we were being deliberately overlooked and this was strange since we had always got on well with the chief smith, who right from the time of our coming to Zululand, had been fascinated by the steel from which my father's hook was made. Now, as he handed over the newly-made hoes he kept his eyes lowered and his lips closed and I got the impression that he didn't want to do business with us and yet at the same

53

time wasn't happy about the fact that he didn't. Anyway, my father told him curtly that the goats would be sent over the following day in payment and we picked up the hoes and left.

My father let me ride on the crupper and we hadn't gone more than a couple of miles before the dusk gave way to darkness. There was no moon but the stars were bright and anyway Violin knew her way home by now with her eyes closed. My father let the reins drop on her neck and we allowed our bodies to relax to the rhythm of her gait. We had been up since before dawn and we were exhausted.

I must have been half asleep because when I heard the shout I jerked upright so quickly I almost sent us both out of the saddle.

'What was that?' I asked.

'I don't know,' my father said. He brought Violin to a halt and we sat listening. We were in our own valley now and the rim of the rising moon was bathing everything in silver. Suddenly there was another shout, almost a scream, that ended in an abrupt gurgle.

'My God!' my father said. 'That's Izak!'

We couldn't make out the direction and as we sat staring about us at the moonlit veld there came a whole series of cries. But they were not cries of anger or fear, they were more like the calls a herdsman makes when he drives cattle. And then we heard the thudding of the hooves and the bellowing of running steers and the thought came into both our minds at the same time.

'Ndwandwes!' my father said hoarsely. 'They're stealing the beasts!'

The north-western end of our valley is shaped like the neck of a bottle and it was obvious that this was the direction in which the cattle were being run. Once through the neck the land gave way to a jumble of low hills and koppies in which a herd could be quickly lost. There was only one thing my father could do and that was to try and head them off.

'You wait here!' he shouted. 'And don't move!'

My feet had hardly touched ground before he was urging Violin forward and at the same time drawing his rifle from the long leather scabbard that hung at his saddle. One moment he was there and the next he was flitting through the grass and trees like the shadow of a fast-moving cloud and I was alone with the night all around me. I stood quite still and waited.

But I had never been out alone at night before. Always there

54

had been Stone-Axe with me so that I had never given a thought to my environment. Now I was afraid.

The sounds of the drumming hooves grew fainter and fainter. I heard a shot; then another; then silence.

I don't know how long I'd been standing still but it was long enough to make the first step an experience of incalculable dread. Here, in this grass that came up to my waist, night-adders would be hunting rats, leopards and lions awaiting the unwary buck, hyenas watching their chance—and *mambas*—what if there were mambas? But standing still was even worse than movement. I could see Ben Mhor outlined against the night sky and I began to work my way through the grass towards it. Bushes became buffaloes, branches pythons, thorns that scratched and tore became fangs. I began to run. But I ran softly, breathing carefully through my mouth so that my ears would pick up the first hint of an attack. They didn't help me, though, because the man was standing quite still under the lip of a donga and if I hadn't seen the sudden splash of white I would have run right into him. As it was I dropped like a falling hawk and lay silent in the long grass. I must have learnt more from Stone-Axe than I realised for he had not even heard me coming.

After a few moments I raised my head and stared at him through the grass stems. I couldn't clearly make out his face but the plume of egret feathers that rose from his head was all the indentification I needed. I had seen them earlier that day at Bulawayo and they had belonged to Dingane. He stood as still as rock with his head canted to one side, listening. Faintly came the sound of a gunshot and then silence settled on the veld again. Dingane turned and padded softly past me in the direction of Chaka's kraal.

It took me nearly an hour of hard running to reach Morile and at first I thought everyone must have evacuated it or been killed. Not a light showed. As I came up the slope I became aware of a shadow next to me and it was Stone-Axe bringing me safely in. The place was in a state of siege. My mother had brought Donald into the front room and was standing at one of the slit windows holding the heavy elephant gun. Cupido was guarding the back of the house and Stone-Axe had the fowling-piece which I knew he would have loaded with his own form of canister.

My mother put down her rifle and held me fiercely for a long moment, stroking my hair and patting my back, and then asked in an unnaturally shrill and angry voice where my father was. I told her what had happened, or at least what I knew of the events up to the time my father galloped across the valley.

Then we heard Violin coming up the slope and my father burst into the room like a wild man. He took in the scene with one glance, picked me up like a terrier grabbing a rat and shook me till my eyes popped.

'I thought I told you to stay put!' he shouted. 'I've a mind to skelp you black and blue!'

Instead he dropped me and went over to my mother and held her by the wrist. 'Are you all right, Fran?'

'Yes, yes. We're all right.' And then in a more strident tone: 'But you shouldn't have gone off like that by yourself! You might have been harmed!' And all the time she was stroking and patting the front of his coat. 'We heard the cattle and the shots.'

'Ndwandwes,' my father said.

'But they've never raided this far south before.'

'I know. Anyway, they didn't get everything. Ran like devils when they heard the gun and I managed to turn the beasts as they were going into the hills. We've lost some, of course, ten or a dozen, but it might have been worse. We'll go after them in the morning, there's no hope now.'

'Father . . .' I began.

'I don't want to hear a single word from you!'

'But Father . . .'

'Are you deaf!'

'Let the boy speak, Jamie,' my mother said. 'Don't frighten him any more.'

'Well, what is it?'

'They weren't Ndwandwes, Father.'

'What nonsense are you at now?'

So I told him everything. What I'd seen at Bulawayo and then later in the valley. As I talked his face became grimmer. When I had finished he said in a softer voice: 'Thank you, son. I'm sorry I shouted.'

'But what does it *mean*?' my mother said, and you could hear her worry and apprehension.

My father shook his head. 'I don't know. I don't know at all. But you're not to get all fashed up. Just leave it to me.' He turned to Stone-Axe. 'Come, we'll look for Izak's body.'

This was the first of a series of events that overtook us in the months to come. Each was scarcely significant by itself but when you put them all together it did seem to point to a programme of attrition. No act was on the same scale as the attempt to run off our cattle and this made us believe at first that it bore no relationship to future occurrences but stood alone. However, when it became apparent that there were distinct motives behind each act we came to the conclusion that there was a link. Those among the Zulus who were irritated by our presence in their country took Dingane's attempt on the cattle as a sign that we were not completely under Chaka's armpit.

And so we would wake up in the morning and find that a boulder had rolled itself into the irrigation furrow or that by magic a fire had burnt down part of the corn or that a heifer had broken its leg on perfectly flat veld; things like that. With each new incident my father's eyes became angrier, my mother's face more drawn.

After one particularly unpleasant occurrence—the putrid carcass of a wildcat was found in the spring that fed the house—my mother appealed to my father to go to Chaka.

'Like a snot-nosed child?' he retorted angrily. 'Leave this to me, Fran!'

It wasn't really possible for my father to go to Chaka. The King was preparing for war with the Ndwandwes and our troubles would only be an irritating distraction. In any event he would already know what was going on. If he wanted to stop it, he could. But why should he? We were the intelligent and well-armed White people whose civilisation was said to be so advanced; why couldn't *we* stop it? Or at least that's how I imagined he would think. It might have been different if my father had told him of Dingane's raid, but even that was doubtful. We were strangers in the land and no one, especially not Chaka, would take kindly to accusations against his own family even if they were true and even if he did not already know. As my father often repeated, this was something we might have expected—since foreigners were welcome nowhere in the world—and we would just have to work it out ourselves.

And then two things happened which both depressed and confused us. The first was that Tanga no longer came over to Morile for his lessons. Since the cattle raid, now that I look back on it, he had cut his visits from three or four times a week to one or two. We didn't think much of it at the time since Zulus are an unpredictable people, but then one day when my mother was teaching me long division she suddenly said: 'Oh dear, what *are* we going to do about Tanga? You're getting so far ahead now.' And we realised that he had not been to visit us for more than a week.

That afternoon I took Stone-Axe with me and went to Ngwadi's kraal to look for him. It was exactly the same as always. The women were pounding the corn in the deep hollow stones, the men were doing each other's hair or working on their shields and assegais. The children were playing between the huts.

I knew several of the adults by sight and most of the children from having played with them. '*Sakubona,*' I said, smiling my greetings.

No one replied. The women stopped their pounding, the men looked up from their work and worst of all the children ceased their antics and stood in a small huddle watching me. Then one of the men laughed and made a disparaging remark about the 'bush-caffre' as the Zulus called the Bushmen. I watched Stone-Axe out of the corner of my eye but he was too careful and excellent a hunter to let angry emotions upset him. We went forward in dead silence to the high stockade that surrounded Ngwadi's private apartments. As we reached the gate he came forward to greet us.

'*Sakubona umlunghu,*' he said with unusual formality.

'*Sakubona*, Ngwadi. I have come to see what ails Tanga.'

His thin face wore a worried frown and he did not look directly at me when he spoke. 'Tanga is away,' he said. 'He is visiting his grandmother.'

But even as he spoke I saw a flash of brown at the doorway of one of the furthest huts and for a second I looked into Tanga's eyes. Then, as quickly, the head was withdrawn.

Later, I told my mother what had happened and she nodded unhappily. 'It's part of a whole,' she said.

The second thing was a visit paid to us by Mgobozi-of-the-Hill. We had not seen him for many months, which was hardly surprising. Chaka had given him permission to marry and Mgobozi had astounded everyone by marrying twenty brides at the same time. To demonstrate the esteem in which he held Mgobozi, Chaka had himself paid the dowries in cattle. However, his action was not as altruistic as it might first have seemed for, hearing of his liberality to a man not of the Zulu clan, soldiers of fortune began to pour into Bulawayo to swell the ranks of the Zulu regiments.

Anyway, the point is that on his wedding day Mgobozi told each of his betrothed that wherever her hut was placed in his kraal, there he would be found. It was trying to fulfil this boast which had kept Mgobozi at home and it was said that not even the Hammer of Chaka could satisfy all of his wives all of the time. He was looking quite a bit thinner and a little peaky around the mouth when he came to visit us. We thought it was just an excuse to leave the multiple marriage bed for a while but this was not so. Mgobozi-of-the-Hill was known for his brave actions and none, I think, was more courageous than coming to visit us at that time.

His presence was announced by a loud whoop from Stone-Axe. 'Behold!' he cried, jumping to his feet and running down towards the visitor. 'It is the Great Fornicator! Terror of the Marriage Bed! Frightener of Virgins!' And then he held up his thumb and forefinger and waggled them under Mgobozi's nose. My father laughed out loud and went to the door. 'Welcome, Mgobozi,' he said. 'Come in and rest yourself, I'm sure you need it.'

At any other time Mgobozi would have enjoyed the joke but now his broad face wore a solemn and worried expression. '*Sakubona*, Iron Hand,' he said. 'I bring you cattle.' At the foot of the hill grazed eleven cows. My father looked first at them then at Mgobozi then back to the cattle. 'Eleven,' he said. 'That's a strange number though I thank you very greatly.'

Mgobozi looked steadily at my father. 'A small enough gift for a friend,' he said. Eleven was exactly the tally we had lost in the raid some months before.

He and my father sat in the cool of the living-room drinking sour milk and at last Mgobozi said: 'I came up through the valley and the land looks fat. The crop is good, the cattle are like Chaka's own.'

My father nodded. 'It could be worse,' he said. This was a grudging understatement, for the fact was that in spite of our setbacks our stock and crops were burgeoning. The main reasons for this were that my father had practised large-scale manure fertilisation, little-known among the Zulus, who dried the cow-pats for fuel, and had developed a form of silage with which he hand-fed the stock in winter when the grass was burnt off.

'It is said,' Mgobozi continued steadily, 'that Claw's cattle are even better than the King's.'

'I wouldn't go so far as to say that,' my father intervened hastily.

'It is also asked why, in this season when the crops are not good and the cattle are not fat, those of the white man are beyond description.'

'Now look here, Mgobozi—'

'Can it be that more rain falls on the white man's land, or that the soil is richer, the sun more bright?'

'I don't care for—'

'Or is it the white man's gods or the white man's king who watches over him even so far from home. Or—'

'Enough!'

I have already remarked that Mgobozi was ill-fitted for intrigue. He was a simple soldier and happiest with an assegai in his hand. But he had seen his duty and nothing was going to divert his purpose. His face wore a look of total misery as he went on. 'Or,' and he pointed his finger at my father, 'or is the white man a wizard.' Even as he said the word his voice developed a quiver of fear.

My father breathed harshly through his nose. 'Is that what they're saying? Is that why they think? The poor fools! Why, if they would only watch and learn—'

Mgobozi held up his hand. 'I have only asked a question of myself,' he said softly.

My father collected himself. 'Yes, yes, I'm sorry. I know you mean well. And thank you for your warning though I think it comes a trifle late.' He told Mgobozi of the other incidents which had plagued us and finally of the foetid wild-cat corpse which had so upset my mother.

Mgobozi jerked upright. 'An *impaka*!' His eyes grew round with fright and one could almost see him go several shades lighter. 'That is an evil thing. There are some who wish you dead.'

'Good God, just because my cattle are fat and my crops grow tall! What sort of people are these!'

'Is there no jealousy among white people?'

'Yes, of course there is. But—'

'I cannot stay longer,' Mgobozi said, rising to his feet. 'The King arrived back at Bulawayo yesterday from attending the

60

death of his foster-father Mbiya. During his absence a *hammer-kop* flew over the kraal and then came a porcupine. A crow was heard to talk human words. Two of the King's herd were killed by lightning. The omens are bad, Iron Hand. There are wizards abroad.' He paused before leaving the house and turned. 'Be prepared,' he said. 'There are times when even the Hammer of Chaka is like a blade of grass.' And with that he was gone.

For the remainder of the day my father kept to the house. He and Stone-Axe heated a mixture of lead and tin in the stone crucible and spent an hour or two moulding a supply of bullets. Then Stone-Axe, with deft fingers, sewed them into small greased leather pouches for easy loading.

'There's nothing to worry about,' my father said when my mother expressed agitation. 'You can't hang a man because his cows give more milk than his neighbour's.'

'What do you know of these people? What do you know of what they can or what they can't do?'

'You'll see, it'll all blow over.'

But it didn't blow over, for later that day Mbopa, the shrewd major-domo of Chaka's kraal wheezed his way to the top of Ben Mhor to tell us Chaka demanded my father's presence the following day and he was to bring me with him.

'I told you,' my mother said fearfully, after Mbopa had gone. 'I said there was something wrong!'

'Don't be silly, Fran. How many times haven't I been summoned to Chaka?'

'But not by the head of his court.'

'The messenger is neither here nor there.' But I knew my father's moods as well as my mother and we were not fooled.

I suppose I was just young enough not to grasp exactly what was happening and therefore what our ultimate fate could be, but children take their worry from their parents and so, as I lay in bed that night I began to grow more and more frightened. My heart nearly stopped altogether when I heard a scratching at the window slit.

At first I tried to ignore it by putting my head beneath the blankets but my imagination immediately became worse than reality. The scratching went on and at last I jumped from my bed and was about to run into the other room when I heard a voice whisper my name. I clambered up to the window and saw a face peering at me through the slit. It was Tanga. He must have been holding himself up by his arms for he was breathing heavily and there was great strain on his face.

'What is it?' I said, bewildered. 'What do you want?'

'Listen,' he hissed. 'There's no time. You go to Bulawayo to-morrow.'

I nodded.

'Remember the mound,' he said. 'Touch it in need. Remember the mound!' And then the strength went out of his arms and I heard him drop down into the grass. I was more confused than ever.

I'm not sure what we expected to find at Bulawayo the following morning but that it was something greatly unusual we had little doubt, for the whole of Zululand seemed to be on the move. As we made our way down the valley on Violin we saw that every path was choked with men, all hurrying towards Chaka's kraal. No one greeted us, in fact no one even seemed to see us. Each hurrying figure was wrapped in himself, unaware of his neighbours. There was a sense of fear over the land.

We left Violin at the gate of the kraal as usual and one of the guards indicated that my father should leave his gun in its saddle scabbard. There was no use pretending now. We weren't just being called to have a chat and a bowl of milk with the King, which is what my father had insisted to my mother, and as we went forward into the arena he dropped his hand on to my shoulder and smiled down at me. It is at moments like this that I like best to remember him.

The first thing to be said is that there were probably about thirty thousand people already in the arena—all of them men—and hundreds more were arriving every minute. Without being told they had formed themselves, like the regiments already there, into great horse-shoe lines facing Chaka. He was seated on the Royal Mound surrounded by his councillors. I could see Dingane, Mdlaka, the King's Army commander, Mbopa, Mgobozi-of-the-Hill and several others, including Jacob Sumbiti, the interpreter.

Chaka pretended not to notice our arrival. His expression, as he looked out over the completely silent multitude, was bleak, and for the first time that morning I felt really afraid.

But Mgobozi had seen us and for the second time in two days he made his position clear. He came down from the group, collected us, and made room for us to sit at his left side, which made me feel better. Although we could not have been more than three yards from the King we might not have existed for all the notice he took. No one else except Mdlaka, a warrior of almost as great reknown as Mgobozi himself, gave us greeting—and then it was only the briefest nod.

All at once Chaka rose to his feet and began to speak. Standing there on his mound with the lory feathers waving in the slight breeze and towering above everyone else, he made a terrifying sight. 'The omens have been read,' he called out. 'There is evil at large in the land. It is evil that seeks to destroy even the King himself.' Then he raised his toy spear and waved it over the throng. 'Let the witch-finders seek out the evil and destroy it!'

As one the people answered with a low fearful moan and then silence again fell on the arena. Almost immediately came a series of frantic shrieks, and three grotesque figures bounded into the centre of the horse-shoe, gyrating and whirling and sending up clouds of dust. At first I could not make them out but as they came nearer I saw they were women, if that simple word can be stretched to the limits of its power to define them. They were monsters, travesties of womanhood, misshapen hags from a nightmare world of freakish extravagance. They were painted with streaks of white clay and wore bladders in their hair and on their arms. Snake skins hung from their wrists and goats' horns from their necks. Each held a switch from the tail of a wildebeeste in her right hand and as they danced and leaped their flat, withered breasts flapped against their ribs like pouches of dried leather.

Like everyone else in that vast space I was horror-struck by their performance and it took me a few moments to realise that their leader was the old woman who had come to us to sell us charms for our crops and whom my father had so brusquely dismissed. And I realised something else : this same malevolent old hag was someone whose name even Chaka had mentioned with apprehension. She was Nobela, the chief witch-finder among the Zulu people, known throughout the country as the Mother of Fear.

Now the three diviners were joined in the centre of the horse-shoe by six enormous slayers, each of whom held a bundle of long wooden slivers in one hand and a club in the other. The smelling-out began.

Slowly, at first, the hags started an intricate dance pattern, one following the other in a series of convolutions and figures of eight which, as their speed increased, seemed to flow into each other like the coils of a moving snake. And all the time they danced they made a hissing noise through their teeth, every now and then bounding high into the air and uttering unearthly shrieks. The dance grew faster and faster and they seemed to be working themselves into a state of frenzy and just at the time when their limbs were flying in all directions and it seemed they must either fall down in exhaustion or foam at the mouth and let the fit overwhelm them, they suddenly stopped dead. Slowly they turned outwards and let their eyes roam over the avenues of people. Terror became an almost palpable thing.

Then, without a word being uttered, they began to chant: 'We are the seekers of evil. We are the *ingosamas*, the finders of witches. We have noses like the jackal and the wild dog and we can smell the smell of evil. We can smell it in the sky and on the ground. We can smell it in the grass and in the trees, on the hills and in the rivers. Sniff . . . ! Sniff . . . ! We can smell it here among us! We can smell a great evil in the land!' And they raised their faces and sniffed all around them and at last Nobela shouted: 'Chant! Chant! We the dogs of Chaka wish to smell! We wish to smell the breath of evil!'

And the whole throng began to chant in a low tone and the diviners moved down the avenues, each taking a different segment of the horse-shoe.

At first they toyed with the people for effect. They stopped in front of individuals and sniffed at their breath, then moved on or came back to repeat the sniffing—an act which often pushed an already terrified man to the brink of collapse—and you could see the diviners were really enjoying themselves. It was only on rare occasions that they could perform their deadly offices before so great an audience and it was in their interest to fix these moments indelibly in the corporate mind, so enhancing the significance of their occult powers.

From where we were sitting, at the higher end of the slope, we could look down upon the serried ranks of Zulus. Sometimes we lost sight of the diviners as they threaded their way in and out of the avenues but it was easy to tell where they were since their presence in a given area caused a stir of movement, like wheat flowing in a gentle breeze.

And then a strange thing began to happen. The throng had

kept up its low chanting right from the first command but at certain moments it rose and fell. I first became aware of it when Nobela stopped before a man called Nokaka, a minor kraal head who lived some miles from us and who was known for his wealth.

As she capered there in front of him the chant almost unconsciously began to swell. Nobela moved on and the volume of sound diminished. She came back to him and once again the threnody increased. Nokaka himself began to tremble. And then, with a tremendous standing leap Nobela hurled herself into the air and jumped clean over his head, touching him with the wildebeeste switch as she did so. This was the signal. Before he could make a move the slayers had gripped his arms and the long sharpened sticks were being driven up his anus.

The executions began. Some were clubbed to death, some tortured, and one man, a farmer who had come to my father for guidance and now used manure on his field instead of buying spells from the diviners, was tied to a post and strangled with a leather thong.

All the time the chanting continued and the diviners scurried in and out of the ranks, sniffing like dogs at their victims. Each time the chant rose a man was killed, each time it dropped the diviners moved on to someone else. It became apparent that, whether they knew it or not, the Zulus were giving expression to feelings of jealousy or envy and the victims were almost all wealthy or clever men. By noon more than twenty bodies had been carted off to the outskirts of the kraal.

My father and I had been watching the dreadful ceremony with a mixture of fascination and loathing but the one thing we had failed to realise was that the witch-finders had been working to a carefully organised plan. They had moved through the back ranks first, slowly making their way to the front of the horse-shoe. Suddenly they had finished their work among the crowd and now faced the court and councillors itself. I heard a low rumble of anger from Mgobozi and saw Mdlaka shift his seat uneasily.

I suppose that until then we had felt partially safe where we were. If we *had* given it any thought we might have considered our invitation to be meant as a lesson in tribal justice, or to show us that there was an added dimension in Zulu life of which we were not aware and not a part.

What I had never thought to see was fear on Mgobozi's face. But as the witch-finders moved along the lines of councillors his eyes grew wide and the great muscles of his thighs and arms began to twitch. I looked hastily around me and found that everyone in the royal enclosure, including even Chaka himself, was, if not actually sweating with fear, at least uncomfortable. They looked almost mesmerised and I remembered both Chaka and Mgobozi saying that there were some things against which even they could not save us. Was that it then? Was this a gigantic charade with only one end in view—our deaths? But it couldn't be! If Chaka wanted us dead he had only to snap his fingers and we would be wiped from the face of the earth.

Or was it a combination of things? I cannot profess to have known the answer then but looking back it would seem that the smelling-out at that particular time was the vehicle for two policies: the first was Chaka's wish to cement the Zulu nation into a single entity in the face of the imminent Ndwandwe invasion. Cleverly he had used the omens as a sign that there was disunity and, knowing the depths of superstition among his people, was aware that fear was the greatest of all binding threads. Secondly, Nobela was using the ceremony to enhance her own power. As long as she did not come into open conflict with Chaka he would give her rein; but where was her line to be drawn?

It was one thing to single out unpopular individuals among the mass of the people, quite another to mount an attack on the heads of the civil and military administrations at that moment gathered around the King. But therein would lie the real fruits of her victory.

Slowly the three hags capered their way along the lines of councillors and soldiers, stopping every now and then to look deeply into their horrified faces and smell their breaths—for even their mouths were open to the throbbing chant. They made their way towards us. They stopped at Mdlaka and the chanting dropped to an almost imperceptible level. They moved on. They checked in front of Mgobozi and this time the chanting ceased altogether for no one was more popular than the Hammer of Chaka. They were almost on top of us now and I could see the hate in Nobela's eyes as she smelled Mgobozi's breath and I thought of him coming up to Morile to warn us and I thought of him taking us under his armpit earlier that morning when we came to Bulawayo. Was he going to die because he had shown us friendship?

At that moment I'm sure if he felt anything at all it must

have been the very wings of death itself for his whole body was shaking and his eyes were locked on Nobela's. And suddenly Chaka said softly : 'Listen to me, Mother of Fear, seek not among my tried and trusted friends for evil or I will begin my own smelling-out and where that will end no man can tell.'

'The mediums of the wizard can be the closest of all, O King,' Nobela replied tartly.

'Mark well what I say,' Chaka growled.

This seemed to infuriate Nobela to the point of frenzy for she leaped angrily in the air three times before coming to land in front of my father. As if in a dream I heard the chant begin again and slowly rise to a crescendo of sound.

They were on top of us now and their rank body smell filled the air. I shrank back against my father and I felt Mgobozi's reassuring hand on my other arm.

Close-up Nobela was the very incarnation of evil. Sweat dripped down her face streaking the white clay. Her eyes were red and mad-looking. Her body was covered in brown dust and as she gyrated her breasts flapped grotesquely in my face. I wanted to scream and bury my head under blankets, to run wildly away into the hills, to jump into a foaming river, to escape forever from manic black bodies and burning eyes; for it was her eyes that were the most frightening thing about her. The purple pupils filled the cavities and were bottomless, so that when she looked at me I seemed to be drawn forward into the very eyes themselves and to fall down . . . and down . . .

And above all was the chanting. Louder and louder. Was this then to be her victory? Would our deaths add to her power?

They began to play with us, grovelling in the dust to smell our ankles, running around behind us to sniff at the backs of our necks. And then they whirled away in skipping steps further up the line to where Mbopa and Dingane were sitting together. But with the sudden fall in the chant they turned and ran back to us and the accusing voices rose again. They did this three times and I could feel my father shift his weight so that he came up on his haunches. His left arm, with the dangerous hook, he held straight down at his side as though hiding the only weapon we possessed between us.

The three witch-finders drew out their moment of triumph for as long as they could, until the droning of the chant had almost succeeded in hypnotising the mass of the people; and then they acted. In a series of incredible leaps the three hags bounded into the air one after the other, each striking my father once in the face with her wildebeeste switch.

What happened next was so fast that it remains now in my mind as a blur. Turning with the speed of a leopard, Mgobozi scooped me off the ground and in a single fluid motion flung me cartwheeling through the air to land in a tangle at Chaka's feet. At the same moment I heard his great roar go out over the throng : 'He has touched the Mound! He has touched the Mound!' In that split second I realised what Tanga had meant the previous evening.

'Father!' I screamed. 'Get to the Mound! Get to sanctuary!'

For the first time in my life, I saw an explosive force revealed. I don't think he could have managed it if the slayers had not been momentarily confused by Mgobozi's sudden and unexpected action, but they were, and by the time they had recovered and come in to take him, my father was ready. What they didn't realise was that here was a man who was not solidified by fear and who would not stand meekly still while his brains were dashed out. Two ran forward and the first was dead with his throat torn out before he knew what had happened to him. The second, my father picked up in his arms and flung at Nobela, knocking her sideways into the dust. In the confusion he made several paces towards the Mound and might even have reached it had he not tripped over Dingane's feet. I still don't know whether this was done deliberately or not but it does not matter, it happened. My father went down and the four remaining slayers ran in for the kill. I saw a club rise and fall.

'Si-gi-di! Si-gi-di!' The tremendous Zulu war-cry rang in our ears and with a running leap Mgobozi-of-the-Hill flung himself into the mass of writhing bodies. He struck left and right sending the slayers sprawling across the ground. He pulled my father to his feet and I could see the blood pouring down from a wound on his head.

Nobela was almost demented with anger and frustration. 'Kill!' she screamed. 'Kill the wizards!'

The slayers swooped in from different angles but now they met a resolute defence. Mgobozi and my father stood shoulder to shoulder. I saw Mgobozi take one in his arms and I heard the crack as a backbone snapped; I saw a glint of bloody steel and heard a scream as entrails poured from a ripped paunch. I saw

Mgobozi take another and lift him high above his head and crash him down on to the hard-baked ground so he lay there shattered and twitching. My father was holding his left wrist in his right hand and using the hook with the strength of both arms. He swung it like a claymore, hacking and chopping and smashing sideways with the back of it.

Nothing could stand in their way and like magic a path opened in the ranks of the councillors, and suddenly they were there with me on the Mound at Chaka's feet and only two slayers were left alive.

As my father and Mgobozi fell face down on the clay a great shout went up from the Zulus who were a fighting race and who had never seen a fight like this.

I looked up and saw Chaka's face and his eyes were alive and smiling. He bent to help Mgobozi to his feet and with his other hand he took my shoulder. 'Hear me, my children!' he shouted. 'They have sought sanctuary as is the custom and it has been granted. They are now under *my* armpit and those who fail to remember it will eat earth. I have spoken!'

'It is the will of the Great Elephant!' the crowd responded.

He turned to Nobela who was squatting like a black bundle of malice where she had fallen. 'Do you agree that they have secured rightful sanctuary according to the laws of the land?'

'Yes, O King,' she said through her teeth.

'What have you to say then? It seems that you wrongly accused the white man and his son.'

'No, Lord, it was thus. These two were the innocent and therefore the most dangerous mediums of an evil wizard but the spirits came to their aid and so enabled them to throw out the witchcraft from their bodies. How else could they have had the power to overwhelm the slayers?'

'Nobela, you have always had a clever tongue, but perhaps it is the only clever thing about you. Did I not tell you to beware of those closest to me?'

'Yes, Lord.'

'Then perhaps your ears are stopped up by the lies you and your fraternity are always hearing. Perhaps they need to be washed.' He turned to the crowd which was now in a state of euphoria. 'Should we wash them for her?' he called, and the answer that came rolling back was unmistakeable. Chaka nodded to four of his bodyguard and the chief of the diviners was carried

69

kicking and shrieking to the river at the bottom of the kraal. About half of the assembled populace ran down to see the perpetration of the final indignity.

I would like to have witnessed it myself; perhaps I might have had a chance to hold her head under water while they really got her ears clean, but at that moment there was a commotion at the gate and a dust-covered warrior ran up through the arena and threw himself down at Chaka's feet. I found out later that he had been running for half a night and a day, for the news he brought was grave : the Ndwandwes were preparing the invasion of Zululand.

I have recounted what happened that day at some length because it was an important turning point in our lives. We had been through the fire and come out unscathed. We were seen to be close to the King and we were accepted as such. It was as simple as that. Or was it?

It was only later, when I began to think about it, that I saw what had really happened that day. We had just been pawns in the power struggle between the secular and spiritual (if such a word can be used to describe a philosophy of superstition) forces within the State. Chaka had known what he wanted and he had achieved it. First he had bound his people by fear then bound them even tighter by removing the fear. And at the same time he had chopped off a great deal of Nobela's power. Had he wished he could have killed the three diviners then and there without transgressing the traditional code, but he was never like that. One day he might need Nobela again.

But one thing remains to haunt me. If we had not known about the Mound, would Chaka have helped us?

Book Two

The King's Man

Strike an enemy once and for all. Let him cease to exist as a tribe or he will live to fly at your throat again.

CHAKA

By 1824 I was in my early youth and in many ways as much a young Zulu as Tanga or the others except for a black skin. I often wished I did have one, mainly I suppose, because boys of that age don't like being different. But there were also more practical reasons. With a black skin you didn't have to worry about the fierceness of the sun in summer. Without one I was made to feel slightly inferior. I remember Chaka once saying to my father that he felt sorry for us; he was convinced that somewhere in the past we had incurred the displeasure of the Spirits and good black skins had been withheld. Tanga was always rubbing his body with mutton fat or butter and it used to glisten in the sunlight. I tried it once but only succeeded in covering myself with dirty streaks and my father said I smelt like a dead jackal and made me go down to the stream and wash. It took several days before I began to smell like myself again.

We had now been in Zululand going on for ten years and we had become part of the landscape. Starting from the time Mgobozi had stood shoulder to shoulder with my father at the smelling-out we had rapidly been absorbed into the Zulu social structure and now it seemed as though we had never known anything else. We all spoke the language fluently, we had all learnt the customs and taboos—so that we no longer ignorantly transgressed good manners—and we had friends. There was Mgobozi, of course, and Ngwadi and Tanga and Mdlaka, the army leader, and Chaka himself, who continued to smile upon us.

Whenever we went to Chaka's kraal we were unable to avoid meeting Mbopa but since the King's public demonstration of affection his attitude had changed to one of fawning camaraderie. Neither we nor our friends cared much for him but there was no denying he was a brilliant administrator and he kept Chaka's kraal running smoothly. We saw almost nothing of Dingane who lived in his own kraal and this suited us very well. Some years after the cattle raid the rumour reached us that he had given the plundered stock to Mbopa. This confirmed my reading of the events at that execution of one of Chaka's 'sisters'.

Zululand then was a secure and viable state at that time. Chaka still ruled by fear and I was still nauseated by the show of power he would often put on for our benefit but I am bound to say that we grew used to the sight of casual executions and with each one the enormity of the act diminished. We did nothing to try and make our position in these matters very clear and I am not proud of that.

There was no question but that my father felt safe in Chaka's domain and I suppose that if safety is not too ludicrous a term to apply to one's existence in a dictatorship where a smile at the wrong moment could mean instant death, then we were safe enough.

However, the Ndwandwes were a bother. In the first war the Zulus, while numerically inferior, had been the marginal victors —though their victory had cost them dear. It had been a tactical triumph for Chaka, and Mgobozi would have a place forever in the tribal memory for his feats of arms, especially at the Battle of Qokli Hill. To hear him tell it you might have thought he did it every day and twice on Sundays just for exercise, and Tanga and I often sat at his feet and made him tell it to us all over again. I once asked him whether it was more tiring fighting in the front line of a Zulu regiment or engaging in the battle of the blankets with twenty amorous wives and he caught me a gentle cuff around the ear which knocked me flat and made my head sing for two days. I only found out later that few of his wives were producing infants at the standard annual rate and that Chaka had jokingly asked him if he'd like one or two of the Belebele Brigade to help him out.

The importance of the First Ndwandwe War was two-fold; it was the first real battle the Zulu Army had engaged in and therefore the first real test of Chaka's military tactics. It lasted for more than two days near the White Umfolosi River to the north of Morile and it was a triumph for the Zulus, whose army of four thousand faced a force nearly twice as large.

Chaka first of all placed part of his heavy regiments at each of the river fords and at the same time got the Zulu women to put food and water supplies on Qokli Hill, some distance from the river, a natural strategic fortress.

When the Ndwandwes attacked through the water they were immediately set at a disadvantage and lost hundreds before they forced a crossing-point. Instead of continuing the battle, as the Ndwandwe leaders expected, Chaka lured them on to Qokli Hill. The battle there was fought the following day in intense heat and by the afternoon thirst was the decisive factor. The Zulus broached their caches of water but the nearest water for the Ndwandwes was the river, and they began to drift there in twos and threes and finally in greater numbers.

At once the Zulus counter-attacked. The chest-and-horns formation was used and Mgobozi, leading the Fasimbas, 'closed the gate' and the Ndwandwes were trapped. Had Chaka more men he might have put paid to the Ndwandwe power there and then but when they broke through the Zulus and took to the hills at least a third of their number was intact. No one quite knew how many warriors Mgobozi had slaughtered. When they finally found him he was blissfully unconscious, almost suffocating beneath a mound of slain.

At any rate the Ndwandwes were very far from being defeated and Chaka's continuing references to their king as an old dried-up foreskin kept their battle spirits up.

In a way it was just as well there *were* enemies who needed fighting every now and then because Chaka had built up several more regiments like the Plovers, the Cockroaches and the Expellers and even one or two women's regiments like the Ripen-at-Noon and the Self-Admirers and often at moments of peace he would sit moodily in his palace and complain at such length that they were eating him out of house and home that you got a mental picture of thousands of champing jaws leaving the countryside as bare as locusts. If the Ndwandwes hadn't been ideally situated over his northern border he would have had to find some other tribe to fight and since no one else was too keen, it would have been trying.

I remember these years as being the only really happy ones of my youth. Though Tanga no longer joined me for lessons—he had early detected the fatuousness of education—he, Stone-Axe and I were frequently in each other's company: hunting, fishing or helping my father.

It was at this time that I nearly had my first sexual experience. It was inherent in Zulu philosophy that both male and female needed sexual release and this was condoned even among children as a natural bodily function. There was nothing dirty about it, in fact it was quite joyous and one casual form of intercourse between strangers was actually called 'the fun of the roads'. And then there was spiritual intercourse mandatory for every warrior who had killed his man in battle. Before he could rejoin his regiment he had to 'wipe the axe'. However, there was no looseness of morals, except perhaps among the King's sisters, for adultery was punishable by death and so was recklessness. Zulu tradition demanded that intercourse between unmarried couples should occur on the exterior of the pudenda. Any man who deflowered a woman was signing both their death warrants.

I learnt about this just as I learnt about the other Zulu customs and it seemed to me then, and still does, an eminently reasonable compromise.

It's all very well to be dispassionate about it now, but then I was just coming into my sexual powers and was as nervous as a bushbaby about the whole affair.

I suppose one reason was that I was very big for my age— almost as tall as my father—and every time we went to Bulawayo and sat in Chaka's hut at least one, or perhaps even two, of his sisters would try to feel me as she slithered about the hut on her hands and knees. It was extremely embarrassing as well as highly dangerous because Chaka would have made her eat earth if he'd seen. My father told me afterwards that it was because there were so many of them that Chaka couldn't satisfy them all, but that didn't help at the time. There's nothing like being interfered with by a woman when you don't want to be for putting you off a thing.

It was probably this that made me backward and it caught up with me one day when Tanga and I were on the road from Ngwadi's kraal. We had stopped at a stream to dangle our feet in the water. It was a hot afternoon with great fleecy clouds in the sky and we were both drowsy from the beer we had drunk at the mid-day meal. We lay down and watched the clouds drifting overhead and then we heard someone laugh and we looked up and saw two young Zulu girls bathing in a pool about fifty yards away. They were quite naked, which ordinarily wasn't anything new at all, but then they started beckoning to us and suddenly their nakedness took on a more sinister aspect. They began to call to us in high singing voices and I heard Tanga laugh.

76

I knew what that singing was supposed to do—it was supposed to excite us.

'Come on,' Tanga said, getting to his feet.

'Come on where?'

'The fun of the roads,' he said. 'It is our custom.'

'I know all about your custom. I'll stay here and throw stones.'

'They will laugh at you.'

'I don't care.' I did really, because I half wanted to go and half didn't.

'They will think white men are ashamed.'

'Ashamed of what?'

'You know.'

'Well, I'm not.'

All the time the girls had been coming nearer and singing and making gestures with their arms and I began to feel rather warm under my leather jerkin and found it difficult to get enough air into my lungs.

'You think I've never done this before?' I asked with a nervous laugh.

The girls really were quite exceptional. They were about fourteen or fifteen and just the right age for a Zulu woman. Their skins were still shining wet from the water and black as ebony. They were smiling quite unashamedly and obviously looking forward to what was going to happen. It really was quite a pleasure to look at them. Anyway, Tanga took his behind some rocks and I walked downstream a bit until we came to an area of soft grass hedged by bush. My heart was hammering in my ears like a woodpecker and my knees felt spongy.

'*Sakubona*,' I said because I couldn't think of anything else.

'You're big,' she said, looking at me like a cat.

She began fingering my clothing which reminded me of the sisters and I thought if she goes on doing this it's going to put me off, so I pulled the jerkin over my head.

'You're brown like the *aBathwa*,' she said, meaning the Bushman.

'It's the sun,' I said, fumbling hurriedly at my trousers.

Her eyes widened with surprise. 'You're red,' she said, pointing. 'Red!' and she gave a delighted laugh and came forward, calling to her friend to come and witness this strange manifestation. I pulled on my clothes and jumped up the bank of the river and ran towards our valley like a hunted kudu. Later, in the secrecy of Tanga's cave I relieved myself in the usual way—and as usual felt frightened afterwards.

This was happening more and more frequently and there was no question but that some new force had arrived in my body that needed an outlet. I think what frightened me was the strength of the force.

I have always looked upon myself as being part Zulu and I suppose the person mainly responsible for this was Mgobozi-of-the-Hill. Ever since as a child I had first tickled his hand to gain the shining pebble there was a warmth between us that I have experienced with very few people. He lived some miles from us in his own separate kraal and it was towards that small community that I was now more frequently drawn.

From this distance I cannot hope to differentiate between his womenfolk, they were so numerous, and I'm not sure whether I could at the time; suffice it to say that when in my mind's eye I try to picture Mgobozi at that time he is framed by a freize of naked buttocks and breasts—all belonging to different owners. In any case, it was as the great Hammer of Chaka that he attracted me, not as a bridegroom. I was of an age for hero worship and no boy could have discovered a better hero outside the pages of a romance. If Stone-Axe knew everything about the world of the veld, Mgobozi knew everything about warfare.

In his own home Mgobozi might have passed as an ordinary citizen—perhaps more wealthy than most, for Chaka was forever sending him presents of livestock. He lived simply as did all Zulus, rich or poor, though his couch was richly padded with lion skins. The floor of his own hut was covered in rush matting and here his wives came by turns to clean, cook and generally care for him, and it was here, in the dark, smoke-stained interior, still smelling of its last dung fire, that I would often come on hot summer afternoons and listen to his talk. It was always of battles or great hunts. The hours would slip away unnoticed and frequently, before I knew it, I would be sitting with the others around the evening porridge pot, using one of the wooden spoons that stuck at intervals in the thatch ceiling. Afterwards I would lick it as clean as I had found it and replace it with care.

As I grew older he used to take me with him for training sessions with his beloved Fasimba regiment. They were all young men, whose energies reached bursting point cooped up in one or other of the huge military barracks, and they liked nothing better than to go on manœuvres with Mgobozi: I say manœuvres, but this hardly covers their activities, since there was little formal training in the Zulu Army.

Mgobozi used to organise dances for the men in which they were able to develop suppleness and grace, two enormous advantages in battle, and on other occasions he would set up a mock battle between two teams and if a few heads were not broken by the end of the day neither the Fasimba nor Mgobozi were entirely satisfied.

Naturally he did not allow me to take part in these skirmishes —nor would I have wanted to—instead he would call me over to his side and let me hold his shield and Chest-biter and sometimes the crack of stick on skull would become so beguiling to him that he was unable to resist joining in and with a bound and a roar of 'Si-gi-di!' the drill sergeant would land among his 'boys' as he called them, laying about him left and right until his own lust for battle had been somewhat assuaged.

But the times I remember best were the training runs. I suppose these could be likened to forced marches in a European army, though there is not an army anywhere in the world which could have matched the Zulus for stamina. I know because he took me with him.

'Are your legs strong today?' he would ask, and I knew what was coming. Sometimes even Chaka came with us for the exercise. It was nothing for the Zulus to run twenty miles in one direction only to be told they shouldn't be there but somewhere else entirely. This other point might be twelve or fifteen miles in another direction. They would go racing off again, perhaps covering forty or forty-five miles, before returning to their barracks, and this over steep hills and through heavily bushed valleys. Chaka himself once covered sixty miles in a single night.

At first I could not keep up and would drop out after five miles or so. But gradually my legs grew stronger and my lung capacity increased until finally I was able to finish one run in three. I could not realise then in what good stead this training would eventually stand me. The odd thing is that the harder Mgobozi drove his men the more they loved him.

In return he gave them everything he had in the way of battle knowledge and fighting. He loved them as a father loves his

79

children and he had the same hopes and ambitions for them, but his real love, with which was bound up his honour and loyalty, he gave to Chaka. Mgobozi was a soldier-of-fortune who had found a master about whom he entertained no doubts whatsoever. In battle it was Chaka's body that he guarded, in peace he tried to do the same. But here things were less simple and the art of kingship was far beyond him. I recall once, much later on, after an attempt had been made on Chaka's life and when he still refused a bodyguard, Mgobozi set out for Bulawayo and in front of all the councillors turned to Chaka, calling him both stupid and thoughtless. In the shocked silence that ensued, he went on: 'Now kill me, for no one likes to hear the truth!'

Instead tears sprang to the King's eyes and he put his hand on Mgobozi's shoulder, saying: 'If I killed you, old friend, I would be killing myself. If it will make you happier I will keep men about me of a dark night. But ask no more. I will not live like a sick child.' And with that Mgobozi had to be satisfied.

Often he would visit us at Morile, talking with my father over pots of beer or bantering with Stone-Axe. Sometimes he would stay for a day or two and we would all go hunting buffalo or lions. I remember him as being as much a part of our family as Stone-Axe himself, and almost as well loved.

I have said that these years were the really happy ones in Zululand and they were—for me. We had been isolated from the world outside, giving no thought to the future but existing from one golden sunny day to the next. We had food in abundance, a good place to live, and a growing pile of elephant tusks which my father assured us would be our fortune in time to come. In that fecund land we did not even have to work too hard. But I was being selfishly happy and it was a long time before I realized that there were others in our little community who were not so happy: my mother and Stone-Axe.

I first became aware that something was wrong one dark winter's day when an icy wind blew down upon us from the snow-capped Dragon Mountains, rattling at the doors and howling mournfully round the corners. My father was away at Bulawayo with Chaka—a practice that was becoming more and more common—and by early afternoon the day seemed too cheerless to be out of doors so I took down one of my mother's collection

80

of books and curled up in the big skin-covered chair by the fire. After a few pages I must have fallen asleep for I woke with a start to hear someone crying. My mother was kneeling at one of the wagon-chests and slight tremors were shaking her back and shoulders. Her eyes were screwed up tight and she was pinching the bridge of her nose with thumb and forefinger as though trying to hold back tears, but every now and then they would spill out from between the closed lids and run down her cheeks. Around her on the floor were what she called her 'things'. I could just make them out in the dim light : the cameos of her father and mother, a locket which contained some strands of Donald's baby hair, a water colour of Paradise—the house at the Cape of Good Hope where she had been brought up—and a small bound volume of Dryden which she had won as a school prize in England. There was also a beautiful Chinese silk shawl which Dr Goodsir had once given her, and one or two other things.

It was obvious that she had no idea I was in the room and as I watched she began slowly to put everything back in the chest. There was a look of such sadness, almost desolation, on her face that I felt my heart turn over and tears spring to the back of my own eyes. I wanted to go to her and put my arms around her and tell her that whatever was wrong I would put right but instead I crouched there feeling a mixture of pity and fear.

After a time she closed the lid of the chest and locked it and slowly made her way out of the room. I sat on in the chair for a long while and eventually I began to shiver, but not with cold, and gradually a feeling of great melancholy came over me and I could no longer check my own tears. I was crying partly for the sadness I had seen in someone dear to me, and partly for reasons of selfishness : my own idyll had been breached.

I see that I have not mentioned my mother very often so far in this account and it is perhaps right that I should do so now. She came of good English county stock although most of her life had been spent in Africa. Her father had been Assistant Secretary at the Cape in the First British Occupation and had been killed in a hunting accident two years after her mother had died of fever. From that time she lived with her guardian, Dr Henry Goodsir, at his house at Paradise near Cape Town and except for the few years when he had sent her to England for schooling, she had been his constant companion, housekeeper and, for all practical purposes, daughter. It was she who had taken my father in after his escape from the convict ship and she who had nursed him back to health. During the next seven or eight years when he grew to manhood on the Frontier, married and sired me, she was accompanying Dr Goodsir on his zoological expeditions, until finally she met my widowed father again in the land of the Bachapins almost at the same time that Dr Goodsir died of recurrent fever.

Since then they had wandered the land together, been married by a proselytising missionary, produced Donald, and finally come to rest in Zululand.

If I had given it any thought at all I would have said that with this background my mother would have been as tough as leather and as hardy as a man. And I would have been wrong. It is difficult to say whether she was beautiful or not because we lived so closely. I loved her very much and so naturally I found her good-looking. If I were to try now and be objective about her appearance I would say she was a woman with golden hair and a fair complexion. Her face was thin and her nose sharp. She had wide-spaced grey eyes and freckles on the bridge of her nose. She was not a big woman but there was a tensile strength in her body.

What I saw that winter's afternoon gave her a new dimension and I perceived for perhaps the first time her soft and feminine core. But it is one thing to see, another to understand. What I couldn't fathom was the nature of her unhappiness.

On the face of it, she should have been happy. Morile had grown now to a small community with Zulu herdsmen in the valley and their wives or daughters in the kitchen. Most of her chores no longer existed and even Donald, who was rapidly growing up, spent most of his time either at lessons or playing with the children of the Zulu servants, so he was no longer a burden.

I could see nothing that one could be unhappy about. However, from that moment I began to look at things with a less self-satisfied eye. It is extraordinary how blind the fully-sighted can be. The cause was quite plain : my father.

He would have been in his mid-thirties at this time; in the prime of his life. He had always been a big man but where I could remember his physique as resembling the springy strength of green wood, now I noticed that his body was thickening and becoming more granite-like. He still wore a full beard and it, and his dark hair, both showed traces of grey. He had never been a man to smile much and this was hardly surprising when one took into account his past, but now he seemed not to smile at all.

This was the first thing I noticed : no one seemed to smile any longer. How long it had been going on I find difficult to say; I must have been more immersed in my own affairs than I realised.

As his body had coarsened, so had his manners. He ate like a Zulu with his own special basket of boiled beef from which he would pick with his fingers, and always had at hand great bowls of specially strong beer which one of the maids brewed for him. Meal times were dominated by long silences in which my father sat, lost in thought, his face grim and unapproachable. Once I passed some innocent remark about Zulu beer, something about liking it better than sour milk, and he looked at me for a long moment out of his bleak blue eyes and said that Zulu children learnt not to talk when adults were at their food and it was a habit he wished I would borrow. I saw my mother open her mouth as though to rebuke him and then she closed it again and bent her eyes to her plate.

Fortunately he was not often home. He and Chaka had become very close and with reports coming in of other white men now less than two hundred miles away to the south-east the King wished his advisers near him at all times. So normally it was just my mother and Donald and I who ate together and at these times the servants and Stone-Axe would often sit on the floor at the far end of the room and take their own meal, especially if it was winter and there were blazing logs in the stone hearth. This is how it had been in the early years when we had been more like a family, welded together out of hardship and united against danger, and less like white people with their servants. But recently my father had changed all that. He had sent the servants back to the kitchen and told Stone-Axe to go with them. This was such an extreme action that even my father felt obliged to make some comment.

'He watches me,' he said. 'I don't like being watched when I'm eating.'

It was strange enough by itself but when one added to it the fact that my father had always said he and Stone-Axe were indivisible, that even as far back as his time on the Frontier Stone-Axe had never liked to be more than a few yards from him at all times, including at meals or asleep, and that this was the measure of his love—something my father had been greatly proud of and touched by—then clearly things were far from right.

Nor did he ever take the little Bushman with him to Bulawayo. This was equally inexplicable. Granted the Zulus were not over-keen on Bushmen but in the old days something like that would never have stopped my father. It was sad to see Stone-Axe moping around the house like a dog without its master. I hadn't noticed it before, but he seemed to have grown much older and there was hurt in his eyes.

But it was his treatment of my mother that I noticed most plainly. I should say his non-treatment. He hardly spoke to her now, or if he did it was just a yes or a no. He wasn't actually brusque, just reticent. Somehow, they seemed to have lost the knack of speech.

Often, now that I had begun to notice things, I would watch my mother at her sewing in the evenings and frequently, for no apparent reason, the lamplight would fall on eyes swimming with tears. Many times I ached to go down on my knees and lay my head on her lap and try to comfort her in some way but instinctively I drew back, as though unwilling to enter a world of adults where so much sadness was unexplained.

It is not a pretty thing to have to say about one's father but the whole house seemed to heave a sigh of relief each time he went galloping off to Bulawayo. Frequently he would stay away for a day or two at a time, letting the farm run itself, and as far as I was concerned the longer the better.

It was about this time that he killed a man.

He had been away, as usual, on one of his visits to Chaka. My mother had asked me to see if I could find her some canna roots, which she boiled up with animal fat to make soap, and Stone-Axe and I had gone down into the valley with a basket. We went through the corn lands and on into the wild part of the valley and almost at once came across the body of a heifer with its throat torn out and its guts spilling on to the grass. The blood was still sticky and we knew it had not been dead more than an hour or so.

Stone-Axe bent down and examined the wounds and the ground around the dead animal. When he looked up I said: 'Leopard?'

'Leopard,' and he pointed through the grass in the direction it had taken.

'Come on then,' I said.

He unslung his bow and I took a stronger grip on the pair of fighting-sticks I usually carried with me. I think both of us were hoping he had not read the scene correctly, but before we'd got another hundred yards we found the second heifer dead like the first.

It was typical of a leopard. Sometimes they go berserk and kill for the sake of killing. Once, a long time ago before our guns had cleared the valley of most predators, a pair of leopards had killed nineteen head just for sport. None of them had been eaten.

Again Stone-Axe circled the corpse to pick up the spoor but suddenly he lifted his head and looked down the valley. 'Claw comes,' he said. Seconds later I heard the drumbeat of hooves on the valley floor.

My father dismounted and threw the reins to the Bushman. Without saying anything he got down on his haunches and stared for a long time at the dead animal. Then he straightened up and turned to Stone-Axe. 'Leopard?' he asked. The Bushman nodded.

'There's one further back too, Father,' I said.

His face grew grimmer, as though a dark cloud had just passed over the sun. 'You're sure it was the same.'

'Yes, just like this one.'

'No point in going back, then. Let's see how many.'

We followed Stone-Axe deeper into the valley.

My father seemed rather strange. His eyes were sunk back in their sockets, the whites flecked with red. His skin had a sort of papery look about it and his hands trembled. He seemed to be sweating a lot. We came on eight more dead cattle in the next half hour, making ten in all, and I could see his anger mounting with each kill.

At last he said : 'There'll be no more after this. He'll have gone up there, and away a good hour by now.' He pointed up a kloof that led to the western ridge of the valley. 'There'll be a next time.' He slid the rifle into the saddle scabbard and then said : 'Now we'll look for Bacela, this was his area.'

It took us another fifteen minutes of searching before we came across Bacela, the herdsman. He was stretched out in the shade of an acacia tree fast asleep. 'That's about what I thought,' my father said softly. He touched the herdsman with the toe of his buckskin boot. Bacela came out of his slumbers rather slowly and with a confused expression on his face. Then he saw who we were and leapt to his feet. His eyes were guilty and afraid. I had never cared much for Bacela. He was a rather dim man of about forty who had come to us from one of the tribes eaten up by Chaka's regiments. There was no use leaving him to his own initiative; he had to be told everything. Perhaps no one had mentioned that herdsmen were not to fall asleep while watching the cattle.

'Good morning, Bacela,' my father said in the same soft tone.

'Good morning, Lord.'

'Does everything go well?'

'Everything is well, Lord.'

'With the cattle?'

'With the cattle, Lord.'

'And with Bacela?'

He tried to smile but it got all lopsided somehow. 'Yes, Lord.'

'Do you find the work hard, Bacela?'

'Not too hard, Lord.'

'I'm glad.'

'Yes, Lord.'

The gentleness of my father's voice must have soothed Bacela for he began to look slightly more confident.

'By the by, Bacela, were you asleep just now?'

The herdsman paused and then dropped his eyes. 'No, Lord.'

'No, of course not. Just resting, then?'

'No, Lord.'

'Well, no matter. Tell me, Bacela, have you heard any lions in the valley?'

'There are no lions, Lord.'

'And leopards?'

Bacela laughed. 'I have chased all the leopards away!'

The poor simpleton couldn't see what was happening to him. I was reminded of a puff-adder playing with a rat.

'Come,' my father said. 'There's something I want to show you.'

We all followed him to the last carcase we'd discovered. Bacela looked down at the torn paunch and throat, and the skin around his mouth became pinched and grey.

'What do you think, Bacela? Leopard?'

The herdsman saw the trap only as he stepped into it. At last he said: '*Amatagati.*'

'Oh, you think so?' He turned to Stone-Axe and me. 'Our friend thinks it's the wizards.' He turned to Bacela. 'Come.'

We retraced our steps, stopping at every carcase. Each time

my father asked: '*Amatagati?*' until the word became a knell ringing in our ears, and each time Bacela said: 'Yes, Lord,' until finally his answers were no more than a whisper. As we came to the tenth dead heifer he suddenly dropped on his knees and said: 'I was sick, Lord,' and he pointed to his head.

'Now you'll be sicker,' my father said, reaching for the *sjambok* which hung from the saddle.

Once or twice before I had seen my father lose his temper with a servant but I had never seen him raise a hand to one. His annoyance, coupled with a warning and backed up by judicious display of his hook, was usually enough to ensure that the same mistake was never made again, but now his anger was of a cold and icy kind. He reminded me of Chaka.

He struck Bacela where he knelt, the shod tip of the rhino-hide lash laying open the flesh on the side of his ribs. 'That is for the first!' my father said, and struck again. 'And that for the second! And that for the third! And that for the fourth! And that . . .' And he went on hitting and hitting and the air became filled with a spray of blood. I looked at Stone-Axe and saw his eyes were sick with shame and I remembered having been told that my father had once saved him from a similar thrashing and that it had been the birth of their friendship.

Bacela had toppled to the dust and still my father went on. There was something almost manic about his actions and I could stand it no longer. 'Stop!' I cried. 'For God's sake stop, or you'll kill him!' I jumped forward and held on to the stock of the *sjambok* with both hands. I think we were equally surprised at my strength.

My father glared at me through his red-flecked eyes. His breath was coming in gasps. 'Get away, boy, or you'll taste it yourself.'

I tried to open my mouth to answer but I was so frightened my tongue seemed stuck to my palate; all I could do was try to hang on and I couldn't even do that for my father suddenly jerked his arms and I felt myself flying through the air.

'That was a bad thing, Claw,' Stone-Axe said, helping me to my feet.

'You too, you little beggar!'

They stood looking at each other, the big bearded Scot with the rhino-hide whip in his hand and the small yellow-skinned Bushman with the bow hanging slackly from his right arm. And then

87

my father dropped his eyes and turned to the mass of tattered and ribboned flesh which lay at his feet. 'That should teach him a lesson,' he said, and he mounted Violin and kicked her into a canter.

We carried Bacela up to the house and told my mother the leopard had got him as well. She bathed the torn rib-cage and put on an ointment of herbs, lard and beeswax but he died before morning. I don't know whether the servants believed our story of the leopard and I'm not sure whether it mattered one way or the other. My father was the King's man and wasn't this how the King lived?

From about that time onward things developed quickly. For my own part I tried, I suppose almost unconsciously at first, to become less like a Zulu in direct ratio to my father's increasing identification. I spent more time with my books and in my mother's company; which no doubt irritated him further because when he was at home I was always under-foot. I hardly saw Tanga now nor went anywhere near Ngwadi's kraal. There was a reason for this. About a fortnight after Bacela's death I overheard two Zulu *indunas* discussing my father. It was not easy to make out what they were saying but it had to do with his frequent visits to Bulawayo and one chuckled and said : 'I wish I had his reasons.'

Later when I repeated this to Tanga and asked him what it meant he looked surprised and laughed and said didn't I know that Chaka had given my father two concubines which he kept in a kraal near Bulawayo. They were said to brew the strongest beer in Zululand.

I felt ashamed for us all and I told no one, not even Stone-Axe though he probably knew anyway. It was easy to understand my father's long absences from Morile and the sunken eyes and the papery skin. I wasn't upset because of his drinking, I liked the beer as well as anyone, but what I couldn't understand was that he should take another woman when he already had my mother. I can see now that this was an ingenuous attitude, but I suppose it sprang from the confusion and unhappiness about my own sexual awakening and there was no one with whom I could discuss it.

Zulu youths of my own age were not in the least confused about sex, why then was I? It was only later I learnt that in their society

88

hings like this were explained to them early by their parents; in ours, or at least in the only society I was familiar with at the ime, nothing was explained at all.

But I was not allowed to brood on these thoughts too long, for he first white men arrived in Bulawayo from the coast. We had known about them through Chaka's spies for some time and my ather had been apprehensive about meeting them. They were eally the vanguard of a trickle of Englishmen and Colonists who nade their way to Zululand in the next few years bartering for vory and land. Most of them came up from the Cape of Good Iope by sea and stayed at the small settlement south-east of us vhich they called Port Natal. Few of them ever visited Chaka and this suited my father very well.

But when the news came to us that the first of them were noving north, my father cleaned and oiled his guns and put Stone-Axe to work casting bullets. His face became even grimmer and we kept out of his way as much as we could. If there was any place we could have gone he would probably have rebuilt the plundered wagons and set off again. But I think he knew we were afer at Morile under the armpit of Chaka than if we wandered but into the wilderness again. Chaka smiled on us; there was no guarantee that another tribal chief would not simply slit our hroats.

While my father feared the coming of other Europeans my nother yearned for it, though she never expressed a hope. It was lifficult for her. She knew there was always a chance, however emote, that the new visitors would be British officials moving the boundary of the Colony ever further north, in which case my ather would once more be a wanted convict. Yet at the same time he needed company.

It was a curious thing to see my father busy with his weapons at the same time as my mother was cleaning the house from top o bottom and spending hours on the verandah staring southwards across the downs for the first sight of the visitors. But as the days passed with nothing on the horizon, her excitement faded. And hen, about midnight one night, one of Chaka's runners reached Morile with the news my father had feared. Three white men vere only a day's march away and Chaka wanted my father at his side.

But in the event things turned out well. It transpired that it vas not the King's policy to let the white men meet my father.

He looked to him as a fountainhead of knowledge, an oracle who could advise him on all matters relating to the subjects of King George. The fact that Chaka could draw on this supply without other white men knowing of it greatly strengthened his hand. And so it happened. My father and the King spent the preceding day in close consultation, not even Mbopa being privy to their talks. For the remainder of the time the white men were to spend at Bulawayo my father was to stay with his concubines at the nearby kraal, only minutes away from the King if his advice was needed.

To us the importance of this visit to King Chaka by Lieutenant George Farewell, R.N., Henry Francis Fynn, Esq., and Mr Petersen, a former boarding-house keeper at the Cape, lies in what happened a few days later. Since my father had left me in charge of Morile I was unable to witness the events so I now borrow again from his Journal.

'From my position in a hut close by the Palace,' my father writes, 'I was able to witness the festivities which the King had organised to greet his visitors. They were greatly similar in nature to those with which he had honoured our own arrival; the massed ranks of Zulu *impis*, the vast herds of matched cattle, the troops of dancing maidens. It was only once these were past that I was enabled to get a clear view of the subjects. They seemed greatly astonished by what they had seen and stood together as though to take courage from each other. The King then ordered two oxen to be slaughtered for them and they returned to their tents which were pitched beyond the gate of the kraal to partake of their repast. On Chaka's instructions I hid in the tall grass nearby to study them and overhear their conversation.

'I listened and observed for upwards of two hours. Their leader was Lt Farewell, a young man of forceful bearing with wide-spaced slanted eyes and a long nose. It struck me from the way he spoke that he was a man of great resolution. Mr Fynn was of more benign demeanour, with an open face and thinning hair. His eyes were shrewd though kindly. Both these gentlemen were in great contrast to the third, a man called Petersen who, it turned out, was Lt Farewell's father-in-law. How such an amalgamation took place is beyond me for Petersen was a portly and foul-mouthed Dutchman, many years their senior, who complained constantly of the journey they had undertaken, of pains in his stomach, of the fact that Chaka's kraal was not completely built of ivory as he had been led to expect, that they had travelled this distance for little or nothing in the way of profit and finally he ended up by accusing his son-in-law of bringing him to this barbarous place to make an end of him.

' "Why don't we eat our supper in peace," Fynn finally said, "and thank the Lord we are safely here, unmolested and unharmed."

' "Amen to that," said Farewell, wishing to make an end to the arguing.

' "I tell you these damned Caffres will have our hides," Petersen replied, unwilling to be mollified.

'And thus it continued and I thought to myself then that they were an ill-matched trio to come seeking riches. After they had eaten, Chaka sent for them but by this time Petersen was groaning with stomach cramps and Farewell told the interpreter Jacob Sumbiti that he must, of necessity, stay with the older man. So Fynn went alone to the Palace in which Chaka was now surrounded by four hundred of his women. I took up a place in the dark shadows of the wall where I could see and hear. Chaka was angry. He had heard from Mbopa that on their journey north Fynn had used medicine on a woman to cure her of fever. Ever since I had given him a bottle of sweet oil and rubbed his limbs with it he had expressed a wish to have more European medicine. Now he turned to Fynn angrily, saying: "I hear you have come from Umjoji. Is he as great a king as I?"

' "King George is one of the greatest kings in the world," Fynn replied.

' "I am very angry with you. I shall send a message to Umjoji asking him to kill you. He sent you to *me*; not to give medicine to my dogs." At this all his "sisters" applauded. "Why do you give my dogs medicine?"

' "It is a practice of our country to help those who are in need."

' "Are you then the doctor of dogs? You were sent here to be *my* doctor."

'Fynn looked about him helplessly. "But I'm not a doctor," he said finally. "Not a real one."

'But Chaka was not to be diverted. "Have you any medicine with you?" And when Fynn replied in the affirmative, the King said: "Then cure me or I will have you sent to Umjoji to be killed."

'Bewildered, Fynn asked: "But what ails you?"

91

' "That's for you to find out," Chaka said triumphantly.

'Fynn had now become enmeshed in the King's illogicalities and he glanced hopelessly around the close-packed throng. For a moment I thought he might have spied me in the shadows but his glance passed, returning to Chaka. At length he asked the King to stand up.

' "Why?" asked Chaka.

' "So that I can try to find out."

'Chaka rose and several of his women held up lighted torches. Fynn examined him closely and pronounced that the King suffered from pain in his legs. I was greatly astonished to hear this because it was true: Chaka had suffered from rheumaticks for several years. The King was equally surprised and stared at Fynn with growing respect. It was either a lucky surmise or he knew more about medicine than he offered.'

(My father could not know then what Fynn had seen. In his own Diary, Fynn writes: 'I looked about his person and, after reflecting on the great activity he had shown during the day, was satisfied he had not much the matter with him. I, however, observed numerous black marks on his loins where native doctors had scarified him and at once said he had pains in his loins.')

'The King then allowed Fynn to return to his camp, where Petersen was worse. The following day the traders presented their gifts to Chaka. They consisted of every description of beads available at the Cape, woollen blankets, brass bars, sheets of copper, a basket of pigeons, a pig, several cats and dogs and a full-dress military coat with epaulettes covered in gold thread.

'It had always been the King's policy never to express open gratitude over gifts but when I saw him later in the day he expressed his satisfaction. In return he presented the party with five elephant teeth and forty head of cattle.

'After several days in which Fynn treated friends of the King for fevers and colicks Lieutenant Farewell and Mr Petersen, whose condition was now greatly worsened, returned to Port Natal, but Chaka insisted that Fynn stay on for a while. And this he did.

'Some nights later there was dancing at the King's palace and Fynn, who had spent the day reading, came to watch. He had no sooner arrived than there was a dreadful shriek from the midst of the dancers and the torches of dry reeds were immediately extinguished.

'At this time I knew nothing of what was happening since I

was taking my ease in my own hut, when Mgobozi suddenly burst through the door shouting: "The King is dying! The King is dying!" I managed to calm him down and get some sense from him. In the confusion of the dance the King had been stabbed. This was all he knew.

'It did not take me many moments to realise that if the King died every white person in Zululand would be summarily torn to pieces. The coincidence of the new arrivals would be too much for the people to support. I ran with Mgobozi knowing that if Chaka was indeed sorely hurt there was little I could do. But what of Fynn? Had he not shown great expertness in the manner of physicks? I told Mgobozi then that this was the only way to save Chaka and we set out to find him.

'The King's kraal was in great uproar. People were running hither and thither, screaming and yelling. Some had fallen down in fits and were writhing upon the ground, others lay unconscious where they had fainted. Still others were dead, trampled underfoot in the great panic which had overtaken everyone.

'It seemed impossible that we should ever find Fynn in such a great mêlée. We made for the Palace and there we found him in the midst of a crowd of women. These were members of the seraglio and they were pulling him from one side to the other, crying and shouting, and in a few more seconds he would have fallen and that would have been the end. Mgobozi leapt in amongst them using his fists and feet to clear a space. He caught Fynn's arm and pulled him away from the place but Fynn, thinking that he was about to be dragged away to his death, continued struggling until I caught his other arm and we ran him through the crowd to a place of sanctuary outside the main kraal where Chaka had been removed for safety. He was greatly surprised to meet another white man there but also greatly relieved. I told him I was an ivory hunter who came from the West and he seemed satisfied with this.

'Chaka was lying on a pile of skins groaning and crying and every now and then blood would gather in his mouth and he would spit it out on the ground. Fynn got to work immediately bathing the wound with camomile tea and then binding it up with clean linen.

'The King had been greatly lucky. The assegai had passed under his left breast, the blade going through the ribs, but had not actually entered the lung.

'Chaka seemed convinced that death was close upon him and he cried lamentably all through the night.

'By morning the crowds had increased so greatly that their shrieking was almost too much to bear. Thousands upon thousands were arriving every hour as the news spread to all parts of his kingdom. Thinking that the King was already dead the people were falling into paroxysms of lamentation. They were pulling each other about, men and women throwing themselves down in every direction without taking care how they fell. Great numbers fainted from over-exertion and excessive heat. The females of the seraglio, more particularly, were in very great distress, having overtaxed themselves during the night. They were suffering from the heat and want of nourishment, which no one had dared to touch, whilst the four brass collars each had, fitting so closely around the neck as to make it impossible for the wearer to turn her head, nearly suffocated them. Several of them died. And then Fynn, who had left the King's hut, came to their aid by pouring water over them as they fell. This helped and after a while the women began giving assistance to each other.

'Now the worst thing of all happened; the people began to kill each other. Some were put to death because they did not cry, others for putting spittle in their eyes to imitate tears, others for sitting down to cry, although strength and tears, after such continuous mourning and exertion, were quite exhausted.

'It was rumoured that the would-be assassins had been seen leaving the kraal and that they were thought to be Ndwandwes from the direction they took. Mdlaka immediately ordered two regiments off in pursuit.

'For four days the King lay sick and Fynn washed and dressed the wounds and covered them with ointment. And all this time the great crowds remained closely by though they were now too exhausted to do much more than lie on the ground. It was only on the fourth day that cattle were killed to feed them and by now hundreds had expired. Their bodies were everywhere. On the fifth and sixth days the King began to improve and at noon on the sixth day the regiments returned from their pursuit. They carried with them the bodies of the three assassins.

'The bodies were placed about a mile from the kraal and their right ears were cut off and then all of the people who had come to the kraal, and there must have been more than thirty thousand, passed by the bodies yelling and crying. Each struck the bodies several times with a stick and thereupon threw the stick down, so that in a little while the bodies no longer remained in view and all that anyone could see was an immense pile of sticks.

'From the moment Chaka had been stabbed the wearing of ornaments was prohibited, nor was anyone permitted to wash or shave his head, moreover no man whose wife was pregnant was allowed to come into the King's presence. A fire was now made in the central arena of the kraal and the ears of the would-be assassins were burnt in the ashes.

'I remained to ascertain that the King was now on the road to recovery before I took horse and returned to Morile.'

As the months passed there were other visits to Chaka by the white people who were trying to gain a foothold on the coast. But the journey was hard and they were very few. In any case, Chaka later moved his royal kraal to Dukusa, a hundred miles or so down the coast, our isolation became even more complete.

The attempted assassination had not passed without its effect on Chaka. He brooded more than ever on his role as creator of the Zulu nation. I think he had a feeling that the Spirits meant him to live forever and he was constantly on the watch for signs and omens which would support this theory. But each time he looked at his mother, Nandi, who was now getting very old, he foresaw his own decaying flesh and this frightened him. With age came weakness and few tribal kings died in their blankets.

The first signs of grey had appeared in his hair and often he would become quite enraged and distraught over this until he heard through one of his white visitors of an unguent—which I later discovered to be Rowland's Macassar Oil—said to restore grey hair to its original colour. At once he fastened on to this as the elixir of life he sought for himself and his mother. If it could do this for the hair, he said, then by drinking it the body too must return to its youthful vigour. For a long time he anxiously awaited its arrival at the hands of the Europeans, but it never did come and I have often wondered how many of his country-men died because of his resultant depression and anger.

This, then, was the state of affairs when Nerissa entered our lives. It is strange now to think that there was ever a time before Nerissa. Seldom can one recognise an exact turning point in one's life, a fork in the road, but on the morning I first saw the wagon moving sedately along the valley floor I sensed its portentousness. This is not as psychic as it sounds since *any* wagon would have been cause for surprise.

'Mother,' I called, running through the corridors in search of her. 'Mother! There's a wagon at the bottom of the hill!'

'What? Show me! Quick!'

We ran through to the front of the house and there it was just as I'd said.

'It is! It is!' she cried. 'Go and call your father, he's down in the lands! And I must change my dress! Your hair! Get the brush quickly! No . . . no . . . don't, there's not time. Do I look all right? Your shoes! Get your shoes on; the new ones Stone-Axe made! And then run for your father!' Suddenly she caught my hands in hers and I could see the high colour in her cheeks. 'Oh, Robbie,' she cried. 'How I've waited for this!'

But when I got down to the lands I found that my father was inspecting cattle in the farthest part of the valley so I sent one of the servants for him and ran back to the wagon. As I reached it two men climbed down from the fore-tree. I could see my mother in a fresh white dress standing outside our front door and next to her was Stone-Axe.

I had a chance to observe the men before coming up with them. They were both dark-skinned but the bigger of the two was obviously a European, burnt mahogany-brown by the sun. He was dressed in soft green corduroy trousers and a white silk shirt with lace ruffles at the wrists and a folded front that left part of his hairy chest open to view. His beard was neatly trimmed and he wore a single gold ear-ring in the lobe of his right ear. On his left hand he wore a gold seal-ring and, on his right wrist, a bracelet of beaten silver. But perhaps the most noticeable thing about him was the scar that ran across his nose squashing it into his face as though there had been a cave-in. He was smoking a long cigar and altogether he was as strange a sight as we had seen for a long time. By comparison his companion was slight and thin-faced with a shaven head and piercing black eyes. His nose was hooked like a hawk's beak. He wore a single garment, with a hole for his head, as though someone had cut the centre of a white cotton sheet and allowed it to fall loosely over his body.

'Good day,' I said, drawing up with them.

The big man turned slowly towards me and let his eyes travel up and down my body as though judging me for weight, then he turned to the other and said something in a tongue I could not understand. There was something in the way he did it that was vaguely disturbing, almost insolent, but I remembered the manners my mother had taught me.

'Welcome to Morile,' I went on. 'We have food and can give you rest.' This time he took the cigar from his mouth and blew smoke in my direction and said something that sounded like water splashing against river rocks. The smaller man came forward and addressed himself to me. It was not the same language as before, but more sing-song interposed with strange explosive noises.

'I'm sorry,' I said, trying to be polite. 'But I can't understand you.'

At this the big man stretched out his hand and took mine and shook it. 'Pereira,' he said. 'Velho Pereira.' I took this to be his name. 'Hamad,' he said, indicating the other.

'My name is Robert Fraser Black,' I said with some relief. 'This is my home.'

'Ro-ber-t,' Pereira said, making fairly heavy weather of it. 'Ro-ber-t. Roberto.' He pointed his glowing cigar in my face. 'Roberto.'

'I Roberto,' I said, nodding. We seemed to be getting somewhere at last.

'Inglis?'

'That's right. I—I mean me—Yes, I'm English. Do you speak English?'

Pereira shook his head as though the thought was distasteful to him.

Then I had an idea. I tried him in the only other language I knew. 'Do you speak Zulu?' I said.

He laughed. 'Better than you,' he said, which wasn't true at all. His accent was vile and it wasn't pure Zulu anyway but a dialect.

'My mother waits to greet you,' I said.

'This is yours?'

'My family's.' He nodded, letting his eyes rove over the rich grain lands and the lush grazing.

'How far is it to Chaka's kraal?'

'Half a day in that.' I pointed to the wagon.

'Then we shall rest here until morning.'

'That's what I've been suggesting,' I said shortly. 'My mother is waiting to give you food.'

He looked up at the figure at the top of the hill. 'This is fortunate,' he said. 'There are things she can do for us.'

I wasn't sure quite what he meant by that but then I wasn't sure of a great many things about them. 'I'll take you up,' I offered.

'Not so fast.' He walked around the rear of the wagon and unlaced the tent flaps. 'Your mother has an additional guest.' He stepped back and said something in his own language, but nothing happened and he stuck his head through the flaps. Immediately the wagon rocked with violent movement and he leapt back with an oath. Two weals on the side of his cheek began to ooze blood.

'Hamad!' he called. They both leant into the wagon-bed and again the bleached canvas shook and trembled until suddenly a third figure appeared, twisting and turning in their arms. I saw it was a woman, a girl rather, and I stood there with my mouth open. She fought them with a savage ferocity, using her nails and teeth but they held her away so she could not damage them and it seemed to me then, as it proved to be later, that this was not the first time they had fought with her. They held her until she subsided. This she did quite suddenly. At one moment she was tearing and scratching, the next she was standing between them, mute and listless, as though all the fire had been abruptly extinguished. And it was the same with her eyes. From the moment she shot from the wagon-bed I had noticed the intensity of her amethyst eyes. Now they were tired and faded.

'What's the matter with her?' I cried as soon as I found my tongue.

'Nothing that a man won't cure,' he said, dabbing at the scratches on his cheeks with an orange silk square.

This was my first sight of Nerissa, although no one, not even Pereira, knew her name then, so I must put down exactly how she appeared to me.

She was tall and slender and dressed in a loose shift of some brown woollen material. I suppose she was a year or two older than myself. Her hair was the black of a widow-bird's tail and her skin was the colour of new ivory. Her mouth was wide and above it high cheekbones seemed to run up to the extremities of her eyes. Her bones were so prominent that they emphasised the shadowy hollows of her cheeks and temples, giving her face added planes and angles which changed constantly with movement and expression. It was a face too arresting for conventional beauty.

98

There was something haunted or haunting about that first sight of it—and I have never been sure which.

'What's wrong? What's happening?' My mother said, hurrying down to us.

I began to introduce the men to her in Zulu. 'Stop talking nonsense!' she snapped at me, brushing Pereira and Hamad aside. 'What have they been doing to the girl?'

'You'll have to speak Zulu,' I said. 'They can't understand.'

'Who are they, anyway,' she said, more to herself than us, 'to be manhandling a young girl so? Leave off!' Hamad stood his ground for a fraction of a second, then I saw Pereira move his head and Hamad dropped the girl's arm. 'I should think so!' I hadn't seen my mother like this for so long I'd almost forgotten how formidable she could be. I found time, even then, to be delighted.

'Come, my dear,' my mother said, taking her by the hand and leading her towards the house. 'You have met my son, Robert, and my name is Frances. Will you tell me yours?' But Nerissa was too dazed to answer and she simply walked woodenly at my mother's side.

'Never mind,' my mother said. 'There'll be plenty of time for that.' It was obvious right then, at the very beginning, that she sensed there was something seriously wrong with Nerissa.

For the next hour I was left on my own with the two strangers. My mother had taken Nerissa to her room and I heard orders being given for hot water and clean linen. In the meantime I tried to find out something about our visitors but instead it was they who questioned me. We had long since exhausted our supplies of coffee and tea so I offered them sour milk or beer and they chose the latter. The injuries to Pereira's face had twisted one corner of his top lip which gave him a permanently sardonic expression and as he drew me out about our arrival and settlement in Zululand it seemed he was mocking me with every question. Since these were the first real visitors we had ever had at Morile it was disconcerting to be patronised in one's own home.

At length he was satisfied which was just as well since I had told him everything I could about ourselves. His own story was brief and I'm sure he left out more than he told. He was an ivory hunter, he said, and he and the Arab, Hamad, came from Portuguese territory hundreds of miles to the north-east of us. He said he was the younger son of a duke who lived in a place called

Lisboã but I didn't believe him then and I don't now. The point is that the way he spoke you could see he didn't care one way or the other.

When I asked him about Nerissa he laughed and said he paid a lot for her because she was a virgin and no young cockerel, that was his exact phrase, was going to mount her. He had heard of a Zulu custom called 'the fun of the roads' and this seemed admirable in many ways except as it applied to her. I replied, rather hotly, that I had no wish even to touch Nerissa, that on the contrary it seemed *they* who were indulging not so much in fun as in cruelty and that I had simply asked an ordinary question concerning her origins.

Pereira looked at me thoughtfully and then drank deeply from the wooden bowl holding the beer. Finally he nodded and said: 'All right. What harm is there? We were hunting in the marshes north-east of here. We found her living in a headman's kraal. How she got there and why we don't know. They say they found her wandering there. She has said nothing; not even her name; not a single word. But I paid two bushels of beads for her and now she is mine. Does that satisfy you, my young friend?'

It didn't, of course, and I knew it wouldn't satisfy my mother either, but there did not seem much we could do.

Just then a shadow fell across the threshold and I looked up to see my father at the door. I had not heard either the horse or his footsteps. He must have come with great care and now he stood between the doorposts, the rifle held loosely in his hands.

'Who are you?' he asked.

Hurriedly, I explained and I saw him relax. He propped the rifle against the wall and came forward with outstretched hand to greet Pereira. They were both so big, standing there, that the room seemed to shrink.

'Robbie,' he said, turning to me, 'run along and fetch the spirits, beer's a poor thing for entertaining guests like these.' When I returned Hamad was coming in from the wagon with a flask of brandy in his hands. 'Now then,' my father said, filling their cups. 'Here's a health to you.' I stood around for a while but no one offered me anything so I wandered out on the hillside in the late afternoon sun. I didn't mind really because I wanted to think about Nerissa.

It took some thinking. Here was the first girl of my own age and race I'd ever seen and she hauled out of a stranger's wagon

100

fighting and spitting like a lynx. And then, as abruptly, turning into a somnambulist! It is a measure of the sort of life we'd been leading that I was more surprised than shocked.

But just thinking didn't seem to get me anywhere since there were no precedents to guide my thoughts so after a while I went back into the house. Dusk was beginning to creep along the walls and the tallow lamps had been lit in the living-room. No one spared me more than a glance as I settled myself in one of the darker corners, so intent were they on the problem of communication. As the level of the ardent spirits fell, so the problem seemed to become easier: my father was speaking in a grotesque mixture of English and Zulu, Pereira was equally fluent in a compound of Portuguese and Zulu, and Hamad, when he occasionally made comment, did so in a trio of tongues, one of which I believe to have been Arabic. The strange thing is that the more they drank the more complex became the language they used, yet the easier they seemed to understand one another.

Soon I, too, became less involved in semantics than in the sense of what they were saying—it is only the sense that I shall try to set down—and I was able, without too much difficulty, to follow the conversation. I realised that my father was covering the same ground as I had earlier but in much greater detail, though he gave no information at all about his past. Pereira, on the other hand, seemed less reticent. I gathered he had been all over the wild parts of Africa in the past twenty years hunting and slaving and he and Hamad had penetrated such remote fastnesses as Angola and Monomatapa and even sold their slaves as far north as Zanzibar and the coast of Arabia. My father warned him of attempting anything similar in Chaka's kingdom and Pereira replied that he had traversed the area even before we came and had realised then that the Zulus would never sell either their own people or the subjugated tribes, as was the custom further north.

'Oh,' said my father casually. 'So you've been here before, have you?'

Pereira nodded. 'Ten or eleven years ago. Some time like that.'

'You couldn't have missed us by long.' He drank deeply of the Portuguese brandy and wiped his lips with the back of his hand. 'Now tell me,' he began. 'What of the girl?'

Pereira smiled. 'You are as anxious as your son.'

My father laughed and turned to me. 'Never show your eagerness to a lassie,' he said. 'That's something you'll have to learn.'

'Perhaps he learns from his father, Senhor.'

'No, no, Pereira. Forbye if what you say is true I'm old enough to be *her* father and in any case I've not yet seen her.'

'Then that is the difference. Your son has.'

'And what are you proposing to do with this paragon who comes from nowhere and whose name you don't even know? Are you for marrying her for yourself?'

'No, Senhor. Nor taking her for myself.'

'Well, what then?'

'For many years I have been in Africa, perhaps too long. It is now time to go. I wish to return to Portugal to live like my ancestors but it has always been a question of money. A common problem.'

'I'll grant you that.'

'I have certain funds—a man trading and hunting as I have done would have been a fool not to keep something—but there has never seemed enough, not quite enough. Now it will be different.'

'But from what you've told me, she's not a penny to her name,' my father said, puzzled.

'It's not what she has, Senhor, but what she is worth that counts.'

'You mean you'd sell her?' There was no mistaking the disgust in my father's voice. 'You'd trade her like a black?'

'Si, Senhor. Remember, that is how I acquired her.'

'And who do you think you'd sell her to? I've already got one woman in my house.'

Pereira laughed. 'Not to you, my friend. I said I was seeking riches.'

'Oh,' said my father, his voice becoming sharp at the implied insult. 'King Croesus doesn't dwell in these parts.'

'But King Chaka does.'

'What?' My father suddenly put his head back and roared with laughter. 'You can't be serious, laddie. Chaka!'

'Indeed Chaka. What is so amusing?'

'Now listen to me: I'm as close to the King as his shadow and I can tell you he'd never touch a white woman.'

Pereira nodded. 'Except this one. For her he will pay me two hundred elephants' teeth and think he has a bargain.'

'You're addled, Pereira. Soft in the head, man.'

For the first time the Portuguese hunter looked angry. 'It is easy to insult a guest in your own house, Senhor.'

'Now, now, don't get your bile up. It's just that I know what I'm talking about. Listen, Chaka's got twelve hundred women of his own. It's doubtful whether he'd thank you for another black maiden, let alone a white one.'

'It is idle to argue when one of the parties is not in possession of the facts,' Pereira replied peevishly. 'Better that you see her first.'

'The first sensible idea you've had,' my father said. He turned to me, slopping the brandy as he did so, and I could see that he had already had too much to drink. 'Fetch her in, Robbie. Let's have a look at this Venus.'

I could hear my mother in the kitchen as I crossed the inner courtyard and I wondered what she would have to say about things. Anyway, Nerissa wasn't in the main bedroom and I found her in my own room, stretched out on my bed, fast asleep. I stood looking down at her, savouring the sudden intimacy of the moment and then I gently touched her shoulder. She came awake slowly and peacefully and then, as her eyes opened and she saw me bending over her she gave a muffled cry and shrank into the furthest corner of the bed.

'It's all right . . . it's all right . . .' I said soothingly, as one might speak to a frightened calf. 'I'm not going to hurt you.'

But even as I spoke the film of blankness passed across her eyes and she became as wooden as before. 'They want you,' I said. 'But you don't have to worry, my father's there and I'll be with you.'

I put out my hand to take her arm and for the first time I saw a flicker of understanding in her eyes. But she pulled her arm away and slid off the bed. She was wearing one of my mother's nightgowns which was too short for her and her long pale legs showed underneath. I should have given her a coat or something to cover herself more completely but at the time I could only think how beautiful she was.

'Come,' I said and she followed me out of the room.

Angry words must have passed between my father and Pereira because they were both looking heated when I returned. 'I've brought her, father,' I said, and stood aside to let her into the room. The light of the lamp above the door fell fully on to her. My father had been in the act of drinking and I saw his hand stop halfway to his mouth, then slowly he set the vessel back on the table. He stared at her as though he was seeing a vision.

'Look well, farmer,' Pereira said mockingly. 'This isn't a cow from your fields. And now see this and consider yourself a fortunate man.' With that he rose from his chair, crossed to Nerissa, placed his fingers in the neck of the nightgown and, with an abrupt downward movement, tore the garment from her body so that it fell in a heap at her feet.

It was so sudden and unexpected that I went quite numb with shock. My father had half started out of his chair and now, with a groan, he sank back, letting his eyes rove over her body. We were all staring; it was like a revelation.

Even now I cannot ever remember having seen anything as beautiful as Nerissa. Her body was long and lean with high young breasts and her flanks were soft and gently rounded. But it was her colouring which overwhelmed us. Under her shimmering black hair her entire body was as white as a winter moon. Even her pubic hair and the hair under her arms had been shaved. She was the pale perfection of marble, except for one blemish and indeed it was this imperfection which gave interest to the rest of her and it was this that was her most important feature. On the right-hand side of her flat boy's stomach, about two inches from her navel, was a black birthmark shaped like a kidney and half the size of a man's palm. And seeing this I knew why Pereira was right and my father was wrong. We were looking at the living incarnation of Chaka's great milk-white war shield, even to the black mark. It was uncanny. I did not need to be told that if he ever saw her he would know she was a gift from the Spirits.

All that time, and it must have been minutes, Nerissa stood quite still under our scrutiny. She made no move to cover her breasts or groin, just stood there like an image.

In the silence my mother's voice cut at us like a *sjambok*. 'Pigs!' she said. 'Animals!' Then she scooped the fallen nightdress and threw it around Nerissa. 'Get out!' she hissed. 'Get out of this house!'

I must have run from the room for the next thing I remember is lying on my own bed with the door bolted behind me. The blankets were still warm from Nerissa's body but even so I felt chilled to the bone and I lay there shivering and trembling with the reaction. Some time later I heard my mother come out of one of the extra rooms, closing the door softly behind her and I knew that Nerissa was probably asleep. I closed my eyes and tried to bury everything in unconsciousness but my brain was a mass of churning images and sleep stayed far away. I wanted desperately to go to Nerissa and apologise for all that had happened and especially for the look in my father's eyes. But what of my own? Had it not been just as cruel?

In spite of my mental turmoil I must have dozed off because some hours later I awoke with a start to hear voices. They were coming from the main bedroom but the walls were so thick I could not make out what was being said or, in fact, who was talking. For a second I thought Pereira or Hamad might have entered the house again and I caught up one of the thick fighting-sticks which stood in the corner and crept out into the courtyard. There was a light under the bedroom door and as I approached I could make out the voices of my mother and father. I moved into the shadows and listened.

'I'm not blaming you,' my mother was saying. 'I'm not suggesting you wanted it to happen, what I *am* saying is that it was a disgusting exhibition and you let it happen.'

'I know, Fran, I know.' My father sounded flat and old. I did not know it then but now I would put his mood down to alcoholic depression. 'I should have kicked them out at the beginning. I never liked the look of them.'

I heard my mother clear her throat impatiently. 'All right, Jamie, let's leave that, then. It happened. The point is, what are you going to do about things now?'

'Do? About what?'

'For goodness sake, are you just going to let them take the girl away tomorrow and sell her to Chaka like a prime heifer?'

'I don't see what I can do to stop them, short of killing them, and I'm sure you're not suggesting that.'

'Of course I'm not! That brigand said he wanted two hundred tusks for her, isn't that so? Well—'

'Now wait a minute! You're not suggesting—?'

'Of course I am.'

'But that's half our store!'

'And what about it! Do you not consider the life of that young girl worth ten times that amount?'

'Now listen! That ivory is our future, our security. Other white men will be coming, traders and the like. You know as well as I that wherever we've been in Africa ivory is like gold. For God's sake, Fran, why do you think I've gone weeks at a time in search of elephant? For the fun of it?'

'I'm not arguing with you, James. If you can't see the difference between owning a store-room full of ivory and saving a young girl's life, then I'm sorry for you. You've changed even more than I thought and what you've become, God knows!'

'See here, Fran, I'm not going to be—'

'Oh, Jamie, what's happening to you and to us?'

'All right,' he said after a long pause. 'All right. But just remember it was you who wanted it.'

As I tiptoed away I remember feeling a great sense of happiness that Nerissa would be staying and at the same time being surprised that my father had capitulated so easily. Now I can see why.

We had long since acquired too much ivory for it to be stored in the main house and my father had built a special ant-proof hut for his treasure. It was built of stone and the massive wooden door was kept locked with one of the big padlocks from a wagon-chest. My father kept the key on a leather cord around his waist and no one ever went into the building unless he was there. When Pereira saw the piles of gleaming tusks his eyes widened.

'I misjudged you, farmer,' he said.

My father, who was recovered somewhat from the night before, replied shortly: 'Aye, and that's not the only way. Now, Pereira, I'm a busy man. Let's see, you were wanting a hundred tusks, was not that the figure?'

'No, Senhor, that was not the figure.' They began to haggle.

By mid-afternoon the deal was closed and the tusks loaded into Pereira's wagon. I can't remember exactly how much was paid, somewhere around one hundred and eighty, I think, but I know the wagon was groaning with the weight. Pereira fished out a bottle of brandy and said something about a celebration but my father just stared coldly at him. 'Now you can get off my land,' he said abruptly.

'You're making a joke, Senhor.'

'I was told once by a better man than you that I was just a mite humourless. Be it so. Now get off my land.'

For the first time, Pereira seemed nonplussed. It wasn't more than an hour or so to dusk, when he would have to make camp anyway and my father's attitude seemed, even to me, unreasonable.

'Now let us be sensible, my friend—'

My father didn't even bother to reply. He looked over his

shoulder and called: 'Stone-Axe! Cupido!' They came from the side of the house where they had been hidden. Each carried a weapon.

'Good-bye, Pereira.'

The hunter slowly poured himself a drink, sipped it, and nodded at my father. 'You are a fool, farmer. And an ungracious one at that.'

'Good-bye, Pereira.'

'You just can't wait to get your hands on her, can you?'

My father flushed and I saw the late sun glint on the steel of his hook as he moved it, but Pereira had turned his back on him and was climbing into the wagon. 'Good-bye, farmer,' he said. 'I don't think we shall meet again.'

We watched the wagon move around the side of the hill and then my father turned to me. 'Take the mare and ride to Mgobozi. Tell him that two of his old hunting friends are in the valley. Just that and no more, do you follow me?'

'Yes, Father.'

'All right, off with you then, as hard as you can go.'

No doubt you will think me uncommonly stupid when I state that I had no idea then who Pereira and Hamad really were; nor therefore did my father's message mean anything at all to me. It did, of course, to Mgobozi.

It was dark when I reached his kraal. He was stretched out on a kaross of lion skins drinking beer from a large wooden bowl and as I spoke his brow furrowed in thought. At first I was sure he understood as little as I did but then when I described the two men to him, and especially the scar on Pereira's face, the bewilderment cleared from his eyes and a frown settled on his features. One could almost see the slow advance of anger. In a moment he swung to his feet calling for Chest-biter and the rest of his armament. Standing there, with his great shield, his two spears and his war-club he made a frightening spectacle. 'Come,' he said. 'Show me.'

One might have thought that with all his wives for pleasure and all the beer he drank, Mgobozi-of-the-Hill would have softened with the years. This was not so. He was still the perfect fighting machine he had been ten years before. Now he ran easily by the side of the horse and it was I who was pressed to keep up. We plunged across the shoulders of hillocks and through the long grass of kloofs, Mgobozi as sure-footed as a goat in the darkness, until after about an hour we saw the light of their campfire. Still I suspected nothing. Mgobozi's arms, if I thought about them at all, need not have signified more than the accoutrements of a formal visit. It was only when we drew near and Mgobozi slowed his pace and began to approach more warily that I had the feeling that things were not as they seemed.

The two men had made their camp on the far side of a heavily-bushed stream and Mgobozi made me dismount and remain on the near side. 'I have a debt to pay which concerns no one but myself,' he said. Then he slipped away down the bank of the stream and I lost him in the darkness.

I tied the mare to a low branch and moved along the bank until I had a clear view of the camp. I could see Pereira and Hamad by the light of the flames. They were drinking together—celebrating their riches, I've no doubt—but the noise of the stream made it impossible to hear what they were saying. They were totally unsuspecting.

And then Mgobozi fell on them. I'm not sure who was the more surprised, the two men or myself. For Mgobozi had circled right around them, trapping them against the stream, and suddenly he seemed to rise out of the ground a few yards from them.

For a moment they sat there transfixed by the sight of this unexpected and ghostly materialisation. 'Look well!' I heard Mgobozi shout. 'Did you ever think to see me again?'

But Pereira was an old hunter and so was Hamad and now they whirled as one, scooping up their guns which were lying at their feet. It was obvious they must seek the protection of the wagon somehow, but things were too far along. I heard the great Zulu war-cry 'Si-gi-di!' roll from Mgobozi's open mouth and saw his throwing spear take Hamad between the shoulders and slice right through him, the point emerging to the left of his breast bone. Pereira swung his rifle up as Mgobozi charged. Later I saw the hole the bullet had made in the shield as well as the furrow it gouged along Mgobozi's rib-cage. At the time it seemed to affect the Zulu no more than a wasp sting. He came forward like a leopard knocking the gun out of his path and exposing Pereira's left side. And then Chest-biter flashed in the fire-light and I heard Pereira scream.

Without even bothering to look at the fallen man Mgobozi let the momentum of his charge take him right through the stream bringing him level with me. His body was shining with water and sweat and his eyes were wide.

'Tell Iron Hand the debt is paid,' he said hoarsely and then he sprang into the air and raced away across the dark veld and I pitied anyone who got in his way that night. He had tasted blood, but not enough. I fled the place at a gallop.

I have given my own part in this murder in some detail because I find it hard to convince myself even at this time that I had been involved unconsciously. But now that I have set it down and seen it once again against its real background my ignorance, naiveté, stupidity—call it what you like—does seem possible. After all, I was no more than a small boy when Pereira and Hamad left Mgobozi to die and it was only later, when my father mentioned it, that the earlier incident came clear in my mind. But at the time of which I write, so many things had happened, and were happening, that I seemed to be moving, or carried along rather, from one peak of violence to the next.

And things did not stop there, for the following morning something occurred which surprised us all. We were about to set off to bury the bodies and bring the wagon back when Nerissa suddenly spoke. She spoke in a curiously accented English, but she spoke.

'Are they dead?' she said.

I heard my mother gasp. Both my father and I stood and gaped.

'Are they dead?' she repeated. There was no expression either on her face or in the tone itself. It was as though the voice was issuing from the lips of a corpse.

'Murdered,' my mother said dully.

'I want to see them.'

'Don't talk like that, child. You want to forget. We *all* want to forget.' Something seemed to have gone out of her.

'I don't want to forget. I want to remember.'

My father and I took her with us. Hamad was lying where he'd fallen with the assegai still driven through him. But there was no sign of Pereira.

'Are you sure he was dead?' my father said angrily.

I had seen the gun swept aside; I had seen Chest-biter flash forward; I had heard Pereira scream. Of course I was sure.

109

We found his tracks, bloodstained and slimy, moving towards the stream. We could see where he entered; and then nothing.

'He'll not get far with that wound,' my father said. But he made no move to go downstream. It was as if he did not want to find the body.

'I wanted to see him,' Nerissa said. 'I wanted to see him dead.' And then she began to cry, almost impassively at first, the tears simply squeezing through the eyelids and coursing down her cheeks, and then her emotions surged to the surface and she began to sob like a child. My father tried to put an arm around her for comfort but she turned away and placed her head against the canvas top of the wagon and we let her alone.

After we had buried Hamad we collected the straying bullocks and inspanned them. All the ivory was intact. I know because my father counted each tusk. On the way home I asked him why it had had to happen.

'Use your head, boy. He was on his way to Chaka. Anyone but a fool can see that. He'd have got payment there too with the news he was bringing—and what do you think our lives would have been worth then?'

And so we left it. There are some things better forgotten. Anyway, he might have been right.

So began the second phase of our residence in Zululand. Until then we had lived a life of total isolation; now it had been disrupted by visitors from the outside world and was never finally to return to its earlier simplicity. In some ways this was good; in others bad. I don't think I ever wanted to sacrifice Nerissa to the memory of the past and yet that would have been the only way to re-enter a time when our family unit was close-knit with love and respect. The coming of Nerissa hastened a process already in motion.

I should like to be able to record that the sudden flood of tears and the surge of repressed feeling had acted like an emetic on her occluded emotions, but it was not as simple as that. Too much had happened to her; there had been too much terror, too much grief, too much physical hardship for an easy cure. But she was in my mother's hands now and if there was a cure at all it was there.

I don't think there was ever a time, at least I can't remember

110

it, when Nerissa sat down and told us her whole story. It came rather in bits and pieces, fragments of a mosaic, and each time she disgorged a fragment she seemed to take one more hesitant step towards recovery. It was months before one could even place these fragments in any sort of order.

She was a strange mixture. Her father had been in the Swedish diplomatic service and during his time as consul in Alexandria had married into one of the most important Coptic families in Egypt. Nerissa had been born in Java and had spent much of her youth in the Dutch East Indies. From there her father had been sent to India. The family had been returning to Europe on long leave before another posting, when their ship, the English East Indiaman *Plymouth*, fifty-three days out of Trincomalee, was blown ashore on the south-eastern coast of Africa.

Nerissa was never able coherently to describe all that happened at the time of the wreck or what happened thereafter but I have been able to fill in the gaps from the *Minutes of Proceedings and Evidence* at the Joint Inquiry in London, especially from the testimony of Thomas Aspin, an eighteen-year-old passenger and one of only twenty-two survivors of a total of one hundred and thirty-one who managed to get ashore. According to Aspin, the wreck must have occurred only a few miles north of Port Natal and it is a sad irony that if the survivors had walked south they would have come, within a day or two, on the small English settlement which had lately been started. But they were not to know and thought the nearest Christian settlement was at Delagoa Bay in Portuguese territory some hundreds of miles to the north.

Aspin told the Inquiry : 'After waiting twelve days for the sick to recover, we set out for Delagoa Bay. Madame Stresemann (this is Nerissa's mother) who had incurred a festering wound upon her leg was borne in a litter by seamen to whom Consul Stresemann paid one guinea a day each. Miss Stresemann walked always by the litter shading her mother's face by means of a broken parasol. We travelled in this way for thirty days skirmishing with the few Caffres we saw and thus protecting our lives. We subsisted upon rice saved from the wreck, and fruit found in thickets. Some of the party were killed by the Caffres and others abandoned through physical weakness. Water was so scarce that eventually a single cup was sold for two and sometimes three guineas. Coin seemed to have little value at this time.

'After another sixty days we came upon a land ruled by Chief

Bika. He was a good man for there is no doubt that there are good and bad in all nations. He begged us to remain, saying that the tribe to the north would assuredly slaughter us if we ventured there. But in spite of his warning we travelled on. Our passage was extremely slow since most of us were weak with hunger and many, like Madame Stresemann, had suffered grievous wounds. This brave lady was now walking by herself with the aid of a stick since the Consul had spent all his coin and there was no one in our party who gave assistance freely.

'We entered the territory of the northern chief and he offered us his hospitality until such time as a ship arrived if we would surrender our remaining muskets and powder and split ourselves up among his numerous villages. Consul Stresemann, who was by this time in charge of the party since all the officers had already died or been killed, yielded in spite of his wife, who cried out: "You lay down your arms, and now I give myself up for lost with all these people!"

'And this is indeed how it fell out, for once in possession of the muskets the Caffres threw us out of their villages with many blows and stripped us of our clothing. Madame Stresemann fought greatly against the Caffres who wished to strip both her and her daughter and she would have died under their hands if Consul Stresemann had not besought her to yield, reminding her that she was, like all of us, born naked and that she should submit to the will of God.

'She covered herself as best she could with her long hair and cast herself frantically upon the ground. There with frenzied hands she dug a pit in which she buried herself to the waist. Then she turned to us and said: "You see what we are reduced to. We can go no further, but must perish here for our sins; go on your way and try to save yourselves, and commend us to God." That is how we left her.'

So much for Thomas Aspin; he could not have known what followed. Nerissa crouched by her mother's side for two days and two nights, feeding her scraps which her father was able to steal from the village dogs. Eventually Consul Stresemann went into the bush in search of wild fruit. He never returned. That night Madame Stresemann died in her semi-grave and the following day Nerissa saw her father's signet ring on the chief's hand. She was alone. Had two things then not fortuitously happened she would have ended up, as other female castaways from earlier wrecks had already ended, in the seraglio of a chief, eventually to spawn a brood of half-caste children. She was saved from his pleasure by the onset of her monthly sickness. Three days later Pereira and Hamad arrived in the village and, after seeing her there naked, bought her.

It was so frightful an experience that she was lucky to recover. But recover she did, though it took many months.

With Nerissa's coming the pattern of our lives at Morile changed; and in the beginning this was all to the good. We had someone now who needed help badly and this seemed to pull us together. It was only when I began washing myself regularly and brushing my hair and seeing that my clothes were neat that I realised what I must have looked like before. My mother even remarked on my new cleanliness which was a striking thing in itself since it was always she who in the past had abjured me to take an interest in my appearance. After a while I found cleanliness no more irksome than many other things.

For my mother Nerissa was like the answer to a prayer. Every particle of maternal instinct, dormant for the past few years, was focussed on her. She made her special foods, sewed her new clothes, decorated a special room for her and generally fussed over her as though she was a long-absent daughter now returned to the family.

I can see now how important was the presence of another woman in a family, and for that matter in a land, of men.

But the biggest change came in my father. He was almost unrecognisable. In many ways her experiences were similar to his own at about the same age and they obviously touched a deep spring of identification. He became more human, even courteous to us. His table manners improved at the same time as his concubines languished, for during this period he spent most of the time at Morile except when Chaka sent for him. The whole household, including Stone-Axe and the servants, seemed to bask in an atmosphere of unexpected though welcome benignity. And the odd thing was that the person who had caused this change was herself seemingly impervious not only to it but to almost everything else as well.

Nerissa spent her days in a sort of numb half-world. She helped my mother around the house as often as was needed and she seemed to do the things required of her with a certain deftness but she did nothing on her own initiative. As meal times approached my mother would say to her: 'Would you like to lay the table, Nerissa?' Or if one of my father's shirts needed mending she would ask: 'I wonder if you'd like to get the needle and thread?' Just things like that, but without the gentle prodding she would never have started. One had the feeling that if we all went out of the house leaving her alone we would come back to find her poised in suspended action.

I once heard my mother say to my father: 'Remember the early days at Paradise after you'd lost your hand? She's very like that.'

'Aye, it'll take time, all right. She's more hurt than ever I was. But she's young; she'll mend.'

Weeks passed without much change in her. She hardly spoke at all and when she did it was just a yes or a no or a thank you. We did what we could but it wasn't enough.

After a longish spell of bad weather in which we'd all been house-bound—which put a strain on everyone, no matter what their intentions—I asked her to come out for a walk. She didn't often leave the house, preferring its safety, I suppose. But anyway she nodded her head and we went down into the valley and circled Ben Mhor. As we walked I pointed things out to her, like an ant-bear hole or a tree which had been struck by lightning, or made her feel the warm patch in the grass where a hare had been lying —just simple things like that which I thought might interest her. And each time she nodded obediently and looked and felt and did everything I asked and yet she didn't actually seem to be seeing or feeling.

All of a sudden we heard a strange bellowing noise quite close, the noise a cow makes when she's in trouble. Nerissa stood stock still and her whole body began to shake.

'It's all right,' I said. 'It's only a cow. Come on and we'll see what's wrong.'

I took her hand and squeezed it a bit just to show there really wasn't anything to bother about and we walked towards the noise. She didn't withdraw her hand. It was the first time she had allowed anyone except my mother to touch her. We came out at the top of a small, steep slope and there at the bottom was the cow. She was struggling to get up but one of her front legs was twisted out at an unusual angle and it was apparent she had slipped down the slope and broken her leg on the rocks at the bottom.

She struggled quite desperately, bellowing all the time and jerking and kicking as though she'd smelt a leopard in the grass. And then I saw why. She was in the process of calving. Already the front feet were through the womb and sticking out of her backside. I knew enough about animals to tell that she was labouring badly and would probably never deliver the calf herself.

'Come,' I said. 'We've got to help her.'

But Nerissa hung back. 'Come *on*. D'you want them both to die?'

'I can't!'

I had a firm grip on her hand and I pulled. We went down the slope together in a slithering rush. 'There's no *can't*!' I shouted.

The labour spasms were coming one on top of each other now but the calf seemed stuck. I bent down and looked more closely. 'The head's twisted,' I said. 'I've got to get the calf round. Look, you hold the legs. I'm going to try and get my hands in and turn it. When I say "Pull," then pull as hard as you can.'

The cow was bleeding badly and it was a messy business altogether so I can't really blame her, but when she hung back a second time I jerked savagely on her arm. 'Look at her,' I said, pointing to the cow's face. She was groaning and blowing froth and must have been in great pain. 'Now get hold of those feet!'

She knelt down in the dust and put her fingers on the tiny legs. 'Not like that! You'll never pull like that. Take a proper grip.'

Then I put my hands into the cow to feel for the head. I was right. It *had* got twisted; in fact the whole of the calf was off-centre. I struggled to get the head and body straight and I could feel the sweat and blood running off my arms like rain.

'All right,' I said. 'Now pull!' Together we heaved on the legs. At first it seemed the calf would never come, but then, once the head was through, it slid towards us in a smooth flow and within a few minutes both it and the after-birth were out.

'It's dead!' Nerissa said, and there was so much dejection in her voice that I looked up abruptly. Her eyes were quite stricken.

'Not yet,' I said in a softer tone, and I lifted the calf, still partially covered in its membrane, and carried it round to its mother. Instantly she began to lick it and in less than a minute the newborn animal opened its mouth and gave a particularly self-pitying bleat.

'It's alive! It's alive!'

'Didn't I tell you? I'll wait here. Go up to the house and tell my father.'

'No. I won't leave it. Something might happen. You go.'

So I went up and fetched my father and when we got back we found she had put the calf next to the udder and was sitting there smiling at it as it sucked.

'Oh, Robbie,' she cried as we got there. 'It's going to be all right,' and she flung her arms around my neck and hugged me. Over her shoulder I saw my father watching us and instead of being pleased for her, his mouth had set in a grim line.

We shot the cow and I carried the calf up to Morile, but I really only carried it for Nerissa because it was hers now. And that was the only name it ever had; it was always just called Nerissa's Calf.

At first we all thought that Nerissa had discovered her own panacea and in many ways I suppose she had. The calf made a great difference to her. She spent hours devising ways to feed it, first by dipping her fingers into milk and letting it suck, and when that didn't work by filling a hollow reed and trying to force it down its throat. Eventually Stone-Axe solved her problem by making a leather milk-bag with its own nipple. As it grew stronger the calf followed her everywhere and if I think of her at that time, it is always close by.

But it soon became apparent that the calf was no cure-all for what ailed her. It had made a difference, certainly, and we were all thankful for that, but I began to notice that there were two Nerissas. When she was out walking in the veld with me or when she was alone with my mother her melancholia seemed to recede. Often she smiled and frequently offered information about herself or just started talking, and this in itself was a new and welcome sign. But it was when we were all together in the house that the veils of blankness seemed to descend and after a while I began to suspect the reason. She was afraid of my father. I suppose she identified him with Pereira and with the men on the long march from the wreck and this must have been unavoidable.

I began to notice little things. For instance, she always sat furthest from his chair and saw that her dress was well pulled down over her ankles. Nor did she ever remain alone in the same room with him. Once I'd begun to notice this I saw how laboured her excuses were and if I had to get up and go outside, even to relieve myself, she would have to go and see the calf or help

116

my mother or fetch her sewing, anything to get through the door. And my father's eyes would follow her every move.

Once, when I had got up suddenly without thinking and gone out to the front to fetch something, I heard my father call her. I looked in through the small window and saw her sitting there like a jackal trapped by dogs. She had already half risen to make her exit when my father spoke.

'Come here, Nerissa.'

'I must—I was just—'

'Come here.' She crossed hesitantly to his chair and stopped a few feet away.

'Nearer, my dear, no one's going to hurt you.'

She took a few steps closer and he reached out and held her arm just above the wrist.

'Why are you avoiding me?' he asked.

'I—I—' She did not seem to be able to form the words and ended by shaking her head.

'I want you to be happy here with us. Aren't you happy, my dear?'

And then her shoulders seemed to slump and the same blank expression came over her face. Hurriedly I went back into the room. He had released her arm and she was leaving by the other door.

'Good night, Nerissa,' my father called, as though nothing had happened. But I saw the sickness in his eyes as he watched her move across the floor. Then he turned to me and growled: 'What do you want?'

'Nothing!' I said. There must have been something in the tone of my voice that got through to him, because he looked up sharply.

'What's that supposed to mean?'

'Nothing.' This time it came out as a mumble.

'My advice to you, laddie, is to step carefully.'

After that I *was* more careful. I tried never to leave her alone with him. And of course he knew. Even a slight change of behaviour is easily detectable when people live on top of each other, and often I would feel his brooding eyes on me. I wished he would leave us alone. I wished he would go back to his beer and his concubines and his long discussions with Chaka.

I had become so concerned with Nerissa that I failed to notice that all was not well with my mother. It must have cost her a great deal to stand up to my father, and then see it all end in ritual

117

killing. It may have been this, coupled with all the new effort she put into making Nerissa feel wanted and at home that weakened her physically. Whatever the cause she suddenly took ill with fever. At first it seemed like other bouts which she had suffered in the past and which she had contracted, so she said, on her travels near the Great River, but this was much worse.

It lasted for more than a week and during that time she was suffering two major paroxysms a day, one in the morning and one in the afternoon. They were always the same and came almost to the minute. First there was the shivering and we put heated stones wrapped in blankets at her back and legs and then that would give way to a spell where she was almost burning hot to the touch. From that would come the sweating. I've never seen anyone sweat like that. It ran off her face and neck in rivulets, soaking her nightgown and pillow, drenching blankets and even the wool mattress so that everything had to be changed four and five times a day.

My father and I, and even the servants, tiptoed about the house as though we were in a place of bereavement. Occasionally we were allowed in to see her, mainly when she was sleeping. I need hardly say that Nerissa was in charge. If anything could have brought her out of herself this was it. She dominated the house. She took charge of everything. Fevers were old enemies of hers, having been brought up in the East, and she was quite used to fighting them. She never left the house in all that time of crisis and I can only remember her coming out of my mother's room to order more blankets, or hot stones, or basins of cold water. She took her meals there, though she didn't eat much, and slept in a cot at the foot of the bed. If it hadn't been for her I'm sure my mother would have died.

Finally a day came when the fever drained out of her body and we were allowed in to see her. Nerissa had dressed her in a clean nightgown and tied a blue ribbon in her hair. The bed was freshly made and for the first time the curtains had been drawn from the window and the bright morning sun streamed in. It should have been a time of great rejoicing but all I can remember is the shock of seeing a stranger lying in my mother's bed. She looked twenty years older and her face was yellow and wasted. I heard my father's sharp intake of breath and I saw the hand-mirror lying next to the bed, and I noticed the look of despair on her face. She *knew*.

Clumsily, my father went forward and sat on the bed. Even as he took my mother's hand I could see his eyes on Nerissa. The comparison was painful.

In another week my mother was taking her first tentative steps in the bedroom and a few days after that Nerissa brought a chair outside and she spent hours sitting on the verandah. We did not have to be told that her convalescence would be a long one. We took it in turns to sit with her and even Donald, who now spent most of his time with Stone-Axe as I had done at his age, voluntarily sacrificed part of his hunting to try and cheer her up. For the fever had left her badly depressed. Gradually the colour came back into her cheeks and her body filled out again and strengthened, but the soft beauty and the smooth golden skin were lost for ever.

With Nerissa it was just the contrary. The responsibility of running the house and looking after my mother had finally healed the bruised parts of her mind and now we began to see what she must have been like before the wreck of the *Plymouth*. She walked with a feline grace and held her head high. She no longer slumped into periods of numbness. She was brisk with the servants but never domineering and she was so efficient in the house that it seemed to run itself. She began to teach the cook the recipes of India and Java and although it is possible that they lacked many of the original ingredients they were different enough to give us a feeling of expectancy as meal times approached.

With the return of her confidence came a heightening of her beauty. Her face filled out slightly and her skin became creamier. The dresses my mother made for her had come from a bolt of plain white cotton and nothing could have enhanced her dramatic colouring more. Sometimes, I recall, she wore a blue or yellow ribbon in her hair and the effect was quite breathtaking. Having gone to school in India her English had been good but heavily accented when she first came to us. Now she was almost perfect and even the accent was fading.

But the most important thing was a new poise in her relationship with my father. She no longer seemed afraid of him. They treated each other as equals and I did not have to worry about leaving her alone in the same room, in spite of the fact that the hunger in his eyes was now more apparent than ever. As a frightened young girl she had been desirable; how much more so as a self-assured and beautiful young woman.

I say that I no longer had to worry about leaving her alone with him and this is true as far as she was concerned. But not so far as it concerned me. I didn't want her alone with *him*; I wanted her to be with *me*. But the only thing I could do, after my mother had gone to bed in the early evening, was to sit with them in the front room while my father talked and Nerissa sewed. He would tell her about his life as a young boy in Scotland and about farming on the Frontier and hunting-trips with Stone-Axe, and all I could do was remain silent since nothing so interesting had ever happened to me. I have to admit he could be both interesting and charming when he set his mind to it.

During the day, when he should have been working or seeing Chaka or drinking beer with his concubines, or doing something, he would find time to walk with Nerissa in the valley or even down to the stream—*my* places. And then one day he came back from a visit to Chaka and told me to get some clothes ready. The King, he said, had suggested I learn some of the Zulu fighting traditions by becoming an *u-dibi* and my father had concurred. I was stunned. The *u-dibi* were boys of fourteen and fifteen who made up a corps in the army. They were the mat carriers and orderlies. It was a Zulu thing; it had nothing to do with me.

Despite the fact that he had clearly been drinking heavily with Chaka, I said : 'I'd rather not go, Father.' It had been on the tip of my tongue to say something stronger, like why didn't he go and live like a Zulu himself, since that's where his women were, but one didn't say things like that to my father.

'I dare say,' he replied. 'And if you've the courage, be sure and tell the King.'

'Tell the King what?' my mother said, entering the room.

He explained. 'So you're starting on Robert now,' she said bitterly.

'Starting?'

'Well, you've made yourself in the King's image; now you'll turn him into a savage too.'

'Rubbish. It'll do the boy good. He'll be with a group of his own age. Don't forget we have to live with these people. It's as well we know the next generation.'

'That's more like it. I know that philosophy well enough. You say it was the King's suggestion. I don't believe it. It was you that sowed the seed.'

120

'All right, then, I admit it. I did suggest it to him. And he was taken with it.'

'Why shouldn't he be? It's easy enough to impress a young lad.'

'I'm damned if I'm arguing about it. Robbie, get your things!'

But I stood where I was. It had dawned on me why he wanted me out of the house.

'There's nothing I can do to stop you,' my mother said. 'He's your son. But you'll not take Donald from me in his turn.' The tears, which were never far away since her illness, now came swimming into her eyes.

'Oh, stop your sniffling,' my father said disgustedly. 'Why should I be taking Donald? He's no more than a child.'

'You're forgetting there's an even younger generation. Why don't you take us all? Why don't we all become Zulus? Why don't we live down there with your other women and then you could play at being king till your heart's content?'

'What's this now! Robert, I thought I told you to get out! What's this about other women, then!' His skin had flushed to a dark wine colour with anger.

'Don't stand there trying to think up a lie to cover it. A kitchen is a fine place for gossip and anyway I could smell them on you. Yes, *smell* them!' Her lips were quivering and her body was trembling. I suddenly saw a new thought come into her eyes; it was one I was now familiar with.

'Of course!' she said. 'You *want* him out of the house. You—'

My father was shouting: 'It was *you* who wanted her here! You! Just you remember that!'

She sank down in one of the big chairs and put her hands up to her face as she cried. I ran to her across the room. 'Get out!' my father yelled at me. 'Get out before I mark you!' This time I went.

I got my things together and picked up my fighting-sticks and then went out to say good-bye to Nerissa. She was down near the stream with the calf.

We sat on a bank eating *imfé* and I told her what was to happen. I didn't make any mention of what had occurred in the house because it was something I was already trying to erase from my mind. Her eyes clouded for a moment and she frowned. And then, as though making a conscious effort, the lines on her brow smoothed out and the worry seemed to disappear. I thought: *She doesn't mind. She wants to be with him.*

'Don't look so miserable,' she said lightly. 'It'll only be for a little while.'

'I don't like leaving you.'

'Me? Don't be silly. Why should you worry about me?'

'You *want* to be alone with him!' I blurted out.

For the first time I saw a flash of anger in her eyes. 'That's an unpleasant thing to say!'

'But it's true, isn't it?'

'Is that what you really think?'

'I don't know,' I said unhappily.

'Listen to me. I'm learning to live with people again. Sometimes I still get frightened. Don't make it more difficult.' Then she leant forward and kissed me on the lips and my heart seemed to turn over.

'I thought I told you to get ready!' said my father harshly, and he caught me by the shoulder and dragged me away from her. He had come up on us with great care.

The fighting-sticks must have been lying at my feet, for in a second they seemed to be in my hands; the left held in the middle as a shield, the right near the end as a weapon. We stared at each other for a moment and then my father said softly: 'Don't bare your fangs at me, laddie, or I'll have to draw them.'

'No!' I said. 'You won't! Don't ever touch me again!'

The anger passed from his eyes and it was replaced by something that seemed to freeze my blood. It was as though he had never seen me before. It was a measuring, calculating look; it seemed to say I was no longer a boy, but an adversary and he was judging me. It was a look which said we were equals and if we fought it would be as equals, and what frightened me most was the thought of the hook. If we fought as equals he would kill me.

I'm not sure what would have happened then if we had not heard a cry from the house. It was Stone-Axe calling to us that a runner had arrived from the King. For the second time the Ndwandwes had crossed our lives at a critical moment. They were invading Zululand from the north.

We left for Bulawayo before dawn on a chill October morning; both of us much aware of each other but not talking. The only thing my father had said to me, since we had heard the news the day before, was: 'I need you with me.' It was still dark when we left and my mother and Nerissa had come out on to the verandah to see us off. We took our leave of them quickly, almost brusquely, and plunged down into the valley. My father was leading Violin, for she was old now and there was no saying what she might be called upon to do in the next few days. Both of us carried rifles, bandoliers of bullets, powder horns, and wallets containing dried meat, hard biscuits and corn for roasting. Our sleeping karosses were rolled and tied behind Violin's saddle and they contained our spare shoes. Both of us were wearing sheepskins against the cold.

As the light strengthened it looked as though the whole race of Zulus was migrating southwards. We could see thousands upon thousands of warriors converging on Bulawayo. I was reminded of the time, nearly ten years before, when we had made our way through a similar dawn to the smelling-out ceremony, except on that occasion our fellow-travellers had looked worried and fearful; now they were joyous. My father had once said that the Zulus were created for war and this was true; happiness to them was the anticipation of a coming battle.

By the time we reached Bulawayo the Meeting Place was already churning with upwards of twenty thousand warriors and the strengthening ceremonies were beginning. Chaka had little time to spend with us then and we took our usual places with the court officials. I had seen the ceremonies several times before at the start of lesser campaigns but this was of much greater importance and Mqalane, the great War Doctor of the Zulu nation, had been called in to preside.

The first day was occupied by a rite known as 'the bringing together of the hearts of the people', which was a strange way of describing it. A great pit had been dug in the centre of the arena alongside of which stood huge pots of foul-smelling brews. Mqalane and his assistants stood beside the pit and each warrior came forward in turn to drink from the pots and then spew up the concoction into the pit. And it was no use pretending to take a mouthful and make gurgling noises in the throat, for the war doctors were waiting with heavy sticks for anyone who did not react correctly. It was a wearisome day, for as the sun climbed in the sky the dust raised by queueing warriors mingled with the foetid stench of the pit, seeming to cover one from head to foot. Finally the last regiment had supped of the brew and brought it up again and the pit was ceremoniously filled in so that no particle of its contents might reach the hands of the Ndwandwes and so grant them supernatural powers over the Zulus. That night I spent at Mgobozi's kraal, my father taking his pleasure elsewhere.

The following day was given over to the Rite of the Bull. In this ceremony a regiment ran one of Chaka's great stud bulls in the cattle enclosure. They kept it running for about three hours until its tongue was lolling from its mouth and it was bellowing mournfully and then they rushed in and threw it to the ground by main force. After its neck had been twisted the war doctors skinned it, cut the meat into long strips, and roasted them. I saw several pieces that could not have come from any bull ever born. One piece had toes.

By mid-afternoon the feasting began, if that is an adequate way of describing it. The warriors formed rank upon rank in a half-moon and the war doctors flung the strips of charred meat high into the air above their heads. Again great clouds of dust rose from the arena as the warriors fought among themselves for the meat. But each man, having grabbed a strip, would only take a small bite before throwing it over his shoulder to be scrambled for again. In this way one bull served for a whole army. The entrails were buried secretly near the King's enclosure and the hole was guarded all night by a watchman. Every other particle of the bull, including bones and hide, was burnt to ash. The war doctors collected up the cinders, took them down to the river, and threw them into a deep pool. Cattle were now slaughtered and the whole populace gorged themselves against the morrow.

Chaka was highly pleased with the ceremonies. As far as he was concerned they had already given victory to the Zulus. There now only remained the matter of the actual battle.

But first the entire army had to visit the grave of Chaka's father fifty miles inland, from which point, by tradition, all Zulu attacks were launched. All this time spies of Chaka's intelligence service were coming and going between the King and what was to become the front line of battle.

This then was the position: the Ndwandwes, under their new King, Sikunyana (his father Zwide had died), were about four or five days march to the north. They had come bursting through the northern borders of Zululand about forty thousand strong. It was almost a migration, for their women and children had come with them and they had brought sixty thousand head of cattle.

After Mqalane had sprinkled the entire Zulu Army near the grave of Chaka's father, the Zulus were finally ready for war.

It is only now that I have read the accounts of the Persian advance on Athens that I have any true yardstick to measure the experiences of the following days. This is what it must have been like to march with Darius or Xerxes.

We moved out on a fine spring morning, the frost winking on the dry winter grass, the sun climbing warmly into the clear blue sky. No rain had fallen throughout the winter and the air was like crystal. The far-off ridges of the tableland in front of us seemed hardly more than a few hundred yards away. For a few brief moments the great army was starkly etched against the lion-coloured veld—and then almost everything became totally obscured by dust. Great clouds of dust rose up from the thudding feet. It was a fine, tawny-coloured dust that clung to the bodies of the warriors, gradually powdering the shining black skins until they became dull and lifeless. Dust caught in the nostrils and eyes and throat; it rimed lips and eyebrows like frosting. From a distance there was no army to be seen at all, just a great moving cloud of dust.

This is how my father described the regiments in his Journal:

'The first division wore a turban of otter skin round the forehead, with a crane's feather, two feet long; ox-tails round the arms; a dress of ox-tails over the shoulders and chest; a kilt of monkey and genet skins made to resemble the tails of those animals; and ox-tails round the legs. They carried white shields chequered at the centre with black patches. Each carried a single assegai and a knobbed stick.

'The second division wore turbans of otter skin, at the upper edges of which were two bits of hide resembling horns; from these hung black cow-tails. They carried red spotted shields.

'The third division wore a very large bunch of eagle feathers on the head, fastened only by a string that passed under the chin. Trappings of ox-tails over the chest and shoulders, and, as the second division, a piece of hide resembling three tails. Their shields were grey.

'The fourth division wore trappings of ox-tails over the chest and shoulders, a band of ox-hide with white cow-tails round the head and their shields were black.

'At first they held their shields down at the left side—and at a distance very much resembled a body of cavalry. Later they

125

were ordered to roll up the shields and carry them on their backs. The first and third divisions marched off making a shrill noise, while the second and fourth made a dreadful howl.'

For this war against the Ndwandwes Chaka had ordered a general mobilisation so that there were some of the older regiments like the Single-Clash and the Look-Outs, men who had married and taken the headrings, and newer ones like the Expellers, the Cockroaches and the Great Affair. Both the Belebele and the Isi-Klebeni Brigades were therefore at full strength.

It is difficult to say how many of us were marching in that frightful dust-cloud but, taking in the young *u-dibis*, carrying the mats and headrests, and the women with the food, my father has estimated the total at more than fifty thousand and he may well have been right. Certainly when we marched across a wide valley the van would be climbing the slopes ahead while the rear were descending those behind. The valley itself would be as full as though it were in flood.

But there was no flood; in fact there was no water. As the sun climbed up to its noon position the army became more and more parched.

Although neither my father nor I had thought to bring water we were still more fortunate than the bulk of the army for we marched in the van near Chaka. He, with Mgobozi by his side, led the first division, Mdlaka the second, and the two flanks were commanded by Nzobo and Ndlela.

Chaka led us into the high mountain country at a cruel pace and even Violin, who was still being led, fretted and stumbled and hung her head in exhaustion. We neither stopped to rest nor checked our pace during the whole of that stifling, burning day.

By early afternoon the beer and milk which the women were carrying had long since been drunk and they turned back, leaving us to our own resources. We were thirstier than ever. I began to march like a sleep-walker. I had tied a kerchief around my mouth and it kept out much of the dust that even we, at the front, were getting, but it could not exclude all and slowly my mouth and throat grew dry and chalky. I tried chewing the thin leather thread of my bandolier to bring saliva into my mouth but after a few minutes I had to stop because it was salty and dried my mouth even further. Every now and then I stole glances at my father and I could see he was suffering too. Both Chaka and Mgobozi seemed impervious to any hardships.

My father and I had been taking turn and turn about to lead the horse, and the reins were in my hands about sunset when suddenly she lifted her head and I saw her nostrils flutter as she tested the air. She jerked and tried to break forward. I held on and she side-stepped, shaking her head at the bridle.

'Can't you hold her?' my father growled.

She was prancing sideways, showing her teeth and shaking her head. She began to drag me.

'Stand still, damn you!' my father said, slamming his fist into her side and then taking the other rein. She whickered and jerked again. And then we reached the top of a rise and I could see what had caused her agitation. A few yards below us bulrushes and reeds marked the banks of a small marshy stream.

'It's the water,' I said. 'You'll never stop her.'

She was bucking and kicking and finally I let her have her head and the three of us plunged down towards the water together.

It is possible that Violin saved our lives at that moment. In her own haste to get at the water she had pulled us clear of the army, for now, as the ranks rose up over the ridge and saw the water, discipline was flung to the winds. I had managed to get a hatful of the warm, scummy liquid and Violin was sipping deeply, when the first black wave broke over us. The Zulus were frantic for moisture and they fell on top of each other to get their faces into the pools. Within seconds a third and fourth wave broke over the ridge until the whole marshy area was covered in bodies and what water there was became churned into mud. But this did not stop them.

As the weight of the Zulus became greater and greater, those who slipped or fell were simply trampled to death. The fact that there was no longer any water did not seem to matter, for the Zulus scooped up handfuls of mud and thrust it into their mouths. Five minutes after our arrival the whole area was a seething, tangled mass of bodies, some fighting to get at the mud, others fighting to get out of it, and above everything were the shrieks of the dying.

I had been pulled across with my father as Violin moved forward and now we stood on the opposite bank and looked back at the scenes of hysteria. For once Chaka and Mgobozi seemed unable to control the *impis* and if it hadn't been for my father the whole of the expedition might have foundered right then.

127

He grabbed his heavy gun from the saddle and fired over the heads of the scrabbling men; then he took my gun and fired again. Both of us loaded as fast as we could and fired the moment the wadding was in. The Zulus nearest us grew silent and soon this spread to the whole army. They looked at each other and at the bodies half buried in the mud and then Mgobozi's great voice rolled out over the throng.

'Shame!' he cried. 'Shame!'

It was just enough. First one man stepped out of the quagmire and then others, until finally the whole army was drawn up on the far side. Chaka, shaking with rage, said nothing; there was nothing to say. As he turned to lead us forward I caught sight of one of the half-buried corpses and there was something about it that looked familiar. I ran back to the marsh to look more closely. It was Tanga. He must have been marching with his father's personal guard in the body of the main army and I had failed to see him. Now in his crushed feathers and mud-smeared finery he was a pitiful sight. I grabbed him under the arms and hauled him from the marsh. My father helped me carry him up the bank and we laid him down gently. His nostrils and eyes were impacted with mud as though someone had stood on his head while he knelt to drink. But his mouth was clear and I thought I could detect faint signs of breathing. I felt for his heart but my own was pumping so loudly I could not be certain of the beat.

'I think he's alive,' I said.

'Here, use this.' My father passed me a twig and I scraped the mud from the nostrils and eyes.

'We should wash it out,' I said.

'What with!'

At that moment Tanga coughed and a large gout of mud which must have been lodged somewhere near the back of his throat blew out on to the grass. He tried to open his eyes but the mud had dried and gummed them fast. We carried him to Violin and tied him on to the saddle and hurried to catch up with Chaka. The vanguard had reached a well-watered kraal and were about to bivouac for the night. We managed to get a calabash of water and I washed out Tanga's eyes and nose and let about a cupful trickle down his throat. After a few minutes he sat up. Later Chaka came to look down at his nephew who was now wrapped up in my kaross.

He stood there for some moments, ignoring us completely, then

128

said to Tanga : 'Those who drink like dogs, die like dogs.' There was not the slightest hint of emotion in his voice.

After he had left Ngwadi came to squat down next to his son. At first he tried to preserve that Spartan indifference to death in war that is the ambition of every Zulu warrior, but this was his son and soon his face softened and he spoke quietly to Tanga, touching him now and then on the shoulder. As he left he came across to me and said : 'From this time forth you are under my armpit.'

On that high, bleak plain there was no wood for fires and about midnight it began to freeze. I crawled into one side of Tanga's kaross and my father wrapped himself up in the other. It was as well we did for by morning our shoes were frozen stiff.

When we marched out over the frosty, crackling veld we passed more corpses, those of warriors who had died of exposure.

Tanga had recovered completely and now he attached himself to us and walked by my side. I'm not sure whether this was done on his father's orders but for whatever reason it was a great comfort. Although I tried not to think of it, we were in fact going to war and I was frightened.

For three days Chaka marched us through the high country until we had covered about one hundred and twenty miles and reached the banks of the Pongola River. This was considered to be the northern border of Zululand and we now found that the Ndwandwes had retreated a day's march further north. They were in fact no longer in Zulu territory but no one was in any doubt that if we simply patrolled the border in a show of force and then returned to Bulawayo, Sikunyana would bring his nation once more into Zululand.

We forded the Pongola and camped in a forest near the En-Tombe River. From here Chaka sent out a platoon of scouts to bring back news of the enemy's position. At their return we found that the earlier reports were in no way exaggerated.

Here we were joined by Fynn who had come to witness the battle and I remember him as being a man of great good humour. He greeted my father as an old comrade and expressed himself pleased to see us. But he did not stay long since he had his writing materials with him and was determined to set everything down.

The following afternoon we accompanied Chaka, who wished

to confirm personally the reports of his scouts. From the top of a hill nearby we were able to survey the ground for the coming battle.

Away to our left stood Ndololwane Hill and it was here that Sikunyana had decided to make his stand. He had drawn up his army, about twenty thousand strong, high on the slopes just below the rocky summit. Behind the fighting lines were the women and children and between the two groups were the cattle.

Chaka at once decided that in spite of his own numerical superiority it would be suicide to launch the whole army in a frontal attack up the steep escarpment, so he ordered Mdlaka to take the second division north-west during the night, coming around the rear of the mountain the following morning. It was a long encircling movement and would depend upon the speed with which Mdlaka could encompass it.

It was dusk when we returned to the forest and the *impis* were making their evening meal of meat and grain which had arrived from the neighbouring kraals. They had survived the march with surprising ease and already it seemed that Sikunyana had underestimated the hardness of Zulu battle training. After we had eaten Chaka called the army together and spoke to them from a slight rise, outlining the enemy's position and explaining the tactics he would use. And then a strange thing happened. As was traditional before battle he called upon champions to lead attacks on the massed enemy ranks and so break up their front and allow the stabbing spears to be used. Mgobozi suddenly leapt up the rise brandishing his shield and spear, stabbing and hacking at imaginary foes, finally coming to a stop before Chaka. He turned to the army, shouting: 'Thus will I go stabbing my way through the enemy! Thus must we all do for our Father!'

I watched a frown of worry and displeasure cross Chaka's face. It was not Mgobozi's function to lead a suicide mission. The Hammer of Chaka would normally have remained with the King to defend his body against attack, but now he had committed himself and Chaka had to support him as a matter of honour.

Later that night as we crouched over a small fire in one of the clearings Mgobozi noted Chaka's sadness and said: 'We must all die sooner or later. If my time has come nothing will hold it back. And, in truth, it is better to die with a spear in one's hand than to fall sick like on old ox at home. You would not deprive me of that, Father?'

'No,' Chaka said sorrowfully, 'but such a parting would be heavy.'

Mgobozi refused another gourd of beer and stood waiting for Chaka's permission to leave. Finally the King nodded his head : 'Go you well, Mgobozi.'

'Stay you well, Father.' He raised his hand to the King and turned away. As he passed me he stopped and looked down. 'Remember well what I have taught you,' he said, 'for these are the games men play.'

The army was drawn up in the bitter pre-dawn cold. Silently the warriors had emerged from behind their leafy windbreaks to take up their parade-ground positions. Chaka always fought a set-piece battle in the same way, sending the army forward in a horns-and-chest formation which allowed the horns to envelop the enemy's flanks before the chest smashed into the centre. We moved out towards the foot of Ndololwane Hill in battle formation. Before we reached the point from which the attack was to be launched the Great Elephant made his headquarters on the brow of a neighbouring hill, taking with him his staff officers and runners. He ordered us to follow. From this point we could look down on the Zulu Army and yet be almost level with the Ndwandwes who were sitting down quite calmly awaiting the attack.

I must make it clear, in describing what follows, that only part of the events were observed by myself, but I spoke with many u-dibi later, and even one of the Fasimbas who, though badly wounded, survived the Battle of the Rock.

Both armies were now quite still and in the bright morning air the scene resembled an old battle print. Then Chaka raised his assegai above his head and the great Zulu force began to move slowly up the slope. Before they had covered half the distance there was a ripple down the length of the Ndwandwe line as warriors scrambled to their feet and closed ranks. From where we watched it seemed as though they had suddenly become one solid black wall, with every here and there the winking reflection of the sun on an assegai blade.

The pattern of the Zulu advance changed. It remained the chest-and-horns formation but now, from the centre of the chest, an arrowhead of men projected, moving slightly faster than the main army. These were Mgobozi and his beloved

131

Fasimbas. Gradually they drew ahead until there were a dozen yards separating them from the front ranks. All this time runners were coming and going from Chaka's headquarters and he was issuing a steady stream of orders.

With less than thirty yards separating the two armies, the Zulus halted. In one fluid motion they swung their shields around to cover their bodies, each warrior gripping the stabbing spear at its point of balance. They waited for the Ndwandwes to charge.

But Sikunyana was no green youth; he had the slope in his favour. The Ndwandwes stood their ground, bunching together even more tightly. Again there was a pause as the armies took stock of each other. There was something sinister about this silent warfare. It was as though the Zulu Army was stalking a prey that was well aware of what was happening and, to my untutored eye, awaiting it with confidence.

All this time Chaka had been standing like a rock, his eyes flicking up and down the Zulu ranks, watchful, alert. Now he frowned in displeasure. Things were not going as he planned. The Ndwandwes formed a living fortress and no one, not even Mgobozi and the Fasimbas, would break up their ranks with an uphill charge. Somehow he had to disturb their solidarity. He looked around him and his eyes fastened on my father. Both he and the interpreter, Jacob, were carrying guns. I saw Chaka's eyes quicken as an idea blossomed in his mind.

'Iron Hand,' he called. 'Can you throw that far?' He pointed to the Ndwandwe army.

My father looked down at his gun and shook his head. 'Not from here,' he said. 'But I could get closer. To that spur.' He indicated a ridge which would put him in firing range.

'Go down,' Chaka ordered. 'Take Jacob with you. See if you can throw well enough to make them eat earth.'

We watched as my father and Jacob slithered down the shoulder of the hill, walked across the ridge and up the further knoll. I was aware of Chaka looking down at me thoughtfully. 'So the young bull has come to make battle. We must find something for him to do.'

Just then we heard the crash of the first shot. I saw the puff of smoke rise first from my father's gun and then came another—first the smoke and then the sound—from Jacob's old musket. We were not able to see if the balls had caused any damage in the

132

Ndwandwes but at that distance it would have been unlikely. The result was immediate and unexpected. The Ndwandwes began to hiss with anger. Coming from twenty thousand throats the noise sounded, in the still morning air, like the rush of a waterfall. As the hissing died down the Ndwandwes began to shout insults. They called the Zulus dogs and sons of dogs. They referred to their mothers' and fathers' genitalia. They spoke disparagingly of their ancestry. They described briefly what they would do to them once they attacked. Then my father fired again.

The Ndwandwes began to shriek their war-cry. '*Ya-ntsini za-nja! Nje-ya . . . ! Nje-ya . . . ! Nje-ya . . . !*' Some, their rage so great, broke ranks, shouting at the others to follow.

This was precisely what the Zulus had been waiting for. '*Si-gi-di!*' roared Mgobozi. '*Si-gi-di!*' howled the Zulus in answer, and the two armies fell upon each other.

The Ndwandwes poured down on the Zulus like a black flood, the impetus of their charge smashing down on the Zulu ranks and stopping them abruptly. For about five minutes they hacked and slashed at each other with the short spears and then the Zulus fell back down the slope to regroup.

The Ndwandwes now held the original Zulu positions and at once they began taunting them again. I had been standing next to Chaka during the first attack and he had remained remarkably cool. He must have expected something like this to happen. But then, when the first clash was over, I saw his face change to an expression of alarm and apprehension. I followed his eyes and saw something I had earlier missed.

Mgobozi, true to his boast, had, with his Fasimbas, hacked a path through the front ranks of the Ndwandwes, but the sudden withdrawal of the Zulus had left him stranded. He and about a dozen warriors were cut off from the main army.

For the first time I saw Chaka lose control of himself. He began to dash about on top of the hill, shouting and raging, sending one runner after another to the commanders in the field, apprising them of what was happening and ordering them, on pain of immediate execution, to renew the attack. By this time we could see that Mgobozi and his young men had scythed their way right through the Ndwandwes and were engaging platoons of hardened veterans in the rear.

'*Si-gi-di! Si-gi-di!*' Once again the Zulu battle cry rolled out over the hills as they charged the slope. But the Ndwandwes stood fast and the panting Zulus were out of breath by the time they hit the front ranks. Again the short spears flashed in the sunlight, again there was a hacking mêlée, and again the Zulus were pushed back to regroup.

'Forward!' Chaka was shouting. 'Attack!' He stabbed the air a dozen times with his spear. But the Zulus remained where they were, looking up at their enemies with a new respect.

Mgobozi and the Fasimbas had fought their way to a great slab of stone the size of a house and now, with their backs to it, they formed a semi-circle of flashing assegais. Here too there was a lull and we could see that the number of Fasimbas was half what it had been only a few minutes before. Again the Zulus launched their uphill attack, again the veterans closed in on Mgobozi. There were now two distinct battles taking place.

Chaka's rage had given way to a curious stillness. He seemed numbed by what was happening; not so much by the ineffectiveness of the Zulu charges but by the hopelessness of Mgobozi's cause. It is said that during the next pause Mgobozi and his now half-dead companions took the chance to lean heavily on their shields and try to regain some of their strength. A dozen yards away their enemies glared at them with a mixture of admiration and loathing. One badly wounded Fasimba turned to Mgobozi and said : 'My Father, we are happy to die with you. Who would wish to live when you are gone?'

The old lion, streaming blood from wounds in his chest and thighs, raised his weary head. 'Your words put a stone in my stomach,' he said, 'for I liked not to drag you to certain death. But now, my children, let us say farewell, for the enemy stirs once more. This will be our last fight. Let us send our final message to our brothers.'

'U-Zulu!' they roared over the heads of the Ndwandwes. 'Bayete!' There was an answering shout from the main Zulu ranks.

'Si-gi-di!' bellowed Mgobozi, and the final clash was begun.

It is said that at this time the curtain of redness dropped over Mgobozi's eyes and the fighting madness overcame him. He went berserk. He sprang at his enemies with such ferocity and abandon that frequently they scattered before him. He became the essence of a battle-crazed Zulu warrior and no one could stand in his way.

At that very moment a movement caught the edge of my

134

vision. I glanced upwards and there on the skyline I saw the faint bobbing heads of warriors at full pace. As I flung up my arm to show this to Chaka he saw them for himself. 'Mdlaka!' he hissed.

In that minute the final outcome of the battle was sealed but Chaka was too involved in Mgobozi's rescue to savour the first taste of victory. He glanced around swiftly for a runner but there was no one near; he had even used his staff officers to carry messages. There was only myself. He looked down at me with an expression of loathing, as though I was responsible for what was happening.

'A child!' he muttered angrily. 'A white child. What can you understand of battles?'

He turned away restlessly but the top of our hillock remained bare of anyone but ourselves. Abruptly he swung around to me again. 'Have you eyes? Can you see?'

It was quite plain. Mdlaka's division was now pouring over the northern skyline. It was obvious that he was aiming to attack the Ndwandwes' right flank, but Mgobozi and what remained of his Fasimbas had cut their way through to the left flank, hidden by cliffs from Mdlaka's sight. It was only we who could see the whole battle-piece. If Mdlaka attacked the right flank time would be against Mgobozi.

'He must be turned,' I said. 'He must come round by the south.'

'Go then and tell him!'

I began to run. It seemed even more important to me that help should reach Mgobozi in time. As I flew down the slope of our hillock I began to plan my route. I would have to traverse the base of Ndololwane Hill, below the fighting, and try to circle both armies, then up the far slope in the path of Mdlaka's advance and stop him before he reached the battle. Once Mdlaka's *impis* were within shouting distance of their comrades there would be no heading them. It became a race.

In minutes I had reached level ground and was running headlong over the veld. The rifle weighed terribly on my right arm and I knew it was slowing me down. I should have left it, but it was too late now.

It was all right while I was on the flat. I could look up and see the gap between myself and the point at which I would bisect Mdlaka's line of advance closing rapidly. But once I took the

135

slopes I began to sweat. The morning sun was baking hot. Above me were the sounds of battle and as I cut slantwise up the slope I came on the bodies of the dead and wounded. They cried to me for water but I could not stop.

I had been keeping my eyes to the ground, springing from rock to rock and now I stopped briefly to look up. I was shocked by what I saw. Mdlaka's warriors were coming down the hill with the speed of baboons. I began to shout. I fired the rifle but the shot was lost in the din of fighting. I saw now that I could never intercept them where I'd planned. I veered upwards to the right, coming closer and closer to the milling armies.

I tore my way up the slope, pulling on tufts of grass, bellowing like a young bull. And then, in what seemed like a matter of seconds, the black lava-flow of Mdlaka's hordes merged with the greater black mass of the armies. I stopped. There was a coppery taste in my mouth and I stood half-way up the slope panting for breath. Slowly each great heave of my lungs turned into a sob as I realised what must eventually happen.

But it had already happened. It is said that Mgobozi's 'children' had already fallen and only the Hammer of Chaka remained. He had returned to his old position against the rock and now, with so many wounds that one ran into the other, patterning his skin with slashes, he awaited the final onslaught.

It is also said that by this time he was no longer living, in the true sense of the word. Life had gone out of his eyes, they were now just two red orbs. His lips were drawn back in a dreadful grimace and bloody foam flecked his chin and cheeks. Blood bubbled out of the great rents in his chest.

He had become more machine than man and this was how he took the last rush. With a shriek the Ndwandwes fell on him. Stabbing and hacking with Chest-biter, he stood his ground until the corpses built up like a wall before him. Again and again the Ndwandwe spear points found his body. Slowly he began to sink and what animal force there was left in him was gone before he reached the ground.

The Zulu Army now broke through the Ndwandwe ranks and scattered them all over the hillside. Their end as a tribe had come. Some tried to fight in small groups, others ran. It made no matter. The fleet-footed Zulus easily caught up with them and everywhere came cries of 'Ngadla! Ngadla! I have eaten! I have eaten!'

136

The whole battle had taken less than two hours and, in an even shorter time, the Zulus swept on up the hill to massacre the Ndwandwe women, children and cattle. By early afternoon the battlefield was a place for flies and silence. Only a handful, led by Sikunyana, made good their escape.

Later Chaka walked broodingly amid the already swelling corpses and stared down at the dead body of Mgobozi. His ostrich plumes still fluttered in the light breeze. The King stood there for a long moment and tears began to trickle down his cheeks. Finally he said, almost to himself: 'I have conquered Zwide's son, but he has killed me in Mgobozi.' And with that he turned away. After the Zulu cowards and the Ndwandwe wounded had been put to death the whole army went to the nearest river and washed away the stain of battle; then began the feasting.

But Chaka sat apart, his face grim and forbidding, mourning the death of his friend. And at this time something happened which has left a more lasting effect on me than even the rivers of blood and the carnage I had witnessed earlier.

A Ndwandwe woman and her small son, who must have been about ten years old, had been found hiding in the forest and Chaka had ordered them to be brought before him. He sent for meat and beer and watched while they ate. They must have been almost starving because they fell on the food with alacrity in spite of the awesome presence of the King; in fact, the woman drank so quickly that she was tipsy before the meal was over.

The King now questioned her about Sikunyana and asked what plans he had made for his escape and she answered quite frankly, although a trifle muzzily, that he had gone to Tembeland. At once the King ordered a regiment to set off in pursuit. The woman must have thought, in her fuddled way, that her treachery had now earned her a place in the Zulu nation. She was wrong. No sooner had she spoken than Chaka said: 'Take them away.'

Mr Fynn had been sitting nearby while the interrogation was taking place and he came to us and said: 'What will happen now?'

'They'll be executed,' my father replied.

'A child? What can a child have had to do with this?'

'Haven't you been up the hill? A thousand dead children lie there.'

'Yes,' Fynn said unhappily. 'I saw. But why this one as well? Can't we do anything?'

'Nothing.'

'For God's sake, try. Tell him I'll take them as servants. Tell him anything you like.'

'Both? You must be optimistic.'

'Just the lad, then. One's better than none.'

My father shrugged and went across to Chaka. They seemed to argue for a few minutes. More than once Chaka turned to glare at me. I did not care, for my own sorrow was great enough.

'You can have the boy,' my father said to Fynn. 'Only get him out of the King's sight.'

'And the woman?'

'No.'

Fynn collected the boy and hurried into the trees. For the first time his mother looked alarmed. She struggled drunkenly to her feet and stood there swaying. The Zulus laughed at her.

My father picked up his rifle and stood to one side of her. 'Where is my son?' she said. 'Where is my boy?'

'There,' said my father, pointing in the direction Fynn had taken. 'Hurry and you'll catch him.'

She started off at a lumbering, drunken trot and when she had covered about twenty yards my father shot her. The bullet had been aimed at the back of her head but she was so unsteady on her feet that at the moment of firing she had swayed slightly out of line, half turning to us, and now the lower part of her jaw was blown away.

She lay there staring up at him, her eyes big and frightened like a dying kudu's. 'Finish her off!' my father yelled at me.

'You bloody murderer,' I said, and I turned away and walked into the forest. I hadn't got more than a hundred yards when I heard the second shot. I began to run. I don't know how long I ran but it must have been several miles, for the forest thinned out and I came into open veld. I remember feeling tired and sick so I slowed down to a walk, keeping the afternoon sun on my right shoulder.

I travelled thus for five days, sleeping rough and eating what I could shoot, until I came to Morile. Something had happened during those five days; something I did not clearly understand. With hindsight it is simpler. I had crossed a dividing line. While I was not yet a man, I was also no longer a boy.

138

Book Three

The Last Journey

The truth is that Shaka was a most unusual product of his race. He was highly emotional and sentimental behind a façade of iron discipline.

Shaka Zulu
E. A. RITTER.

Some months after the Battle of Ndololwane Hill Chaka decided to move his royal kraal from Bulawayo to Dukusa, about sixty miles further away to the south-east, and we were left alone on the top of our hill. There was one main reason for the Great Elephant's decision: to be nearer the white settlers of Port Natal. In Chaka's mind there were only two great kings, himself and Umjoji and although in many respects he looked upon Umjoji's people as sadly inferior to his own he was intelligent enough to realise there were many things he could learn from them. According to Zulu mythology the Great One, the *Unkulunkulu*, had created us all by breaking off the tops of reeds in a great reed bed and allowing us to emerge. But the white man had waited until all the black men came forth and then only emerged after scraping up the last bits of wisdom contained in the reeds. Chaka wished to be closer to this wisdom.

There were now more than a dozen traders at the Port and several had built quite substantial dwellings. Mr Fynn, whose medicinal skill had made him a favourite of the King's, had built his own kraal south of the Port and was living in the fashion of a Zulu benedict. At first this had disturbed my father but when he saw that his countrymen were interested less in his own existence than in the ivory and land which they hoped to obtain from the King, he became less apprehensive. He even went so far as to establish trading relations with Mr Fynn and for the first time in many years we had tea and coffee and wheaten flour in the house. My mother was able to procure bolts of cloth and we wore cotton shirts again instead of leather jerkins. She made dresses for herself and Nerissa and even table-cloths and new curtains.

My father never encouraged visitors and he would travel either by himself or with me to Mr Fynn's kraal for the purpose of barter. It was a long journey and we would take the ivory in Pereira's wagon. We never went to the Port.

Once Mr Fynn asked how we had come to Zululand and my father looked at him for a long moment. 'Pulled,' he said finally. 'By oxen.'

Mr Fynn nodded. 'Capital form of locomotion,' he replied dryly and never mentioned the subject again. It is a fact that here, in what to the white people was a form of no-man's-land, it mattered less what a man's past was than how he acted in the present. Slowly my father came to understand this.

Our isolation at Morile was now complete. In a sense this was what my father and mother had sought all those years ago as they travelled the lonely areas of Southern Africa: a place where they could live in peace, safe from King George's laws. Well, we had it at last and instead of experiencing the sweet fruits of ambition fulfilled there was nothing in our mouths but a sour taste. We had everything we wanted; yet we had nothing. We no longer even had each other. Perhaps it was the very isolation itself which had caused our decay; perhaps it is impossible to cut oneself off from the stream of life as we had done; whatever the reason the departure of Chaka's court—barbaric and dangerous as its presence was—left us in a vacuum. Morile was a house filled with strangers and the only one who seemed unaffected by it was Donald, who did his lessons and hunted with Stone-Axe and became friendly with Tanga's younger brother, Kopo. In fact, his life was a duplicate of mine at that age. I wondered when he would notice, as I had noticed, that he was living in a private world of happiness, an island in a sea of trouble and grief. I hoped for his sake that he would remain insensitive, for things were far worse now than they had been when my own idyll was shattered. We spoke only when spoken to, never from pleasure.

How Nerissa managed to survive in this atmosphere after her own nervous upheaval was miraculous. Hers was the most difficult path to tread. Compared to us she was cheerful and outgoing and had taken over much of the running of the house from my mother, who had never fully regained her strength after the fever. At the time it was Nerissa's serenity which was perhaps the most valuable asset we had. She was like the calm eye of a storm around which we, the turbulent winds, revolved.

We watched each other. My mother watched my father; my father watched Nerissa; I watched the three of them; Stone-Axe watched us all. We seemed to be waiting for something, an overt act, a sign, just a spoken word, something that would throw us

142

out of balance to go whirling and crashing—God knew where. And since we were only a fraction away from destroying everything we had created we were doubly careful. As I say, we spoke only when addressed. But when we did we were careful to make the tone neutral, the words inoffensive. Our habits were meticulous; our actions bland. We led our individual lives, careful lest they encroach on others. When a family exists like this, tension is a living force; it ate with us at meals, sat with us in the living-room, slept with us in our beds.

It was only at night that we were free of each other's eyes and yet instead of being able to relax, the tension seemed, if anything, to increase. I know it did for me. Since my mother's illness she no longer slept in the same bedroom as my father and night after night I could imagine, as an extension to my own thoughts and circumstances, the four of us lying awake in our blankets wondering . . . wondering . . . And dawn would come as a relief and we could watch each other again.

In a sense we had developed into the miniature counterpart of a Zulu kraal. Over the years Morile had expanded to become a tiny state within the State. We had our King, our Queen and our courtiers—and this is how we lived. We had always been mainly self-supporting. Now, apart from the few things we got from Mr Fynn—and which we could have done without—we were a wholly private kingdom.

I no longer spent much time in study. The arable areas of the farm were constantly being extended and there were small dams to be built, water furrows to be dug, ploughs to mend, cattle to be inspected, hoeing to be done—and building, always building.

The central homestead was no longer recognisable; it had spread in all directions. It seemed as though my father had a fixation about building; as though only by building could he stamp his mark on the country; put down his roots; proclaim through stone and mud that here he was and here he was to stay. Walls were always being torn down and rebuilt; rooms were extended or added, outbuildings put up for grain stores, a guinea-fowl run, a milking shed, a new ivory store, a laundry, a baking oven, a store for ploughs and harnesses. And pits were dug for silage and huts were put up for the servants. From its original conception as a strategically placed farmhouse Morile had become a fortified manor.

We had plunged back five hundred years in time and all we

needed to complete the picture was a moat and drawbridge. We already had the serfs. How long we could have gone on in this fashion I cannot tell for in the event something happened which was to change our lives drastically : the death of Chaka's mother.

No woman in Zululand was more revered than Nandi—especially by her son. She had fought to help him become the greatest potentate in Southern Africa and had continued the fight to keep him there. Chaka loved her with a ferocity quite unmatched by his feelings for any other human being, including even those he had held towards Mgobozi. He had elevated her to the highest position a woman could hold, he had designated her the Female Elephant. Now she was dead.

As soon as we heard the news we hurried to Bulawayo where she had spent her last days. The whole of Zululand was in uproar. Chaka had brought his army with him and everyone not too sick to walk or crawl had come out of the hills to converge on Bulawayo. There was no such thing as grieving in seclusion; grief had to be seen. The dismal lamentations were already in full flow when we arrived. Fynn had been treating her and now told us she had died of dysentry only a few hours before.

At that moment Chaka emerged from his Royal Hut. I would hardly have recognised him. His face was contorted with grief and his eyes swollen with weeping. He walked slowly towards the hut where Nandi's body lay. Mdlaka and the other principal war chiefs were already drawn up outside the hut and Chaka joined them. He stood there for perhaps twenty minutes, head bowed on his great white shield, tears streaming down his cheeks until finally, after three deep sighs, he suddenly let out a series of frantic, almost hysterical shrieks and the crowd, which had grown silent, broke into lamentations once more.

It was a scene similar to that which my father has described in his Journal when Chaka was wounded by assassins. It seems that the Zulus can only endure a crisis by sharing it with as many as possible and within hours of our arrival there must have been more than fifty thousand mourners in the arena. And it was only then, as I witnessed their treatment of one another, that the true horror of my father's description was borne in on me. Once again, in an attempt to out-do each other in grief, they began to riot and by morning more than a tenth of their numbers were dead. The stream that ran below the kraal, that very stream in which we had bathed before our first meeting with the Great Elephant, became choked with corpses until its waters ran red.

However, it was not so much the death of Nandi, but the effect on Chaka, that was important. In the days and weeks that followed the pattern of the future began to emerge. We were immediately affected by the mourning decrees, which seemed unnecessarily harsh. No cultivation was to be allowed for a whole year, no milk was to be drunk, in fact it was to be poured on to the ground as soon as a cow was milked; no sexual intercourse might take place and all women who became pregnant in the following twelve months were to be killed with their husbands. Luckily Nandi had died in early October and the crops were already in. But it did mean that there could be no weeding and this in itself meant that the corn crop, for instance, might not be half as good as in a normal year. We should be able to exist, but what of the ordinary people?

Instead of returning to Dukusa, Chaka remained brooding in Bulawayo. We travelled there almost every day for months, not because we wanted to, but because it would have been dangerous not to, for the killings were still going on, in fact were even increasing. Anyone who had not shown the deepest feelings of sadness and loss was executed immediately. Even rumours from afar that so-and-so had lacked respect or that so-and-so had not mourned with sufficient intensity brought Chaka's rage bursting out again and squads of slayers were sent to the furthest parts of the kingdom to bring the King's vengeance. In this way it became easy for Zulus to pay off old scores and revenge themselves on almost-forgotten slights. It only needed a whisper in the right place for an enemy to be eaten up.

In these circumstances it was politic for us to know what was going on and to let the King witness our sorrow. He was going through a period of bitterness towards all white people—had they not an elixir of life which might have saved Nandi?—and it would have been quite possible for him to have ordered the annihilation of us all.

The thing I remember most clearly about Chaka at that time was his daily walk to the top of the hill which overlooked the kraal. There he would sit in the shade of a tree, chin resting in the palm of his hand, deep in the grip of melancholia. Often his eyes would fill with tears and they would spill down his cheeks unnoticed, leaving slight marks on the dusty skin.

'I have conquered the world,' he would say over and over again in a voice filled with sadness, 'but lost my mother. Bitter aloes fill my mouth and all taste has gone out of my life.'

At times one was even tempted to feel sympathy for him, so deep seemed his sorrow, but before such feelings could mature he would do something so grotesque that they would be replaced by horror and detestation.

Bulawayo had truly been named the Place of the Killing. It seemed that a kind of madness would descend upon the King in which he had to kill and kill and kill—if only to bring the same degree of sadness to everyone around him. No one was safe in his presence. A nod of his head was sufficient to terminate a life; and this, added to such idiosyncrasies as taking his meals lying flat on his stomach, which meant that everyone, including ourselves, had to do the same, made this period a complete nightmare for us all.

I recall one morning, after he had taken his daily bath and was sitting slumped in his great carved chair, he called for Nandi's ladies-in-waiting to be brought before him. I think there were six of them, all ancient crones who had served his mother well during her life-time.

Chaka looked up at them from beneath furrowed brows, his eyes changing abruptly from maudlin self-pity to hot rage. 'I left her in your care!' he screamed at them. 'How is it that she died and you live!'

The women fell to their knees and one called out: 'She was old, Father. Her time had come.'

This made him even angrier. 'Take them!' he shouted. 'Let them feel the flames!'

Their hands were tied behind their backs and thatching grass was fastened to their bodies. Chaka ordered the slayers to light the grass and drive the women upwind. As the flames caught and licked up the bundles the women ran screaming across the arena until finally they became fast-burning human torches. As each dropped, the slayers bounded up to crush her skull.

As if the people did not have enough to put up with from Chaka's waking mind, they were now pilloried by his dreams and nightmares. He confided to my father that in his dreams he would often be visited by his foster-father, Mbiya, and they would talk of Nandi and share their sorrow. But in the dreams the dead Mbiya gradually began to exert his influence on the living. In

146

one dream in particular Chaka was warned that the women in his seraglio were being unfaithful to him. On waking he called a secret meeting of his councillors and recounted what Mbiya had said. The council agreed that all the guilty sisters should be put to death. But first they had to be caught in the act, so Chaka pretended to leave Bulawayo on a pilgrimage to his father's grave. At midnight he returned unexpectedly. His guards surrounded the women's palace and took eighty-five warriors and their mistresses in varying stages of love play. Some were beaten to death with clubs; others strangled with the women.

This massacre was generally approved of and in fact redounded to Chaka's credit. But when he had the entire *u-dibi* regiment massacred because some came to peep at his own love play the Zulus experienced a sense of horror and waste. After all, these were only young boys—had my father pursued his plan I would have been one myself—the very buds from which the future Zulu Army would flower.

And so it went on. Even the Zulus' lust for blood and destruction became sated. They began to avoid Bulawayo, turning in on themselves, becoming morose and unhappy. These qualities were just the contrary to those which had fused them into a great nation and there were many, like Mdlaka and Mbopa and even Dingane who began to look upon this devastation with thoughtful eyes.

I knew what they were thinking because similar thoughts were constantly going through my own mind: were we all to be destroyed, and with us the State itself, to assuage the Great Elephant's insane grief? But none was brave enough to try and end it.

And perhaps it would never have ended; perhaps the State would have disintegrated and the countryside become barren of all but fly-blown corpses and whitening bones if Chaka had not overstepped even his own wide latitudes of sadism. He had brooded long on the fact that he had been cuckolded by his own warriors and even the murder of eighty-five of them did not seem to satisfy him. So one morning, more than half a year after Nandi's death, he ordered that the Fasimba regiment should parade without its prepuce-covers in the main arena. None of us knew what he had in mind until we saw a regiment of young girls, the Ngisimane, about three thousand strong, draw up in front of them. This was a newly-formed regiment and contained the youngest and most beautiful of all the Zulu girls. They were naked except for the scantiest of belly-strings. On Chaka's orders they began to entice the Fasimbas, moving forward then back, swaying and gliding, beckoning with their arms, undulating their thighs and buttocks. They formed lines and advanced with a high-stepping walk until they were almost touching the front ranks of the Fasimbas, only to recede again. They were singing, in high-pitched but pleasant tones, the songs of enticement which precede the fun of the roads.

Chaka had taken his place on the Royal Mound and the slayers were gathered at his back. His eyes swept up and down the lines of Fasimbas, watching for signs. After six months of enforced celibacy, it was an inhuman thing to do.

'There!' he shouted, pointing to a man. 'And there! And there!' The slayers ran forward with their clubs and the warriors began to fall. All the time the girls moved voluptuously back and forth, back and forth.

'Look at their fighting-sticks,' Chaka roared. 'Instead of pointing down in sadness they stare brazenly up into my face! Have you no shame? Have you no respect for the Female Elephant? Kill the disgusting brutes!'

In less than fifteen minutes the whole of the first platoon was dead on the ground and that is what my own fate would have been had I been among them. But then I saw what the back ranks were doing. They were using their fists to hit themselves in the testicles. It was a dreadful thing to have to do, but it saved their lives, for when the slayers reached them the symbols of their manhood drooped in sadness and respect. For several days I kept on seeing Fasimba warriors with swollen parts walking bow-legged—but at least they walked.

The wanton massacre of nearly a hundred young warriors because they were tempted to do what every man in Zululand was desperate to do, made a deep impression on the Zulus. And this last obscene act of Chaka's, coupled with over-grown and weed-choked fields, starvation rations and a general air of decay, produced a champion. I had never seen him before, nor did I ever see him afterwards, but for just that one moment when he took Chaka to task he will live in Zulu history.

His name was Gala of the Biyela clan and one morning, after Chaka had taken his bath, he marched fearlessly up to the King's enclosure and began to shout at the Great Elephant.

148

I heard the commotion and went over to see what new terror Chaka was perpetrating, and instead heard the King berated in a fashion that sent shivers of fear up my spine.

'You have destroyed your own country,' the man was shouting. 'Who do you think you're going to rule? Are you going to create a new race? Are we all to die because your mother died?'

At the mention of his mother's name Chaka emerged from the Palace and stood looking at Gala. Ordinarily, I have seen great warriors faint clean away at a glance from the King, but not this peasant from the hills. He gave back glance for glance. 'Your father died,' he said angrily. 'And your grandfather died. Yet none of these things were done to us. If this continues the country will be inhabited by other kings, for we will have died of starvation and will no longer exist. The fields are no longer cultivated, the cows no longer milked. For myself, Father, I say you are already dead, killed through this mother of yours. Why don't you take hold of yourself, put a stone in your stomach? This isn't the first time anyone died in Zululand.'

He finished and stood there waiting for his death. Chaka stared at him for several minutes and then opened his mouth and roared for Mdlaka and Mbopa. They came hurrying to his side.

'Did you hear that?' Chaka bellowed at them. 'Did you hear what this child of my grandfather said? Did *you* ever tell me to stuff a stone into my stomach? No, never! What use are you to me?'

We all stood around in utter amazement as Chaka sent for two fine bullocks. 'Take them,' he said to Gala, who was now more astonished even than we were. 'They will repay you for sound and inspiriting advice. And when you reach your kraal assume the headring and command all your ward to do the same.'

This was the turning point. The mourning decrees were rescinded, Chaka moved off to Dukusa, we went back to Morile, and the country settled down once more.

I say things settled down, but this is only partly true; it seemed to become quieter only in comparison with the reign of terror we had experienced. Even the Zulus seem to have a point at which they become saturated with the need for harsh and eccentric rule and this had been reached some time before. It is one thing to make examples of cowards or to cauterize rotten parts of a society, another to practise wholesale slaughter for no more reason than a personal whim. But the most serious aspect was the food situation. The crop which was finally gathered was less than one-third its normal size and nearly everyone in the country was soon on short commons.

Under Chaka's reign the Zulus had been used to living well, they had forgotten what hunger was like. It was natural for disaffection to breed in these circumstances. In all the time we had been in Zululand we had never heard overt criticism of the King, now there were mutterings and rumblings of discontent wherever we went. But so wrapped up had we become in our own affairs that we had little time to speculate or to listen to complaints. We did what we could; we shared our surplus food with the neighbouring kraals; but that was all.

If we could have forced ourselves out of our own slough of suspicion and mistrust we might have registered that Chaka's star was now on the decline and that since we had identified ourselves so closely with it, ours must be sinking too. Had we realised this we might have been able to avoid the catastrophe that followed; but we didn't. And the reason is that something occurred to us at that time which pushed all extraneous thoughts from our heads; my father tried to force himself on Nerissa.

It must be apparent that it was to this point that our lives had been building and yet when it came we were as greatly shocked as though it had never been in our thoughts : the measure of our self-delusion, I suppose. It was the reason I had watched my father, it was the reason I had lain awake at night, it was the stain of mistrust at the back of our thoughts.

For my own part, I had dreamed waking dreams about it many times. I had seen it enacted in the open veld in a bower of tall grass, or by the river or in the cave. I had seen the satyr-like figure of my father gripping the unwilling girl until her back bent like a bow, moulding her body to his own forward curve. Then the dream would become blurred and hazy and when it cleared it was no longer my father but I who held the girl, nor was she unwilling. The savagery had been eliminated from the scene and we touched each other with tenderness and love. I would come out of these dreams sore and stiff in my loins. I cannot tell what dreams my father had, but I was his son.

I remember the day as though it were only last week and not more than ten years ago. I shall probably remember it as long as I live. It was in the autumn of 1828, some time in late April as I recall, and the weather had been unseasonably hot. Storm

150

clouds had gathered each day for a week, and each day they had passed us by, leaving behind a wilting and panting land. On the eighth day the wind changed and began to blow out of the hot inland deserts, returning the great blue-black clouds still heavy with unshed rain. By noon it was dark enough for the lamps. All around us was the flare of lightning and the crash of thunder, but the rain held off. In a matter of hours everything became dry and brittle; hair felt crisp, skin was hot to the touch. With it the wind brought dust.

None of us could eat our mid-day meal; my father did not even bother to try. Instead he called for a jug of cane spirit and took it with him to the sheltered side of the house. He sat there drinking and watching the lightning play on the surrounding hills. After the meal we all went to our rooms and I remember lying on my bed yearning with every fibre of my body for the clouds to open and the fresh rain to fall. I must have slept for about two hours and when I woke I was feeling thick in the head. My clothes were clammy with sweat. The skies were somewhat lighter but still the rain held off. I began to think about the river and the coolness of the water but the effort of getting off the bed and walking down the hill seemed too great. Just then Nerissa knocked at the door and resolved the impasse.

'I've *got* to swim,' she said. 'I feel as though I'm being scorched.' Her pale face was flushed with the heat.

'All right.' I swung my legs from the bed and stood up, feeling dizzy. 'Slept too long,' I said.

'Let's go out the back way. We'll get some shelter from the trees.'

The house seemed dead. Nothing stirred. We went out past the kitchen and it was dark and empty. As we went through the trees down the shoulder of the hill Nerissa said : 'Listen!'

'What?' I could only hear the wind rustling among the dry leaves.

'To the silence. Even the birds have stopped.'

The dark clouds had passed to the east and the sky was now the colour of phlegm; beneath it the land was a livid yellow. We paused at the bank of the stream and looked at the water. It was black and the wind sent ripples running against the current. The pools seemed murky and menacing.

We swam naked, in separate pools, and the unease of the dark water sent me climbing out on to the bank sooner than usual.

All the time I was in the water I was fearful of touching some-thing—something I couldn't see—like a water leguaan, or a snake, or worse, something that I had never seen before and which only rose from the depths on days like this. Five minutes after we had dressed, our hair was as dry as dead grass and the wind burned our faces; I felt that I would never be cool again. And then I remembered the cave.

We walked upstream until we came to the cliff on the far side, crossed by big stepping-stones, found the half-hidden path that cut along the base of the cliff and finally came to the cave itself. There was so much thick bush round the entrance that it would never have been seen by anyone on the opposite bank, nor indeed on this one, until one was almost on top of it. I led Nerissa through the maze of tangled stems and we passed from the sul-phurous light of the afternoon into the dim gloom of the cave. A spring trickled down one wall giving the place an earthy, damp coolness and we lowered ourselves gratefully onto the sandy floor.

'I never knew about this,' Nerissa said.

'No one does, except Tanga. He showed it to me years ago.'

'A secret cave.' She smiled. 'It's like something in a child's fancy.'

'I don't often come here any more,' I said quickly.

'If it were mine I'd come here every day.'

'Why?'

'Because it's secret. In India I used to have a secret place. A tree on the far side of the garden and everyone said there was a cobra living in the roots and I used to take bowls of milk, but it never came. So it became *my* place.'

'What did you do there?' I said, picking up a handful of small smooth pebbles and flicking them one by one into the bush outside.

'Sometimes I would take my books and read, or else paper and charcoal and try to draw the garden flowers, but most times I would lie on my back under the tree and watch the clouds go by until my mother—until my mother called me for tea.' She paused for a long while and finally said : 'Everyone should have a secret place.'

'Tell me about India.'

'What is it you want to know?'

'Everything.'

She recovered herself and laughed. 'I don't know everything. No one knows everything about India.'

152

'Tell me,' I said, 'or I'll pull your hair.' I was lying down look-ing up at the roof of the cave, my head cradled on my hands, and she was sitting by my side, her arms encircling her knees. Now I reached out and caught one of the long black tresses and let it slip through my fingers.

'If you pull my hair I'll never come here again.'

'Will you if I don't?'

'I'll see.' But she made no move and I let my hand rest on her back.

'Tell me about India.'

She told me about the great cities of Calcutta and Bombay, and about Hindus and Muslims and Diwali and Rhamadan and about her family and their servants and their carriages and their books and food and how they drank from shining glasses and wore clothes of cotton and worsted, and as she spoke a great yearning came over me. It must have been something that had been lying very deeply, for now it came rushing out on to the surface and I knew that this above everything was what I wanted to do: I wanted to go away, to leave Zululand and all the wild parts of Africa and go where there were streets and people and shops and live in a house where you drank out of sparkling glass and see and do all the things I had never seen and done and was unlikely ever to see and do here in the heart of the Continent. And sud-denly it seemed to me that this was an ambition that *had* to be fulfilled.

'Nerissa,' I said, breaking across her nostalgia. 'I want to leave here, to go right away. Will you come with me?'

'It's just my talk. It does that to me sometimes, too.'

'No, it's not just that. It's something I've been thinking about for a long time,' I lied.

'But go where?'

'Anywhere. The Cape.'

'And how would we get there?'

'By ship.'

'Ship?' The word was chill with meaning, but I chose to dis-regard her.

'From the Port. They're not regular, I know, but Mr Fynn says that they come every now and then. We could stay with him and wait until one comes. Once we got to Algoa Bay there are other ships to the Cape. Mr Fynn says so, and he knows.'

'And then? What would we do then?'

'Well . . .' I tried to think.

'You see, Robbie.'

'No, wait. We could go to my mother's home. It's called Paradise and it's near the town itself. She's told me of it many times.'

'And what would we live on?'

'Why, we'd . . . we . . .'

'Robbie,' she said gently, 'when you live in a town you can't just take a gun and shoot your food and make your clothes from skins and live like a Zulu. You have to have money to buy things. Where would we get the money?'

'I could work.'

'At what?'

'My mother says I argue enough for two lawyers. That's what I could do. I could be a lawyer.'

'But you can't just *be* a lawyer. It takes years. You have to train for it.'

'You won't come?'

'No, Robbie. You're too young—'

'Don't say that! You make it sound as if—'

'I was going to say that we're *both* too young.'

'You don't trust me,' I said brutally. 'You think it'll all happen to you again like it did when the ship sank. Well, it won't!'

She looked at me very seriously for a moment. 'If there is anyone in the whole world I trust,' she said, 'it's you.'

'Do you mean that?'

'Yes. I do. And one day we'll go. You'll see.'

I felt a moment of blinding happiness. I sat up quickly and put my arm about her shoulders. 'I love you, Nerissa,' I said. 'I know you think I'm too young, but I love you. I'll never love anyone else! Never!' I felt so choked up I was almost crying with love and joy and excitement.

She leant against me and put her cheek against mine and I could feel the heat of her skin. And then we began to kiss and after a while she lay down by my side because it was more comfortable that way and we touched each other's bodies. I think it was the first time for either of us and so everything was new and exploratory and unfamiliar. I had touched her hand many times before but now, as it stroked my arm or my face it was a different hand, an intimate hand, a hand that had a separate meaning and would always have a separate meaning.

First we kissed chastely, the kisses our mothers had taught us, and then by experiment they gradually became less formal and our lips became wet and our tongues touched and we tasted each other. Every moment was totally new and every texture unexpected. I touched her breasts and her nipples and her thighs and she held me and that was enough for us both.

In between kisses we would lie close and hold each other with great tenderness and talk of all the things we would do in the great future that was still to come. We gave no thought to time. We only realised that the afternoon had slid away when my stomach rumbled and the spell was broken. I've always had a noisy stomach but it had never mattered much until that moment. Nerissa had her head on my chest and her ear was so close it must have sounded like an underground stream, but she simply laughed and said : 'I can hear a voice in there calling for food.'

We sat up. The cave itself had been so dark that we had not seen the gradual change in the day. It was night. At that moment there was a great stab of lightning and an immediate clap of thunder and the rain began to drum down on the bush outside. We went to the mouth of the cave and stepped out into the rain and stood there holding each other's hand and letting the lukewarm drops soak into us until our clothes were dark and wet like a second skin.

'We'd better cross,' I said, 'before the river comes down.'

The stepping-stones were already slightly lower in the water as I led her across. The rain was so heavy that it made one continuous noise like loose dry corn being poured onto a wooden floor.

At the foot of the hill Nerissa tugged on my hand. 'Let's run,' she said, and we ran through the rain, sliding and stumbling and laughing.

We were very young and very happy and when I asked her if she would come again to the cave she said she'd think about it—which meant yes, of course—and I knew I could endure the friction and unhappiness at home. The whole future had suddenly brightened and one day—the urgency seemed already to have diminished—we would leave Zululand completely and go into a new and wonderful world together.

'Where have you been!' My father's voice came harshly from the shadows of the verandah. It was thick and slurred with drink. His clothes were as wet as ours and I realised he'd been out searching for us.

155

'Swimming,' I said.

'At this hour! Why, it's past supper-time!' He took a step towards us. I was still holding Nerissa by the hand and now I moved her behind me. 'You've been hiding somewhere.' His mouth was working strangely and his eyes glinted in the light that fell through the open doorway.

'I said we'd been swimming. We have.'

'Don't you talk like that to me, boy!'

'How d'you want me to talk then? What do you want me to say?'

'I want the truth!'

'It's true, Mr Black,' Nerissa said. 'We did go swimming.' Her voice was frightened and I took a stronger grip on her hand.

'You're a liar! Both of you! I was down at the river to look for you.' His voice had been steadily rising. 'You filthy brats! You've been together somewhere! You've been doing things—filthy things! Don't deny it. I can see it in your faces!' He came close to us, his face almost touching mine. I could see the hook on the left stump half-raised as though to strike and the hair on my scalp began to prickle in fear.

Around us the thunder was rolling and the lightning crashing and the rain was pouring off the thatch roof in a solid sheet of water. I wished desperately that my mother would come but she'd probably gone to bed and she'd never hear us in all this.

'You'll not do it again! Never again! I give you my word on that! You'll do no more filthy things together, do you understand? Answer me! Do you understand?'

'You're wrong, Father,' I began. 'We did go swimming. There's nothing filthy in that. And then the storm broke and we waited for the rain to stop.'

'You're lying!' His jealousy had almost unhinged him and his voice had risen to a shriek. 'Filth!' he cried. 'Filth! Touching each other! Go and wash your hands! I order you to wash your hands, do you hear me?'

'Go quickly,' I whispered to Nerissa. 'I'll try to calm him.' She squeezed my hand once and then slipped through the door and was gone.

'Father,' I said, 'you're making too much—'

'I'll settle you! Do you think I haven't been watching you? D'you think I don't know what you've been planning? My own son! God's love! My own son!'

156

'And where d'you think I get it?' I said fiercely. 'Where do I inherit it? You're a splendid one to talk. D'you think you're the only one to do any watching! D'you imagine we didn't know what you've been thinking about and sweating for! D'you think mother doesn't know what's been going on in your brain! And you call *us* filthy! You! Why, you're old enough to be her father!'

'That's enough!' he shouted. 'I say that's enough! Stop or you'll regret it!'

'I've said what I wanted.' I turned to the door. 'I pity us,' I said more softly. 'I pity all of us with your blood in our veins.' He stood watching me go and there was a wild look on his face. He caught up the jug of rum and held it to his lips.

Nerissa's door was closed and I let her be. I passed my mother's room and there was no light under the door. I took a taper from the wall-bracket in the hallway, crossed the inner keep and lay down on my bed. The storm still rolled around the hills and it was a dramatic background to my thoughts. There was no question about it now : I—we—had to get away. Our life here would become totally eroded. We had to leave before something dreadful happened. But how? My father would never let Nerissa leave now, I was certain of that. Which would mean running away. But it was more than a hundred miles to the Port, and that was as the crow flies. We would have to take a less travelled road, for it would not only be my father searching for us. I had no doubt that he would ask Chaka for help and this meant that almost everyone's eyes would be looking. So I would never be able to risk a gunshot. And if I couldn't use a gun how would we feed? My brain probed the problem from every angle but there seemed no clear way to success. And yet the Port was the gateway to the outside world.

Although the rain had cooled the earth the air within the house was warm and humid. I had changed out of my wet clothes and the fresh ones were already damp with perspiration. I was very thirsty. I crossed the keep to the kitchen and stood in the back doorway leaning out to scoop water from the rain barrel with the calabash dipper. As I did so there was another roll of thunder, but this time it had a curious, flat sound to it. It was more of a thud or a thump. It came again and I realised it wasn't thunder but a noise from within the house itself.

I picked up a billet of wood from the pile near the oven.

Everything was quiet. My own room was as I'd left it. I paused outside my mother's door but could hear nothing. I went on. Above the noise of the rain I thought I could hear a sound of voices. It seemed to be coming from Nerissa's room. Gripping the length of wood tighter I ran quietly to her door. Almost immediately I realised what had caused the thumping noise. The wooden bar which kept the door locked from the inside was splintered and broken and the door was slightly open. Slowly I pushed it with my hand. I could hear my father's voice now. He was saying the same thing over and over again. 'Forgive me, Nerissa. Forgive me. Please forgive me.' As I pushed the door further I noticed something lying on the ground. It was his hook. It had either been ripped off as he flung himself at the door or else he had taken it off. It lay there with its straps and its black leather sheath like some huge metallic spider. I stepped into the room. 'I only want to touch you,' my father was saying. 'That's all. Just to hold you, as he held you.' Nerissa was standing in the corner of the room and he was on his knees in front of her. He was fondling one of her breasts and she was making no attempt to stop him. It was as though she did not know what was happening, that same wooden look was back on her face. 'I'll be gentle,' he said. 'So gentle.'

He must have heard me then because he half-turned as though to rise. He raised his left arm to ward off the blow and I saw the obscene and hairless skin of the stump. I hit him on the side of the head, just above the ear, and it sent him sprawling back against the bed. He rolled over on his arms and knees and began to crawl towards me. I raised the billet again. He stopped, his head hanging far down between his arms like an exhausted horse, and then, with a slight moan, he pitched forward unconscious.

'So it's finally come to this!'

I whirled and saw my mother standing in the doorway. Her face was old and sick with pain.

'I had to,' I said.

'Help me with him.'

We dragged him out of Nerissa's room and put him on his bed. His breathing was ragged and his face was grey. He reeked of the sour liquor.

'I must see to Nerissa,' my mother said. 'God knows what this has done to her.'

'I'll stay with him.'

158

'No, you go to your room. I'll be back.'

'But . . .'

'Go to your room!'

'Mother,' I said, as she turned to go. 'He hadn't done any—I mean—'

'I know,' she said softly. 'I saw. I've been waiting for it. I suppose we all have.'

I lay on my bed looking up sightlessly at the thatch, wondering whether I'd killed him, and the dreadful thing was I didn't seem to care. All I could visualise was Nerissa standing there like a statue, expressionless, emotionless, while his hands were on her body. And my mother, old before her time, her heart almost broken. Everything was falling apart around us.

Later my mother came and sat at the foot of the bed. 'She's sleeping,' she said. 'She wouldn't let me touch her. It's even worse than before.'

'I've got to get her away,' I said.

She shook her head. 'She couldn't travel. It would kill her.'

'But you don't want her here, not after this!'

'You're right in one way. But I love her, too, you see. This isn't her fault.'

'He doesn't love her!' I said savagely.

'I wasn't meaning your father. I've got eyes, Robbie.'

'I told her today.'

'I'm glad. She'll need all our love if she's to get well again.'

'She'll never get well if he's here, not while we're all like this.'

'I know. I've thought about it. There's only one thing to be done. Take him away, Robbie. Take the wagon and go into the mountains and let him find himself.' Her voice was filled with sorrow. 'He wasn't always like this, you know. He was a good man; kind and strong and good. Until we came here. It's this place that has rotted him. He used to say he was looking for a land flowing with milk and honey; I suppose he thought he'd found it. But there's no such place, Robbie, no such place at all.'

I felt an angry resentment at the thought of parting with Nerissa even for a short time. 'Why me?' I asked. 'Why should I be made to suffer for what he's done?'

'Oh, Robbie, think a moment.'

'I am thinking!' I stepped on to the floor and began pacing restlessly up and down the room. My anger was mixed with self-pity. Why, just at this moment, had things to turn against me?

'Not really. You can't have thought of Nerissa. You say you love her.'

'I do. I told you.'

'Then you'd want to give her a chance for recovery. You wouldn't want to see her destroyed.'

It was like being caught between two flooded rivers. 'Couldn't he go by himself?' I said bitterly, already half-accepting the inevitable.

'No, he couldn't. That would be sending him away.'

'Do you really think you can make him go?'

'Not only me, *us*.'

'But what happens if he doesn't—get well?'

'We must pray for that. He was always better when we were travelling; always happier when he was looking forward rather than back.'

'How is he now?'

'He's been sick. His breathing is better.'

'I thought I'd killed him. I didn't seem to care.'

She put her hand up to my face and stroked the hair away from my forehead. I could feel my eyes filling with tears. She pulled my head down onto her breast and held me gently. 'Don't blame yourself,' she whispered. 'I think we've all felt like that. That's why you must take him away.'

And so began my father's last great journey; though we did not know it then, it was to last more than five months.

I find it almost as difficult now to embark on this journey as I did then, though I am clearer about motives than I was. That night, when my mother spoke to me, things finally seemed plain enough : Nerissa was badly shocked and unlikely to get well again in an atmosphere dominated by my father's presence and the conflict between the two of us. So that either Nerissa had to be removed from our influence or we from hers and since my mother was obviously right about the danger to her if we tried to take her even as far as the Port, it *had* to be the latter.

But the more I thought about it, the less simple it became. What if my father refused to go? We couldn't tie him up or force him at gunpoint. I suppose that if my mother really tried she could have made his life at Morile unendurable—but it would have to have been a long programme of attrition which would have been unpleasant for us all and clearly impossible for Nerissa.

And then again where were we supposed to go on this pilgrimage? And what were we looking for? And would we know it if we found it? What guarantee was there that my father would not try to rape her the minute we got back from wherever it was we were going?

I should have trusted more in my mother's instinct or intuition or knowledge of him. There was no trouble about our leaving at all. In fact he had not quite recovered from the blow to the head.

Neither my mother nor I slept much that night and I helped her gather stores in the front room. Long before dawn I sent Cupido to bring the bullocks from the home camp and the servants loaded Pereira's wagon. By first light the oxen were inspanned and we were ready.

'It's time,' I said. 'Do you want to go in alone?'

'No,' my mother replied. 'Come with me. I need your strength.'

My father was lying on his side with his back to the door. The room smelt strongly of vomit and stale drink. I could see the weal on his head where I'd struck him. It had bled a little and the dry blood was now crusted on top of his ear.

'Father,' I began.

'He's not asleep.'

I followed her around the bed. His eyes were open and he was staring vacantly at the wall. In the grey light his skin seemed to have shrunk onto the bones, his eyes were gaunt dark hollows. He did not register our presence at all.

'Jamie,' my mother said, taking him gently by the arm. 'Everything's ready.' And I realised that at some point during the night he must have regained consciousness and she must have told him.

Slowly, like someone rising from a sick bed, he managed to get his feet on the floor.

'Robert will help you.'

I went around and took his other arm. We helped him up from the bed and held him while he got his balance. He shuffled forward, an old man's walk, and we all moved into the keep. The servants were standing in one corner, silent and frightened, and they dropped their eyes as we passed. Only Stone-Axe watched us, his face twisted with grief. 'Where Claw goes, I go,' he had said to me half an hour earlier, but I had ordered him to stay. I would never have gone without the knowledge that he was there to

F*   161

protect those we left. We went on through the house and down the slope of the hill. My father's steps were weak and shaky and we supported him all the way.

The eastern sky was streaked with orange cloud and the walls of the house were a warm apricot colour. After the rain of the previous night the air was clear and cool and there was a strong smell of newly-turned earth. I could not remember a more beautiful morning. We got my father onto the box. I gave a last check that the guns and provisions were securely in place and then I said good-bye to my mother.

'Come back when you're ready,' she said after I had kissed her. 'Not before.'

I took down the long-handled wagon-whip and cracked the lash above the front bullocks' rumps. '*Huk-yeah!*' I cried. '*Huk-yeah!*' Slowly, like some great cumbersome machine, we began to move forward. My memory is of an old grey-faced man hunched above the front wheels, staring unseeingly into the future, and of a woman, standing stiff and straight, her hair and dress billowing slightly in the dawn breeze. Her mouth was set in a straight line and her jaw was firm but she was betrayed by her eyes. It seemed that the pain that lurked there was now a permanent condition. Where she had found this strength I could not tell, only that when she needed it, it had been there. But it must have been the last of her reserves. She had not even trusted herself to say farewell to him. I did not see Nerissa, but she was in my thoughts.

Until the wheels were actually rolling I had still not decided which direction to take. I suppose I had been unconsciously waiting for my father's command. Now I realised I could expect nothing from him at all. He was a human being who in some way had been shattered. It was I who would have to make the decisions. So I indulged myself. I did not want us to founder on the great dry plateaux to the north, nor did I want to go anywhere near Chaka. I had never been to the south-west and it was in this direction that we now turned.

It is in the nature of a journey such as ours for much of it to be monotonous. Certain things such as inspanning and outspanning and watering and collecting fire-wood and cooking meals all have to be done in their correct turn at similar times each day. For the rest, one takes one's pace of life from the slow steps of the bullocks. Time becomes meaningless, distance is measured by the growing nearness of a range of hills, the infinitely slow materialisation of a black speck on the far landscape that finally becomes a tree. It is important that you reach this range or that tree and then, when you have creaked slowly past, it is equally important that you fix another range, another tree, as your goal. Without this tiny ambition you would get slower and slower and finally stop altogether.

I kept no diary of this journey, nor did my father. In fact, his Journal had stopped some months before, just run down like an old clock and petered out. So I can only recall isolated incidents.

I remember on that first day we had not travelled more than five or six miles when the hot sun began to affect my father. He had not spoken at all since we left Morile but now he said: 'Did you bring the spirits?'

'No, only water. It's in the bag behind you.'

He unhooked it and took a long drink. When he'd wiped his mouth with the back of his sleeve, he said: 'Stop at a kraal. We'll get beer.'

Walking behind the oxen in the heat of the day I conjured up a picture of a huge bowl of beer and it seemed infinitely desirable. Abruptly I buried all thoughts of it; there would be no kraal and no damned beer. 'I'll watch for one,' I said briefly. And I did. Periodically I would move away from the wagon on to higher ground and search the countryside and whenever I spied a kraal in the distance I would change our direction just sufficiently to pass it by on the far side of a rise. Soon, of course, there would be fewer and fewer kraals because, although I didn't know it then, we were moving into country completely depopulated by the migrations which Chaka had started.

That night after we'd eaten and bedded down I awoke about midnight to see my father hunched over the fire. His body was trembling and shaking and every now and then he made a noise like a moan. It was cold out here on the bare veld but nothing like cold enough to warrant such shivering.

'Can I get you something, Father?' I called.

He didn't even look up and for a moment I thought he hadn't heard me. Then he half-turned and said: 'A drink is what you can get me, boy, and if you've none of that, go back to your sleep and leave me be.' It was the longest sentence he had spoken the entire day.

Even now, looking back on it, we seemed, in those first weeks of travel, to be two chance acquaintances instead of father and son. We spoke to each other only when necessary and at no time did either of us mention Nerissa. I could not remember what had happened without a flush of rage coursing through my body so I tried not to think about it. At that time I wasn't even sure whether my father knew what had happened, including the fact that I'd struck him.

During this time I did most of the work. I would get up before him in the morning and make the breakfast, have my own quickly and while he was eating his bring in the bullocks and inspan them. This was a lengthy and difficult job in spite of the fact that they were hobbled at night. We did without a mid-day meal and ate again at dusk. Needless to say, I cooked after I'd watered the beasts. All my father did was climb into the wagon after breakfast and climb down again when I outspanned. I was dead tired each night as I crawled into my kaross. I need hardly add that the occasional hare or guinea fowl we ate fell to my fowling-piece.

All this time we had been climbing gently towards the Dragon Mountains and one day after a particularly tiring trek we only reached water in the late afternoon. There was one thing I had learnt long before and that was never to make your camp in the dark. I still had to water the bullocks and I knew that by the time I'd finished it would be too dark to collect wood for the fire. I asked my father if he would get the wood while I attended to the beasts. He had climbed down from the wagon and was seated on his kaross smoking his pipe and staring blindly at nothing. Slowly he took his pipe from his mouth and turned to me : 'The prisoner declines with thanks,' he said.

'Look,' I replied hotly, 'this was no idea of mine.' I felt the resentment building up again that I was there at all.

But he'd turned away and I knew that there was no time then to argue. I watered the bullocks while they were still in their yokes and hobbled them. On the way back to the wagon I picked up what wood I could find in the half darkness. My father was sitting in exactly the same position. I remember then experiencing not so much a feeling of anger but one of despair. In a wave of self-pity I thought that this was too much to bear. I suddenly saw myself caught in a situation for which I was not prepared and yet the responsibility for which I had been asked to shoulder.

I'm not clear what would have happened then had he not pushed me beyond self-pity into cold rage.

'The prisoner wishes his supper,' he said.

'All right,' I replied, holding myself on a tight rein, 'he shall have it.'

I'd shot a duiker the day before and the small haunches were hanging in the wagon. I took them down and placed one at his feet. 'There it is,' I said. I moved off about ten yards, built my own fire-place with three large stones, got the wood going and grilled my own meat. When I'd finished I purposely allowed the fire to die and climbed into my kaross. During all this time he had sat quite still watching me. Neither of us spoke a word.

Breakfast was the same. I cooked my own corn porridge and ate the rest of the meat cold. When I'd finished inspanning he was sitting on the front box and I knew he had taken nothing but a little water. By evening he was looking weak and drawn and he staggered slightly as he got down from the wagon.

'If you want any supper,' I said shortly, 'you'll have to fetch your own wood.'

He disregarded me completely. He spread out his kaross and climbed between the skins. 'You're learning,' he said after a while.

We kept it up for two more days until, on the evening of the third, he fell as he was climbing from the wagon and couldn't get up. I pulled him into his kaross and made a hot broth from a brace of partridge and fed him. By this time I was frightened that I'd gone too far and that he might not recover. The following morning I fed him the rest of the broth which I'd thickened into a gruel with crushed corn. We rested in camp that day and had another meal at noon. He seemed to have recovered somewhat, for he asked for his pipe and lay in the kaross for the remainder of the afternoon sleeping and smoking. As the sun went down behind the western hills he got up. 'Hatred is like anything else,' he said. 'You want to do it properly.'

It took me a moment or two to understand his meaning. 'But I don't hate you,' I said. 'Perhaps I haven't learnt well enough.'

'Then more fool you.'

He wandered away from the camp into a nearby kloof and was back in about half an hour. He had a bundle of kindling under one arm and was pulling the dead trunk of a thorn tree with his good hand. He came right up to me and dropped the wood at my feet. 'If it's imprisonment *with* hard labour you're wanting, so be it.'

This time it was I who ignored him; we seemed to get on better that way.

We journeyed on. The prospect began to change slowly. We were moving into the high country now and ahead of us reared the great slab-sided Dragon Mountains. The weather still held fine and the landscape was spectacular. Instead of the bush country through which we had been moving this was wide grassland, russet in the autumn sun. The air was cool and clear and in spite of the unease of our relationship I was young enough to feel the exhilaration of day after day of frosty mornings and golden sunlight and the huge light-blue dome of the sky above us.

I began to notice a change in my father. It was now nearly a month since we had left Morile and in all that time he had not drunk anything stronger than water. Physically, he seemed to have filled out into his earlier proportions. His skin no longer had its sallow tinge and no longer hung flaccidly from his bones, his eyes were clear and his hair had lost its deadness and shone as though he was smearing it with axle-grease. A couple of days after he had elected to help me with the wood he pulled out the fowling-piece from its hooks in the wagon and strode off into the veld.

We'd had no real meat since I had shot the duiker and both of us were hungry. After a while I heard two shots and about an hour later he walked down to the wagon carrying two magnificent knorhaans. He hung them inside the wagon and climbed back to his usual place on the front box. 'If I'm to work my passage I need the strength,' he said dryly.

He'd shot the two bustards about mid-morning and every time I passed the rear of the wagon I could see their swaying corpses. I began to think about the rich savoury smell of their cooking and the sweet juices began to flow in my mouth. We outspanned early and after I'd watered the bullocks and he had collected the wood we sat down in the afternoon sun, not talking but in a sense not quite so uneasy with each other. I began to think about supper. I didn't want to make the first move since he had shot the birds and if he felt like it I suppose he could have done what I had already done : told me to get my own. But I noticed his eyes swing around at intervals to stare at the wagon. From where we were sitting we could see the bustards against the white canvas tent. Both of us were swallowing more than usual. We lit our pipes but for once the tobacco did not seem to take the edge off my hunger.

'Father . . .' I finally began.

'Tough,' he said longingly, as though he had just been waiting for someone to break the silence. 'Very tough bird, a knorhaan. Should hang for a week at least.'

I swallowed a mouthful of saliva. I wasn't sure how we were going to live with them for a week.

'No good spoiling them,' he said.

'It would be a pity.'

We lapsed into hungry silence again. After puffing at his pipe for a while he said : 'No sense in being hasty.'

'We'd not enjoy them.'

'All game birds should be hung,' he said. 'And that's that.'

'You shot them,' I said.

'Aye. I shot them.'

'So you decide.'

'Aye, I'll decide.'

'Right, then. I'll get the corn out.'

'The corn.'

'That's all there is, Father.'

A look of great distaste crossed his face. He swallowed again and suddenly he said : 'Boy, how are your teeth?'

'Excellent.'

'Well, get the pot on !'

He was on his feet in a moment and was half-running to the wagon. By the time I'd got the big cauldron boiling he had skinned both birds and jointed them. We cooked them with salt and wild garlic. The smell was stupefying. We let them stew for three hours and then we couldn't stand it any longer. We speared the pieces with sharpened sticks and ate them boiling hot. He was right, the meat was tough, but it was gamey and rich and just about the best food I'd ever tasted. A bustard isn't a small bird and we ate until our bellies were distended and our faces shiny with grease. There was very little left when we finally stopped.

We lay back belching and groaning. 'Oh, God,' my father said with reverence in his voice, 'the beautiful wee feathered creatures !'

After that he was out with the guns every day, sometimes the rifle, sometimes the fowling-piece, and we began to eat like kings. It got so we were even able to become choosey. If he shot a buck, for instance, we would only eat the kidneys and liver, the rest

167

we'd cut in strips and dry in the sun. The rear of the wagon began to look like a poulterer's. There was no need to eat tough birds now and at any one time there would be quail or guinea fowl or partridge or even wild duck, hanging until my father judged them ready. We shot the duck from the reed-fringed pools of the mountain streams and often at noon we'd halt the wagon for a few minutes and strip off and plunge into the icy, rushing water. The thing my father liked best was to go out into the middle of shallow rapids and hang on to a boulder with his hook letting the water rush down on his head and neck. Afterwards we would blow and stamp in the sunshine to get the circulation back and right then begin to think of supper.

It was a wide and empty land, like a huge wrinkled lion skin, and we were the only people that moved across it. Everywhere there was evidence of the migrations. Kraals that had once held hundreds of Caffres were broken and decayed. Between the ruined huts lay the bones of those who had inhabited them. The gardens had run to seed long ago but there were still corn-cobs, caffre corn, pumpkins and beans to be had if one searched carefully enough.

All this time we had been trekking south-west, keeping the Dragon Mountains on our right. I had given no thought to our eventual destination, nor even whether a destination existed. I suppose I had just surmised that one day we'd simply turn the bullocks around in their tracks and go back the way we'd come. How I would recognise that day I had little idea. It sounds foot-loose—and it was. I had too much to do every day to dwell on the future.

On the surface we seemed to be getting along better with each other. We were actually talking now, not simply answering yes or no or discussing the state of the commissary. Of course there was not much time for communication during the day but the evenings now became times to which I looked forward.

The days had shortened considerably since we had left home and winter was almost upon us. In the mornings the grass was white with frost and spiders' webs would glint and glisten in the early sun. At noon-time on these still, golden days of late autumn the air was warm enough to bring out sweat patches on our clothing but by mid-afternoon one could feel the chill creeping into the air. Dusk came early, turning the veld a smoky grey. By five o'clock in the afternoon there was steam on our breaths, by six it was almost dark and the flames of our fire would throw up sparks to the crackling stars above. We would huddle near the fire in our big sheep-skin coats, covering our legs with the karosses and eat the game stews from wooden bowls. Afterwards we would smoke our pipes and sometimes my father would recall the days of his youth and the journeys he had made as a young man before he had married my step-mother. When he wished he could tell things more vividly than anyone I've ever heard. He was able to impart a feeling for the land he had traversed and for the first time I realised how large it was and how varied. When he spoke of herding cattle and sheep in the Snowy Mountains or travelling the desert floor in the Bachapin country there was a longing in his voice that reminded me of something my mother had said just before we left. She was right; he was a travelling man.

But I should not like to give the impression that our differences were forgotten. We had not returned—and perhaps never could return—to the intimacy of a father-and-son relationship. Too much had happened; there had been too much friction. Nerissa still lurked just beneath the surface of my mind and I assumed the same for my father. No, we were like two distant cousins, bound by slender ties of blood, who find, in spite of all they have suspected of each other, a certain area of common ground.

Nor should it be thought that one only had to put my father into a wagon, take him out into the veld for a few weeks, let the sun shine on his head and the long winds blow in his face, and suddenly there he'd be, all miraculously re-designed. I have never yet found this to be so with anyone.

True, he had started to take an interest in our voyaging. Where earlier he had simply existed he now took part in what we were doing and seemed to enjoy it. But there were days on end when the old blackness would descend on him and he would be as far away as ever. Days when he would sit hunched on the wagon-seat, the guns in the back forgotten; nights when he would eat his meal in silence and then roll over in his kaross without a word. I didn't mind, since I didn't expect anything of him. That had been my philosophy from the beginning.

I remember one day he took down the rifle and stalked away from the wagon. It happened soon after we had inspanned. Usually he was never away for more than a couple of hours but this time he had not returned by noon and I began to get apprehensive, not that he didn't know the veld—he had been Stone-Axe's first pupil—but one had little defence against accidents. He could have slipped and fallen and even now be lying with broken limbs at the bottom of a kloof wondering when I was going to arrive. By early afternoon I realised I couldn't go on so I out-spanned and went to look for him. About five miles back along the trail I found him resting against a boulder staring vacantly at nothing, his thoughts if he had any, in some other world. I had heard no shot the whole morning and now I saw that the gun wasn't even loaded.

I came right up to him and he did not see me.

'Father,' I said, 'are you all right?'

He jerked, as though coming out of a dream. 'Oh, it's you. What is it?' he said.

'I was worried. You've been away for hours.'

'Have I now?' He got to his feet and began to walk along the furrows of the wagon wheels. That was all he said.

By the following day this black mood had passed and he was normal again. That evening he spoke more animatedly than ever about his journeys and then abruptly he broke off and looked across the fire at me. 'Where are we going?' he asked.

Where indeed? I shook my head. 'Just going,' I said. 'I don't know where.'

'I'm glad you're not a sea captain.' He paused for a moment. 'Still, you're not to blame. This was your mother's scheme. But I'll tell you what, son. D'you see those mountains?' He pointed backwards with his thumb. In the distance I could make out the square tops of the Dragon Mountains like a faint shadow in the moonlight. 'What d'you say we go and look at the other side? There's a kingdom there somewhere. I've heard tell of it. The Land of the Basutos, they call it. A whole tribe that lives on a hill called the Mountain of the Night, ruled by a king name of Moshesh. What say you we pay them a call?'

I felt a sudden excitement at the thought. 'But what about the mountains? We'll never get across them.'

'There'll be passes, boy, be sure of that. I've never seen a range yet that couldn't be crossed. Well? What d'you say? You're the captain, or the gaoler, or whatever you like. What do you say we pay them a visit?'

Both of us were suddenly alive with animation. 'Do you think we'd make it?'

'Of course we would!'

And so, for no other reason than an urge to see what lay beyond the furthest range, our journey added a dimension; it began to have a purpose. Now, as I look back on that evening, I wonder if this is not what my mother had had in her mind.

For nearly a week we travelled south along the escarpment looking in vain for some break in the wall of steep, flat-topped mountains. Then on the afternoon of the sixth day my father called me to him and pointed to a kloof that cut into the side of the range. The mountains folded around it and we could not see its outcome. 'We'll try it in the morning,' he said. As we cooked the meal that evening a breeze blew the smoke into our eyes. It was the first time there had been wind for some weeks.

The following morning the sky was a dirty grey and the wind was blowing hard; it was very cold. We started an hour earlier than usual. By the time I'd finished packing the wagon my father had the bullock whip in his hands. 'Take the leading *riem*,' he said. 'And keep up on the right-hand side of the shoulder.' It was the first time he had given an order since the trip began and I felt a sudden release. I ran along the span to the front oxen and took hold of the *riem* that was fastened to the horns.

'*Hey—! Hey—! Hey—!*' he called, and the *voorslag* cracked in the air.

I led out, keeping as he had told me, to the right side. We began to climb immediately. We kept the kloof on our left, using the flat shoulder as a road-bed. The wind howled down from the slopes and I bent my body against it, keeping one hand on the leading-rein and using the other to guard my eyes from dust. Every now and then I could hear my father calling to the bullocks by name and then the crack of the lash. Although he was no more than twenty yards behind me his voice was faint in the wind.

There was no chance of telling if we were pointing correctly since the mountains were obscured by grey cloud, but we kept to the shoulder which wound into the range like a wide road. What we would do if the sides of the kloof steepened or the buttresses closed in on us, forcing us towards the edge, I did not know. But I wasn't worried; my father had taken over.

Under the dark grey sky what I could see of the landscape was infinitely drear. This has always been my experience of Africa. Take the sun away and all life seems to bleed out of the veld, leaving it barren and depressing. Rocks, trees and grass blend into a dun-coloured whole. All the morning we pushed on, climbing towards the summit of the pass. The kloof on our left had deepened considerably and there was now a drop of five hundred feet or more if one of the wheels slipped. On our right the mountain walls towered above us. It was about mid-day that I felt something cold sting my cheek. I looked up and saw white flakes swirling in front of me. I'd never seen snow before but I knew what it was and I stopped in my tracks holding out my cupped hands in delight as the flakes gathered in my palms.

'It's snow!' I yelled back delightedly. I turned to share the moment with my father but so thick were the flakes I could hardly see him. He was crouched at the back wheels desperately turning the brake handles. In that second I realised what was happening. We had begun to slide down and sideways towards the drop. It was my fault for stopping.

'Get on! Get on!' he was shouting. 'Keep those bullocks moving, damn you!'

I grabbed up the *riem* and began tugging at the leaders' heads. I saw them take the strain, saw their feet begin to slip a little on the wet grass.

'*Hey—! H-e-e-y!*' My father's voice was hoarse with the effort. Crack! Crack! This time the *voorslag* bit into the bullocks' rumps and then I heard the thud as he used the butt of the whip on their ribs.

'Come on, pull them out!' he shouted, coming up to me and taking the *riem* by my side. Gradually the bullocks found their footing and we began to move slowly forward.

'Don't ever do that again!' he said as he ran back to the brake handles. We struggled on into the white wall of snow, unable to tell whether the next few steps would plunge us into the abyss, unable to stop lest we never get started again. On either side of us the snow began to pile in drifts, making the brown winter grass look even dirtier by comparison.

I don't know how long we battled upwards. It felt like days, though it was only hours. Behind me I could hear the heaving lungs of the oxen; my own felt raw and torn. And then, as suddenly as the snow had started it stopped and we burst through a mist of swirling cloud to the top of the pass. On either side of us rose snow-capped peaks, ahead lay a great basin broken up by hills, valleys and streams. In the clear light we could see per-

172

haps fifty or sixty miles and everything was covered in a light dusting of snow.

'We'll camp here for the night,' my father said. His eyes were glittering with success.

That was the coldest night I ever remember. There was no wood to make a fire, nor could we dry out the bullocks' dung pats. We ate an odd mixture of meal and water which my father called drammach and crawled into our karosses. All night the wind howled through the pass with the strength of a hurricane. By morning two bullocks were dead, frozen solid where they lay. We managed to find some tufts of dry grass in the lee of a rock and when we had them alight we thawed out the axle-grease. We didn't wait for breakfast but started the descent immediately. By mid-morning the clouds broke up and the sun came out and soon all the snow had melted leaving the land wet and glistening. We made camp early on the banks of a snow-fed stream and I worked in the sunshine, feeling the cold gradually thaw out of my bones. We stayed there for two days resting the oxen.

It was a strange land in which we found ourselves. Behind us lay the mighty spurs of the Dragon Mountains, ahead other ranges ran north-south. None were as high as the ones we had just crossed but their sides were steep and treeless; we were in a world of mountains and canyons and had it been left to me I should not have known which direction to take.

'It's not difficult,' my father said as we set off again. 'We'll go where we can go and won't go where we can't. It's no good fighting the country, it'll win in the end.' So we kept to the valley floors, meandering along the banks of streams, looking always for the easiest, if the longest, route. I say longest, but it wasn't really a case of long or short, since we didn't know exactly where we were going. When we met up with a Caffre tribe—as we must do eventually—we would take our directions to the kingdom of Moshesh from them. In the meantime we slowly moved deeper and deeper into the unknown.

We had been travelling for nearly three weeks when once again the black mood descended on my father. I had been waiting for it and after he had been absent from the wagon for some hours and I had not heard the sound of a shot, I tied the span to a boulder and went off in search of him. I had not been gone more than half an hour when I heard voices. They came from the far side of a small rise and I hurried in their direction. I'm not sure what made me suddenly change my approach to one of caution but it was as well I did.

As I came to the top I dropped down on my knees and crawled the remaining few yards, invisible in the high grass. I could see my father in the hollow of a *donga* surrounded by about a dozen Caffres. Another group of about twenty stood some distance away. A small flock of goats grazed nearby. Well, we'd found our tribe —or rather, they had found us—and now it only needed a friendly exchange of presents and they would point us in the true direction for Moshesh's kraal. I was about to push myself up and call down to them when I noticed another figure who had been obscured by one of the Caffres. He was a white man. When I looked closer I felt a sudden seizure in my stomach. I was staring down at Pereira. There was no doubt about that. He was wearing different clothes, all made of skins, but there was no way of hiding the crushing scar that cut his face in two. I dropped down into the grass again, wondering what I could do.

'And some people would have it there's not a God in Heaven,' Pereira was saying. 'Yet here you are, farmer, and it's long since that I gave up any thought of seeing you again. Did you never wonder if I might not come calling again?'

'No, I did not.'

'Why should you? You sent your slayer to put an end to that.'

'What would you have done?'

'The same, I think. And like you I would now be paying the price.'

'Rubbish, man, what's this talk of price and payment from a rogue like you? Do you deny you were on your way to the King? That what you'd have told him would have brought destruction on me and my family? You might even be living in my house right now! Would *you* have sat by lightly?'

'You are not so dull as you look, farmer. It was in my mind, just as you say. But as you reverse our roles so let me put it to you that you would have done the same.'

'I'd never have sold the girl in the first place.'

'That's what you think now.'

'I'm no slaver, Pereira.' He nodded towards the furthest group of Caffres and for the first time I noticed that their hands were bound behind their backs. 'It's filthy work.'

'No worse than sending off to have me killed. And let me tell you, farmer, that you are wrong. These are not my slaves, they are no one's. They are simply cattle that belong to the tribe.'

'Cattle?'

'Yes, like your Zulus own cattle, we own men.'

'And you say they're not slaves!'

Pereira shrugged. 'You will see. But to go back a while; did you not think to look for me? I was sorely hurt. You might have finished the work right then.'

'I reckoned you could not have lived. Not from what I heard.'

'But I did, farmer, and that is to your sorrow. Your slayer was too eager, he did not find the heart. I lay for two days near that stream before a woman found me and cared for me. She had been taken in adultery and was fleeing from death, and when I was strong enough to walk we travelled together. How long we journeyed I cannot say but after a time we met these people,' he indicated the Caffres standing around them. 'They took us in. They had never seen a white man before nor a gun.' He smiled suddenly. 'They worship me like a god.'

'They're not Moshesh's people?'

'No, no. Mine. They're my people, and his will soon be mine as well.' He got to his feet and looked down and frowned at my father. 'You come at an awkward time. I could have you killed this instant but it would not suit me. Now, where are your companions?'

'I have no companions. My servants died of fever six weeks ago.'

'Your wagon, then.'

'It was lost in the mountains.'

'Perhaps we can find it for you.'

He and my father had been conversing in Zulu but now he issued a series of quick commands in a tongue I could not understand. The meaning was clear enough. I knew they would find the wheel tracks within a few minutes so I stayed where I was. I had a rifle, powder and ball, and dried meat in my wallet.

It worked out as I had expected. They found the tracks and then the wagon and by early afternoon the whole group was moving north-west. It was good country for stalking and I could follow them easily without giving myself away.

One thing I noticed at the time was to become clear in a terrible fashion sooner than I thought. The bound Caffres were indeed like cattle. Herdsmen kept them in a group and they

175

drifted across the veld like so many cows in a pasture. They neither spoke among themselves nor even looked at each other. They kept their eyes upon the ground like men condemned to the gallows.

Even at this distance I find it hard to describe what followed; I have thought much about how to set it down and have come to the conclusion that it may be better for me to express my revulsion now, and then simply record what I saw, leaving my own feelings and state of mind to the imagination.

They camped on the open veld that night and I had no way of getting close to them so I slept rough and cold, envying them the warmth of their fires.

The following day the country changed appreciably, the mountains giving way to isolated, flat-topped hills which rose from the plains like enormous watch-towers, their crests guarded by steep cliffs of sheer rock. It was to one of these that Pereira now led the party. I'd had to drop a good way back because the cover was poor and I watched them outspan the oxen at the base of the hill and drive them, and the goats, and the human cattle straight up the side as though to force them to scale the cliffs. Abruptly everyone, including the animals, simply vanished from sight. It was so sudden that for a moment I thought there must be a hole in the centre of the hill into which all had fallen until, after about twenty minutes, I saw tiny figures emerge at the crest to be etched for a second against the skyline. Then I realised there must be a deep cleft in the side which gave access to the summit. It was mid-afternoon and I waited where I was until the sun began to sink towards the horizon and my side of the hill was in deep shadow. I began to move through it with all the stealth that Stone-Axe had taught me. As I reached the bottom it became clear that unless one knew which way to approach the hill, its summit was almost unattainable.

In the shadow it was already bitterly cold and I struck upwards to where I imagined the cleft to begin. Without the bullocks' spoors to guide me I should never have found it, nor could I have entered but for the fact that my father's arrival with Pereira must have engaged the guards' attention, for a great wall of interlaced thorn trees nearly thirty feet high and half as wide which, when placed in the mouth of the cleft must have closed it as securely as a cork in a bottle, had been pulled aside and never replaced.

The cleft was in reality a rock chimney that must, through the centuries, have become more and more eroded, until it sliced down the heart of the mountain, offering an easy incline to the crest. I stepped into it warily, holding the loaded rifle ahead of me. On either side the rock walls were devoid of hand or footholds.

As I neared the top I heard singing and shouting but it seemed some distance away so I eased myself out of the cleft and, like a mongoose emerging from its lair to test and probe the air, raised my own head cautiously above the surface.

I was not prepared for what I saw. The top of the hill was flat and circular and about six hundred yards in diameter. It consisted of grass and rock and in the centre a village of seventy or eighty huts had been built. On one side was a stone-walled goat-pen, and nearest me there was a second. In it were about fifty men and women, their hands bound behind their backs. Their faces bore the same look as I had seen before : dull and lifeless apathy. In the dusk they stood or sat as though cut from stone, seeming not to feel the cold at all. It was only later I learnt they were already dead, not physically, of course, but in their own acceptance of their inevitable end.

Just then I saw two figures coming towards me; my father and Pereira. I cast around quickly for cover, but everything was bare and open. I slithered like a snake towards the nearest enclosure and scrambled over the stone wall.

I found myself among the prisoners. The stench from the pen was appalling, a mixture of excrement and rotting food. For all the notice they took of me I might not have existed. I recall tramping inadvertently upon the hand of a plump youth about my own age. He did not seem to feel it and made no move to pull it away.

I crouched down below the top of the wall and watched the two men come nearer. They stood on the edge of the cliff and Pereira pointed towards the north-west. 'That is where Moshesh lives,' he said. 'About thirty miles from here. They, too, live on a hill, but greater than this. They call it the Mountain of the Night and one day soon I shall be king there.'

'And a very noble one you'll make, too,' my father said dryly.

'You will never know whether that be the case or not, farmer.'

'Man, for someone who's got kingship on his mind you do a deal of havering over trifles. Ever since yesterday you've been talking about what's to happen to me: my days are numbered, I haven't much time, I'll not see this or I'll not see that. That's not how a king talks, Pereira. Why don't you have done with me once and for all and set your mind at rest?'

I shivered to hear such talk from my father until I realised how he must be thinking. He must know I had followed. Even now he must expect to hear the roar of a gun and see Pereira topple down the cliffs. And it would have been easy. We could be down the cleft and away before anyone realised. But if so, why did he not simply hurl Pereira over the lip himself? I looked more closely and saw the reason. My father's hands were also bound behind his back and a thong of leather dropped down from his wrists and was fastened around his ankles.

'You know well why I don't kill you now,' Pereira said, stepping back from the cliff as though reading my thoughts.

'I can guess.'

'You must not blame them. They have always sacrificed before a battle.'

'And I'm to give them victory, no less.'

'The spirits will give them that. You go to the spirits on their behalf. Don't you understand, farmer, there could be no greater sacrifice than a white man? A demi-god's life *must* give them victory. And anyway, I have promised them.'

'When's the great moment to be?' my father asked, as calm as a pond.

'Soon . . . soon . . . Come, first you will be feasted.'

As they passed the prisoners I ducked down again, pushing myself into the midden.

They had not been gone for more than a few minutes when half a dozen spearmen came trotting past and disappeared into the cleft. I assumed they were going back to replace the thorn gate and take up their positions. It was full darkness now and a bitter wind blew off the high mountains. I still had no plan in mind, but of one thing I was certain, I couldn't stay where I was. I could already feel my muscles contracting with the cold and it would not be long before I stiffened up badly. Then I would be no use at all. It occurred to me to wonder how the people in the pen survived the exposure. Later I was to discover that it mattered very little whether they survived or not.

I dropped down on to the grass and crawled towards the huts.

178

If I could find which one my father was in I might have some sort of chance at his release for these were not built like Zulu huts. They were completely conical in shape, the thatch coming down to the ground on all sides, giving them the appearance of a halved orange lying on its broad base. It would have been impossible to cart enough mud up to the village for stouter walls.

The cold had driven everyone into the huts and I was able to gain the shadows of the nearest without seeing or hearing a villager. In the centre of the group stood a larger dwelling and this I assumed to be Pereira's. I wriggled on my belly across the open clearing and came around the back. The darkness closed over me like a thick, impenetrable blanket. I heard a commotion and ducked down. Two Caffres passed out of the entrance to the hut and hurried in the direction of the prisoners. Within minutes they were back and had a third man with them.

Meantime I had taken out my big hunting knife and begun to work softly at the thatch and withes that made up the rear wall. They cut easily and my only difficulty was in gauging the thickness of the wall so my knife blade did not slip through, causing a noise. I cut each stem carefully, removing as many as I could, gradually working the hole larger. The wall was about an inch thick and having cut away all but the thinnest of screens I slowly removed those on the inside as well. My fingers were numb with cold. Now I could lie flat and disappear in the shadows or raise my head and peer through the hole as circumstances dictated.

I put my eye to the hole and got my first view of the hut's interior and it was, without doubt, the most terrible scene I have ever witnessed. It was crowded with Caffres. To one side sat Pereira and next to him my father. There was no furniture of any description that I could see but there may well have been objects outside my line of vision. The whole scene was lit by the flickering flames of a wood fire in the centre, over which a huge black pot was bubbling. Yellow smoke filled the room like sea fog. All eyes were turned towards a group in the middle of the hut and the leaping flames and shadows gave faces a demoniacal appearance. It was a nightmarish sight.

At first I could not make out what was happening, and then I realised that a man was being strangled. He was being held by one Caffre while a second twisted a leather thong around his neck. Just before his thick tongue protruded from his lips and his face became distended beyond all recognition I saw that he was the plump young man from the pen on whose hand I had trodden.

As soon as he was dead his paunch and entrails were removed and then he was butchered. His arms and legs were jointed and an axe was used to split his torso into manageable pieces. The flesh was then shared out among the Caffres, some of whom dropped pieces into the cauldron. Others took their share and went out to their own huts. I watched the whole operation with a kind of dread fascination.

There must already have been something cooking in the pot, for the last thing I remember seeing was the emergence of a swollen hand, the black skin split in places to show white, cooked flesh beneath.

I could not help my father then for the vomit came up of its own accord and I lay with my cheek pressed to the earth; it was hot against the frost.

I cannot remember thinking out a plan at that time; I was incapable of thought. It must already have been fixed in my inner mind, for I suddenly found myself running hard towards the 'cattle'. They were lying in bunches, huddled together for warmth. I leapt over the wall and landed among them, hacking at the thongs which bound them. They seemed dazed, unable to comprehend what was happening.

'Go on!' I was yelling at them in a mixture of English and Zulu. 'You're free! You're free! Get out! Run!'

But still they didn't move, only cowering away from me, trying to force themselves into the corners of the pen. I knew the noise of my voice would bring out the others. If the prisoners stayed where they were we were lost. I began to kick and cuff them, trying to make them angry. But it seemed nothing would move them. I heard voices from the huts. In a last desperate measure I put the gun to my shoulder and fired into the sky. At last they acted. Terrified of the gun, they began to scream and mill about. Then, realising that their hands were no longer tied, they threw themselves at the wall and tore their way to the top. Within seconds they were running in all directions. Some down to the cleft, some towards the hut; none seemed to have any motive other than to get clear of the gun.

Hurriedly I reloaded and raced towards Pereira's dwelling.

Everything was in confusion. Women and men, prisoners and Caffres were totally unhinged. I heard Pereira's voice shouting orders but he might have been trying to talk down a buffalo stampede for all the good it was doing.

'Robbie!' The voice was a hiss in my ear.

I whirled. My father was crouched against the wall of the hut. 'Quick, lad!' I slashed at the thongs binding both wrists and ankles. 'I thought you'd left it too late!'

'This way!' I said, leading him at a run towards the cleft.

It was a pitch-dark night and this saved us. It was not possible for the cannibals to recognise each other, much less their intended victims who were still screaming and running all over the top of the hill. Spears were flying but how many were finding their mark was impossible to say. We saw several bodies near the huts.

We dropped down into the cleft. Here the noise was frightening because it was funnelled up to us. 'Steady,' my father said, putting his hand on my shoulder. 'We're almost at the barrier.' We rounded the last turn, keeping to the shadows, and saw a writhing heap of bodies fighting to break down the gate. At least three of the guards were still alive and we could see the flash of their spear points. We were not able to tell how many prisoners were there for some had died from wounds and others had been trampled to death. Some fought to scale the barrier, others were heaving at its base. Suddenly it gave, toppling forward with a crash.

'Now!' my father said, and we raced forward. We slipped and slithered over a carpet of bloody and mangled flesh. I felt the thorns tear at my legs as we crashed across the barrier and then we were through the mouth of the cleft and our feet were on grass and the wind blew fresh in our faces. And in that moment, as we burst through to freedom, I felt a searing pain in my side. It seemed like several seconds before I heard the sound of the shot.

I stumbled, fell, regained my feet, and went on running. 'Are you hit, lad?' my father said.

I put my hand to my side and felt a wet warmth. 'I must be. Here, you take the gun.' I remember nothing more after that.

There now came a long hiatus in my life. For nearly a month there is only blankness, as though it has been excised from my personal history, and so I have had to put together the events of

181

which I now write from the taciturn answers which my father later gave me and the shreds of information I was able to understand in my talks with Moshesh.

I have often wondered how we ever survived the flight from the cannibals, for it was thirty miles to Thaba Bosiyo, which is called the Mountain of the Night, and we reached it soon after dawn. In many ways I am thankful that the memory has been erased. I often asked my father to describe what happened and invariably he said: 'Sometimes you walked and sometimes you didn't.' I had always known him to be a powerful man but the thought of him carrying me across the veld in the blackness of the night added new dimensions not only to his physical strength but to that of his purpose as well. Even when we reached Thaba Bosiyo and the Basutos made us welcome he fought to carry me the five hundred feet to the top of the hill and only gave me up to fresher arms after he had fallen twice.

We were lucky in our hosts. There is a parallel to be drawn between Moshesh, the King of the Basutos, and Chaka. Both were self-made men, both created a new nation from the remnants of others, but while Chaka absorbed them by power, Moshesh did so by offering haven to the countless refugees made homeless by the Great Migrations.

They were of similar age when I knew them, but there all similarity ceased. Where Chaka raged, Moshesh was reflective; where Chaka was cruel, Moshesh was kind; where Chaka wore elaborate finery, Moshesh dressed simply in a cloak, armlets and neckband which contained a knife. In place of Chaka's great head-dress, Moshesh wore a single feather.

Where Chaka was headstrong, Moshesh was guileful; where Chaka conquered by force, Moshesh triumphed by diplomacy. It is even said that once a Zulu regiment under Mzilikazi tried to take Thaba Bosiyo by storm and when he failed, laid siege to it. But it was the Zulus who starved and when Moshesh sent down cattle to them from the great herds which grazed on the summit, they were so grateful that they left in peace and swore not to molest him further.

It was to this Chief of the Mountain we now came in our extremity. We could not have reached a safer haven. Later, when I grew strong again, I walked all over its top. It was about two miles long and a mile wide and elliptical in shape. At one end Moshesh had built his kraal, the remainder was flat tableland of waving grass and bubbling springs. Here the flocks grazed. It was a world entirely on its own and none of his people need ever go down to the rivers and gorges that patterned the surrounding countryside. The hilltop was completely surrounded by cliff and there were only three known paths to the summit. At the top of each of these were collected great mounds of boulders. Moshesh always liked to be prepared.

I neither saw nor knew anything of this the morning of our arrival. Willing hands carried me up the slopes and I was placed in one of the King's own huts. And there I lay. Pereira's ball had blown a hole in my side the size of a clenched fist and no one thought I could live—except my father. If there is any memory I have of that period at all it is the sight of his face, worried and tired, hovering above me as I lay on the skin pallet fighting for life.

Moshesh had offered the services of his best medicine men but my father would have none. He nursed me himself, making hot poultices of crushed corn to try and draw out the poison and when these failed he used wet cow-dung and, later, spiders' webs.

I am somewhat cynical about the effects of these home remedies but the fact is that I did recover. Whether it was the intensity and care of the nursing or the natural strength of youth I do not know, but I like to think it was the former.

As I lay in the great kraal on Thaba Bosiyo, as close to death as it is possible to be, Moshesh questioned my father about our recent past. It appeared that cannibalism was a sickness which lingered among many long after the need for it—during the worst part of the Migrations—was over. Moshesh had heard of Pereira but he did not know that the Portuguese had been in touch with other cannibal bands for a radius of a hundred miles, nor that he was trying to weld them into a single fighting force, the object of which was no less than Moshesh's overthrow.

During the next few weeks Moshesh sent his own armies throughout the land to clear it of the danger. Then they laid siege to Pereira's hill. At the end of a fortnight they gained the top and slaughtered the cannibals that remained. Of Pereira there was no sign, and since no one lived to tell what had happened his end must be left in doubt. But there is one thing that may be offered in evidence. Above the entrance to the largest hut the Basutos found a grinning skull. It had been fixed there by leather thongs. It was quite unlike the skulls found in the great pile of

183

bones which were discovered below the cliffs on the furthest side. For one thing it was smaller, for another the bone of the nose bore an old scar. It is possible to wonder whether the cannibals, cheated of my father, had turned on Pereira himself and sacrificed him during the final battle. We will never know.

Spring was early that year and with its arrival the last of the poisons in my body seemed to disappear and slowly I began to regain my strength. It was at this time I realised how much my father had contributed to my recovery. He was at my side for most of every day, and at night slept on a pile of skins at my feet.

My first memories of the slow recovery were those of weakness. I was not able to rise from the pallet to perform my bodily functions, nor was I able to feed myself. My father cared for me as though I were a baby. I learnt later that for the first three days he had not slept at all—and this even after bringing me there—until on the fourth he had collapsed.

One of the difficulties that had obsessed him early on was how to feed me. Finally he had solved this by sewing a soft leather nipple on a goat's bladder and letting me suck a mixture of blood and milk. When I grew stronger he hand-fed me with a spoon made out of horn.

As the snow on the high peaks melted and the sun grew daily warmer I was allowed to sit outside the hut, sheltered from the breezes by a high reed fence which surrounded each hut in the kraal. My memory of this little yard and of the hut itself is dominated by a sense of cleanliness and neatness, and I later discovered that this was so of all the Basuto dwellings.

It was now that I came to know Moshesh. He often visited me when I was sitting there in the sunshine and we would have long, strange conversations in which we might only understand one word in five. I think what I remember most about him is the courtesy and dignity with which he did everything. He was a well-made man, I suppose in his mid-thirties then, with a moustache and a small beard and large, sad eyes which belied a deep and quiet sense of humour.

We had been talking—if that is how I may describe our language struggle—about the history of cannibalism in his country, when he told me that once some of his own chieftains had urged him to take vengeance on a gang of cannibals who were believed to have killed and eaten Moshesh's grandparents.

'But we were weak then,' I understood him to say. 'The land

184

around us was filled with eaters of men. Here on the top of Thaba Bosiyo no man could attack us, below we might have ended our struggles in their pots. But these men of mine were headstrong. And there was much right in what they said, man must revenge his own.' He smiled grimly. 'I told them I must consider well before disturbing the sepulchres of my ancestors.'

Moshesh laughed softly at the memory and my father laughed with him.

'But,' I said, puzzled, 'you couldn't let them go.'

He shook his head. 'Let me tell you. It was a time of great famine and so we waited. When they had eaten half their own number we came down from the Mountain and killed them!'

I was now on a diet of beef and milk and almost daily I began to feel stronger. My legs, which had seemed as thin as a newborn calf's when I had first got up, had now filled out to something like their previous size. I was still weary at the end of a day and I would often creep into my skins after the evening meal and sleep until the following noon. I spent hours picking at the scab which had formed on the wound. Slowly it, too, disappeared leaving a patch of wrinkled skin, livid purple in colour.

It would have been near the beginning of August that I began to notice a change in my father. He seemed restless, and on edge. Often he would look at me, take a breath as though to say something, then shake his head slightly and close his mouth. I could not divine what ailed him until one day I saw him working on the wagon which the Basuto regiments had brought back with them to the foot of the Mountain. He was making new *riems* and cutting *jukskeis* to replace those we had lost. He worked with great intensity and did not hear me as I came down the slope to him. I watched for a few moments before greeting him. He worked with the economy of a craftsman, using his one good hand with a deftness that would have shamed most men with two.

'When are we leaving?' I said, making a joke. But he looked up so quickly that I realised I had inadvertently hit on the thing that worried him. He was wanting to leave and yet was not certain of me.

'Will you do, son?' he said. His face wore the same anxious expression I had seen so often in my waking dreams.

'Yes, father, I'll do.'

'Are you sure now? You're still gey thin.'

'I can run up and down this Mountain twice a day. Would you like me to show you?'

'No, no. I'll believe you.'

He went on with his work for a few moments and I said: 'Where to this time? The Cape of Good Hope?'

'No, son. Home.'

I felt a sudden chill around my heart as he mentioned it. Home was where Nerissa was. But home was also where our family had nearly foundered. I wondered if either of us was ready to go back.

Four days later we left. Moshesh had given us a span of eighteen bullocks and after three days of training they were ready for the yoke. He also sent an army regiment with us to escort us over the passes and show us the easiest route from his country. In many ways I was sad to be leaving.

The journey back was quite different from the slow, healing voyage that had taken us into Moshesh's country. Now that we had a purpose, a point at which we were aiming, we travelled as quickly as we could. And the first thing that seemed to seep away was the feeling of camaraderie which had taken so long to establish. The closer we came to Zululand the less we spoke and the more uneasy we became with each other. Our true world awaited us; all that had happened between us these past months seemed now to dwindle in the memory. Ahead of us lay reality, and unconsciously we seemed to be adopting our former colouring. This was the saddest thing of all; it seemed we hadn't really changed.

I looked back on the outward journey now with nostalgia, recalling the long still days of autumn, the fight to reach the summit of the pass, the eventful wandering before we reached Thaba Bosiyo, the strained and anxious face that hovered above me as my father nursed me back to life. It seemed like history now; recent history if you like, but history none the less. I tried, perhaps out of sheer gratitude, to bridge the ever-widening gap between us, but my father appeared to have withdrawn into himself. Conversation was limited to the mechanics of the daily trek, at night we ate our meal in silence, then retreated to our karosses. It should have been different. Spring was bursting from the land, my strength had returned, my father looked ten years younger. It all went for nothing.

Only once did we come together, and this on the most delicate of all grounds. It must have been about mid-September when we were within a few days of Chaka's Dukusa kraal. Suddenly one morning, right out of nothing at all, my father came to walk beside me. In itself it was an unusual act and I waited for him to speak. Several times I heard him clear his throat as though to start and each time he gave a slight cough and remained silent.

Eventually, just as I was beginning to think he had nothing to say after all, he turned to me and in a quiet voice asked: 'Do you remember that night? The night before we . . . ?'

'Yes.' I held my breath. We had never touched on this.

'Did I—I mean—did anything—?'

'Nothing happened, Father.'

'I see. Thank you.' He turned away and went about his business.

I should not have allowed it to remain there, still half-buried, but if I had inherited anything from him it was his inability to resolve things by discussion. The walls were too high and too many and only a miracle would have brought them down.

We were within ten miles of Dukusa before we noticed that things were not right in the land. We should by now have been among the outlying kraals where we could have expected great hospitality. Normally a sub-chief would have slaughtered a cow for us and had beer and sour milk waiting for us as soon as we hove across the skyline. Now the kraals were deserted. In a few we even saw the inhabitants leave as we approached, streaming out into hiding places in the bush rather than stay to greet us.

'Something's happened,' my father said grimly. 'Let's push on.'

It was already nightfall but the way was clear and the moon shone down on the silvery veld. We pressed forward with great apprehension. By midnight we were at Dukusa. It was totally deserted. We left the exhausted bullocks at the perimeter and made our way through the central arena. Even now I cannot think about the eerie loneliness of those two thousand empty huts without experiencing a prickling sense of fear. It was as though a sudden plague had snatched away every living thing. Our footfalls were loud in the silence.

We held our guns at the ready, though what we were to shoot, other than ghosts, I could not tell. Without talking we hurried to the King's quarters but they were as empty as the rest. Then we heard a noise, as though of wailing, and hurried towards it.

It came from a point about fifty yards from the seraglio. As we drew near we could make out the crouching figure of a woman. She was swaying to and fro and from her open mouth were coming hoarse cries of sadness. In the moonlight we could see what looked like a bundle of skins on the ground beneath her. I recognised her as one of Chaka's women, and was about to ask her what had happened when my father, who was a few paces ahead of me, jerked to a halt and stood staring down at the object on the ground.

'Christ!' he said, his voice shaky. 'It's the King himself!'

He tore down a bundle of thatch from a nearby hut and set it afire, holding it near the ground to get a better view. The King lay on his side with his cloak thrown over him. My father raised it slightly and we saw the wounds. There was one in his arm, one in his side and one in the middle of his back. His lips were drawn back in a post-death snarl and his mouth and teeth were caked with blood. Darker patches on the sand below him showed where his life had flowed away.

My father had dropped to his knees and was staring helplessly down at the torn body. His hand had begun to tremble badly and the shadows from the torch danced weirdly about us. 'He's gone,' he muttered, as though unwilling to believe his eyes.

'Father . . .' I began. The atmosphere of the place was beginning to affect me and I could hear the fear in my own voice.

'This is the end . . . the end . . .'

I caught him by the sleeve. 'Let's discover what happened,' I said, 'before we judge.'

But he remained in his state of trance and I left him and crossed to the girl. I was unable to get much sense out of her—the only one of them all who had stayed to mourn him.

I have since been able to put together, if somewhat sketchily, his ending. Some hours earlier, as the sun was going down, he had been attacked by his half-brother, Dingane, another half-brother Mhlangana, and his own major-domo, Mbopa.

The killing had occurred while Chaka sat watching his royal herd being driven in from the veld for milking. The three assassins had come up as though to pay their respects when Mhlangana suddenly struck sideways at him with his assegai. But instead of the point entering Chaka's chest it caught on his cloak and sliced into his arm. He whirled away only to feel Dingane's spear thud into his side. He staggered, pulled himself

188

together, turned, and stared into the murderous eyes of his brothers.

'Children of my father!' he cried. 'What is wrong? What have I done that you should kill me thus?'

Blood began to trickle from his lips and he let slip his cloak. He turned from them and began to stagger back to his Royal Hut. Mbopa followed closely and after letting him go a few yards plunged his assegai into the King's back. Blood spurted from his mouth and he fell to the ground.

None of this we knew at the time, but we were able to get the names of the assassins from the almost hysterical concubine and that was enough for my father. He stood there for a few moments deep in thought, then he turned away from the body.

'We've got to hurry, lad,' he said, pulling himself together with an effort. 'He's only the first. There'll be such a blood-letting as even Zululand hasn't seen!'

'They'll attack Ngwadi!' I said, seeing the beginnings of a civil war.

'Aye, and not only him, but what lies on his doorstep!'

'You mean Morile?'

'Of course I do! Dingane has no love for us! We'll have to leave the wagon and bullocks. They'll be no use to us, anyway. It'll have to be done on foot.' He looked up at me quickly. 'Are you strong enough, son?'

I suddenly felt desperately afraid for us all. The King was dead, Mgobozi was dead. Under whose armpit would we shelter now? 'Yes, yes,' I shouted. 'Come on!'

We flitted through the ghostly kraal like hyenas and were soon swallowed up in the immensity of the bush.

Never have I been more thankful for Mgobozi's hard train-ing. Had it not been for those long runs in the hills, the days of forced marching across harsh mountainsides which, all unknow-ing to me, had built up strength and stamina, I should have foundered like a spent horse. We had more than one hundred and twenty miles to cover and we had no time for weakness.

We travelled only at night, lying up in the daytime in thick cover, our only diet some pieces of dried meat we had brought with us from the wagon. Apart from our rifles, bandoliers, powder horns and wallets, we carried nothing else. We were lucky in the weather: the nights were clear with a good moon. We made fast time.

189

If I have one lasting memory of that time it is of numbness, of planting one foot in front of the other, of keeping a rhythm in spite of rocks and slopes and bush-covered gullies. We jogged and walked by turns and every two hours or so we would rest for ten minutes. Thorns sliced into our clothes and flesh, sharp rocks cut our shoes, the stocks of the guns became scarred and chipped as they clattered upon countless boulders. And we sweated. We became saturated in our own sweat so that when we stopped our clothes stiffened and stank. We covered all that dreadful distance in three nights.

We were too late. The word had travelled ahead of us. As we came into the bottom of the valley on the fourth morning we heard the sound of gunfire. My father stopped in his tracks as though checked by a blow. 'It can't be!' he said, and for the first time I heard real despair in his voice. 'They *couldn't* have beaten us!'

That was the worst moment; the moment when our brutal journey seemed to have been for nothing. I remember thinking; *if he gives up now, we're lost.*

'It's probably Stone-Axe hunting. Nothing more than that. Come on!' He staggered after me as we ran through the tall grass. But when we came in sight of Ben Mhor we could see that he was right. And yet it was not as bad as it could have been. Morile itself was under attack but there weren't more than twenty or thirty Zulus on the hill and already I could see the black humps of corpses in the grass.

'This isn't an army!' I said fiercely. 'It's a rabble come for the pickings. We're still ahead of them! They haven't beaten us yet!'

He seemed to gather himself again. 'You stay here. I'll skirt the bottom. When you see me wave come closer and we'll get them in cross fire.' I nodded and he ducked down and made off to the right, going through the grass like a leopard. Every now and then I heard the crash of a gun from one of the loopholes at the house and the frenzied yells of the attackers. In less than ten minutes I saw his hat move quickly back and forth and I went down on my belly and crawled quickly into range.

We began to fire simultaneously. At first the Zulus seemed confused. They withdrew slightly from the house, looking from side to side as, one after another, our bullets began to claim victims. Then one turned and stared down the slope and saw the

190

black swirling smoke from our guns. He gave a frightened yell and dashed to the side of the hill and my father killed him on the skyline. By that time panic had spread to the others and they began streaming away on the far side, ducking and weaving to avoid the bullets and in what seemed like only a matter of seconds the hillside was bare except for the corpses. We waited where we were in case they returned but when I saw them as black specks racing up the far slopes of the valley I rose to my feet calling for my father.

It is a measure of the vitality that still remained that we ran up all the way to the house. A blur of faces: my mother, Nerissa, Donald—growing now, and flaxen-haired like our mother— Stone-Axe, Cupido; arms clinging; tears, sobs of relief, cries of joy. All was movement and confusion and smoke and the acrid smell of burnt powder. We were home.

I remember holding Nerissa and feeling her tremble under my hands. We were whispering to each other things that had no meaning and made no sense except to the two of us at that very moment. But what they were I have no memory. It was enough that we were together. I looked searchingly into her eyes and face but there was no trace of the old sickness. 'I'll never leave you again,' I said. 'Do you understand that? Never again.' She nodded through her tears and we held each other more closely.

There was no time for explanations. My father took charge and I saw the sudden look of happiness cross my mother's face. First he made Stone-Axe climb to the apex of the roof. 'Wau!' the little Bushman shouted, his eyes shining with pleasure. 'The Great Bull Calf has returned!' He shinned up the walls like a baboon. Next my father made the two women get out of their dresses and petticoats and change into some clothes of Donald's: leather trousers and jerkins. Next he made us pack up the store of dried meat in the larder. 'Only what you can carry in your pockets and one hand,' he kept on saying. 'Take nothing that's heavy.' Cupido and Donald were casting lead bullets in the mould as fast as they could. I started barricading the doors.

'Don't be a fool!' my father shouted as he passed me. 'We can't defend this against the whole army!'

'What then?'

'We're moving, lad. Getting out.'

'But where to?'

191

'Don't ask silly questions. There's no time. Have you saddled Violin?'

'Not yet.'

'Hurry, then!'

As I ran to the door I heard him shouting to Donald and Cupido to bring all the guns into the front room. 'We'll need water bags,' he called to my mother. At that moment, as he was coming through the door, he bumped into Nerissa. She had been coming full tilt the other way and he had to grab her arms to save her from falling. I stopped, holding my breath, but he looked at her as though she was a stranger. 'Help my wife,' he said, shortly. 'Don't let her bring all her fripperies. We can't carry them.'

'Yes, Mr Black. Where are we going?'

'I'm not sure yet.' He made to turn away and then he seemed to remember her. He took her by the arms again. 'Are you all right, Nerissa?'

'Yes.'

'Well, don't worry. We'll look after you. Nothing will happen to you, d'you understand?'

'Yes.'

We worked feverishly for more than an hour when we heard Stone-Axe calling from the roof. I ran out with my father. The Bushman was standing at the apex pointing to the south. 'They come, Claw! They come quickly!' It was a few seconds before I could make out the faint black snake of the first Zulu regiment as it breasted the hills to the south of us.

'Damn them!' my father swore.

He whirled and shouted at Stone-Axe. 'All right, down! Fetch the horse.' Then he turned to me. 'Robbie, I charge you to look after the women. Donald and I with Stone-Axe and Cupido will try to hold them back.'

'But where am I to take them?' I asked, bewildered.

'Ngwadi's kraal. Where else? We'll make a stand there. He's got his own small army and with our guns it might make all the difference.'

'Father, it's too late!' I pointed to the west where another regiment had suddenly emerged. 'They'll cut us off!' He looked south and then west, moving his head like a trapped animal. Finally he said, 'You're right. We need darkness. If we could hole up until then we might have a chance.'

'I know a place.'

'Where?'

'A cave by the river. No one knows it but me . . .' I hesitated. 'And Nerissa.'

The implication was lost on him. 'All right. We'll try it. There's no other way.'

We went down the hillside in single file. Each of us, except the women, carried a gun, ammunition, powder and food. They carried more food, as well as water. Over my mother's shoulder she carried a heavy draw-string bag. 'Leave it, Fran,' my father said just before we left, thinking she had delved deeply into her chests. 'They'll be no use to us now.'

'I've got Uncle Henry's Journal and your own,' she answered quietly. 'And I'd rather leave the water.'

There was no time to argue. My father brought Violin along by her head reins. I led and Donald covered the rear. Right at the back came Stone-Axe. He had a wattle branch in his hand and was wiping out the faint spoors we left.

'What about the horse?' my father asked as we began to cross the stream.

'There's thick bush around the mouth. She won't be seen in that.'

Now Stone-Axe ran to the front and gently parted the thick bush stems so that we could pass through without breaking them and marking our passage. Later he went all the way over the trail, brushing and covering until he was satisfied that only one of his own race could ever read our signs.

The cave was as I remembered it, wide and gloomy, and on the spring day rather cold.

'Excellent,' my father said as we moved into it. 'We've a chance.'

We got the women settled and the horse hidden and then he called me. 'We've got to know what's going on. Is there some place we can watch from?'

'Above in the cliffs.'

'All right, I'll follow you.'

We scrambled up through the fringing bush and came onto the dark iron-stone *krantzes*. There were hyrax droppings everywhere and the place smelt of urine. Half-way up we came to a ledge overhung by a bushy tree which hid it completely from view. Here we lay.

We could see across the stream and had a clear view of Morile. It looked sadly bereft and defenceless in the mid-morning sun. I experienced a sudden ache over the heart. This was the first home I had ever known. I knew I would never see it again.

'See them?' my father asked, pointing.

The regiments were much nearer. 'I can't believe Mdlaka would attack us,' I said.

'Perhaps he's dead too.'

'They're not keeping much discipline, anyway.' The Zulus were streaming in on the house from all directions but there seemed to be no order. They looked like a mob dressed up as soldiers.

'Can you recognise the shields?'

'They're too far. But I've never seen a regiment march like this.'

They paused at the foot of the hill and began shouting up at the house. We could not hear what they were saying but I remembered the Battle of Ndololwane Hill and knew they'd be calling us white dogs or other insulting phrases.

'They're frightened,' my father said. 'They think we're waiting.'

It was not a very big force, perhaps a few hundred at the most, and they were obviously apprehensive.

'We should have stayed,' I said. 'A couple of shots and they'd be over the hills and away.'

'You can never tell. Perhaps the main army is already at Ngwadi's kraal. We'd have been trapped either way. When I built the house I never expected it to stand this sort of siege.'

Some of the bolder spirits were now making their way cautiously up the slope. 'Look at them!' I said with derision. 'If Mdlaka was there some of the cowards would have died already.'

The first of them reached the walls and, seeing they were unharmed, began to hack at the doors with their spears.

'They're brave enough now,' my father said grimly.

It didn't take them long to batter down the front door and as it fell we heard a great shout from the rest of the army and it surged up the slope until the house was completely surrounded by shrieking Zulus.

It is still painful to think of what happened next. First they brought out all the furniture that had taken so long to make

194

and smashed it to bits. Next they carried out the skins and blankets and tore them to pieces, some carrying parts of a sheet or floor-skin on the points of their assegais like tattered banners.

'The fools,' my father said. 'They could have used all those.'

When they had ransacked the inside of the house they turned to the outbuildings. The ivory store with its heavy padlock took them some time to breach but eventually we saw the tusks carried out and piled into a heap on the ground. As we watched, my father's face grew harsh with bitterness. I held my tongue. Finally they set fire to all the buildings and the oily black smoke plumed upwards in the hot noon air.

The Zulus had been almost transported with frenzy as they wrecked our home and now, as though exhausted from the catharsis, they sprawled down on the grass to watch the fire eat into the timbers. Just then I heard a lowing and from the bottom of the valley I saw our cattle being driven towards the hill.

'Those, too,' my father said. 'It was to be expected.'

Throughout the afternoon the Zulus slaughtered the cattle and built their own fires to cook the meat. Later, as the sun sank redly below the hills, many of them came down to the stream to drink. Not one gave any sign of seeing our tracks, nor even caring whether there were tracks or not. They'd had their day of victory. As we climbed down the cliff my father said : 'Say nothing to your mother. I'll do the telling.' For the first time in my life I saw tears in his eyes.

But half-way down the cliff I felt something strike my shoulder and then rattle on the rocks. It was a small pebble. I motioned my father to stop and we froze to the cliff-face. I looked round carefully but could see nothing.

'What is it?'

Crack! This time a stone struck the rock in front of my face. I managed to turn, planting my back firmly against the wall, and raised the rifle. In the bush below there was the faintest stir of movement. Suddenly a face materialised from the branches of a thorn tree. It was Tanga and he was beckoning to us.

'It's all right,' I called to my father in a low voice. 'It's Tanga.'

I slid down the few yards that remained and greeted him warmly.

'When I saw the smoke I knew you would either be dead or in the cave,' he said.

'Do you know what's happening?' I asked.

'All Zululand knows what is happening. I've come to bring your people to my father. It's safer there.'

My father nodded. 'We were going to come in the night.'

'How would you have come?' Tanga asked me.

'The usual way. Upstream and across the valleys.'

'It is good that I found you now. There are *impis* above and below. You would have been taken.'

'What other way is there?'

'The *krantzes*.'

'What, here?'

'Further up.'

'But they're even higher!'

'It is the only way.'

We went into the cave and told the others. My mother was the first one to mention it, though it had already crossed my mind. 'What about Violin?' she said.

Darkness had come and it was as well we could not see each other's faces. In a way the mare, old and tired as she was, had more links with the past for at least my mother and father, and even Stone-Axe, than the house itself. Without her our lives might have been very different.

At length my father said: 'We'll have to leave her.'

My mother shook her head. 'No, we'll not leave her to them.'

'What then?'

'Shoot her.'

'We can't risk the sound of gunfire.'

I heard my father fumbling at his belt for the great Hereneuter knife that he always carried. 'I'll do it.' He was about to turn to the entrance of the cave when I saw a shadow detach itself from the wall. Without a word Stone-Axe gently prised his fingers from the knife-handle, touched him gently on the forearm and slipped out into the night. We stood there holding our breath, waiting for the cry of the doomed animal and the thrashing of frenzied hoofs.

We should have known better. To a Bushman all living things possess a soul, an animal-person within the animal. And now he released the horse-person in Violin with all the skill and compassion of his tribe. All we heard was a low whicker of greeting that changed abruptly into a gurgling sigh and the faint crackling of underbush as she subsided. We should have felt moved and sad and perhaps we did but the time was not right. As soon as

Stone-Axe returned Tanga led us fifty yards along the river bank until we came to our climbing point. The *krantzes* were not high, not more than a few hundred feet, but they were broken up by gullies, trees and huge rocks and it was two hours before we reached the top. All of us were scratched and tired; I was drawing on reserves I didn't even know I had.

Ngwadi's kraal was prepared for a siege when we reached it. All around the palisade I could see the glint of spear points. Thorn-bush had been cut and piled on the outside to try and strengthen the defences but I wondered just how long it would take determined attackers to sweep it out of the way. As the gate was closed behind us I remember feeling a sudden sensation of being trapped. The Chief himself came to greet us and I saw a look of relief pass across his face when he saw how well-armed we were and my spirits sank even further. Ngwadi was adequate enough for campaigning with Chaka but there was no evidence that he himself was anything more than an average warrior. This was when we needed someone of Mgobozi's stature. However, I was not able to pursue these melancholy thoughts and perhaps it was just as well, for he came forward and gave me an especially warm greeting—he had never forgotten my part in saving Tanga from suffocation in the mud—and anyway I was too tired to think clearly.

The women were taken off to the female apartments and I followed Tanga to a hut reserved for the men. A meal of boiled beef and sour milk was awaiting us and we sat on the grass mats and helped ourselves, too tired to talk. When we had finished my father went off to consult with Ngwadi, returning about half an hour later, just as we were preparing for sleep.

'It's not as bad as it could be,' he said. 'We're not going to be fighting the army proper at all. The main forces are north of here with Mdlaka. They'd left on campaign some time before the murder, so no one's sure of their loyalty. Ngwadi's sent runners to find them. It'd be no bad thing if Mdlaka took over the State. He could do it, too, with the army behind him.'

'So we were right,' I said. 'They *were* rabble.'

'Old men and young boys. Mbopa's leading them. It's not even sure they'll come this far. Ngwadi thinks they'll lose heart when they see the defences.'

197

'I'm not sure about that.'

'Nor am I. But there's nothing we can do now except wait. You never know, Mdlaka could be on his way south at this very moment.'

One reaches a state of exhaustion where nothing seems real any longer. All I wanted was sleep. Whether the Zulus attacked and killed us as we lay was a matter of total indifference to me.

All the next day we rested, waiting for the attack. Ngwadi had sent out spies early in the morning and they reported that Mbopa's forces were still encamped at Morile. 'It won't take them more than a day to finish off the herd,' my father said.

It was a strange time. There was nothing we could do but wait. None of us seemed afraid; there was an inevitability about what was happening to us, as though our very existence in Zululand had been leading towards this point. Nor, I think, did we seek to find cause or apportion blame. It would have been easy enough to blame my father, he had brought us here in the first place and it was because of him that we had stayed. And yet was that really so? There had been good things, too, and in these we had shared.

This is not to say that I felt no sadness. I felt sad for myself; India, the Cape of Good Hope, cities, streets and people, were remote enough to be insubstantial and, in our present circumstances, artificial. Perhaps I would never see such things and in a way I minded. But I was sad, too, for my mother and Donald and Nerissa, but perhaps most of all for my father. He bore us all on his shoulders and for once they seemed too narrow to hold us. I think it was watching the destruction of Morile that finally put the pain in his eyes. It had taken a long time, but he had begun to suffer.

So the day passed in a curious poignancy. It was cool weather for late spring and the sky was grey and overcast and all the colour had gone from the surrounding hills, leaving them barren and bleak. We all sat together in one of the huts staring into the yellow smoke that rose sluggishly from the dung fire. And then I noticed an odd thing. Without any planning at all we had split into groups. Stone-Axe, Donald and Cupido were looking to the guns, my father sat with my mother on the far side of the fire and I with Nerissa opposite. We leant against the wall of the hut and I held her hand as naturally as if we had long since been lovers.

When we spoke at all it was quietly and to each other. I could hear my father's low tones across the hut but not what he was saying. Perhaps he was telling my mother about our journey, perhaps about what we had seen the previous day. She listened and nodded and sometimes touched him gently as though absolving him from all that had gone before.

Once or twice she caught my glance and smiled at me through the smoke and it was a smile at once touching and reassuring and I realised then where the very heart of the family lay. We seemed to crystalise in her. And the smile said more, or seemed to. Perhaps at times like that, when emotions are near the surface, it is too easy to read meanings, but it seemed to me that she was expressing her gratitude that I had brought her man back to her, just as she had known I would. If only she had really known that it was he who had done the bringing. But again this is exactly what she might have meant. There were corners of her mind that were always hidden from me.

But if I was sad for us all I was worried about Nerissa. What reserves did *she* have? There was nothing much I could do or say. I could have said: 'Don't you worry, you'll be safe,' or 'I'll look after you and see that nothing happens,' as my father had done before we left Morile, but this would have been so patently absurd that it might have made matters worse. Above all, this was a time for truth and since the truth was apparent there was little point in either stating it or minimising it. So I just squeezed her hand and felt the tightening of her own fingers in answer and hoped that if it came to it I would be near her with the rifle.

She did say one thing that gave me a surge of bitter-sweet happiness. It was late in the afternoon and a wind had risen and was blowing dust across the kraal. She brought my hand up to her face and laid it against her cheek and said: 'If we come through this I will cherish you.'

By dusk my father was too restless to remain in the hut. I walked the perimeter with him. 'They should be here,' he said. 'If they're coming they should be here.' But the relays of scouts which Ngwadi had been sending out all day reported that the two regiments, now identified as the U-Hlomendlini (The Home-Guard) and the Izi-Nyosi (The Bees) were still encamped at Morile. That night we began to hope. Perhaps Ngwadi was right, that the defences were good enough to encourage hesitation— for we had no doubt that we too had been under observation by Mbopa's scouts—or they could have learned of our presence with guns or Mdlaka might even now be only a few miles distant. It could have been any one of several things but the simplest was that they might just have decided not to attack at all. But we were mistaken; they came before dawn.

Tanga woke me and as I came, heart-a-flutter, to consciousness, he clamped a hand over my mouth. 'They are here,' he whispered. 'Come quickly but be silent.' My father and Stone-Axe were already stirring and Donald had gone to guard the women. We crept out into the chilly darkness.

The kraal, which was encircled by the tall wooden stockade, was about one hundred and fifty yards in diameter. For the sake of simplicity my father had divided the circle into four segments and Ngwadi had agreed that this seemed best; one gun would go into each segment. My father, Cupido and I had rifles; Stone-Axe had one fowling-piece and the other we had left with Donald. As we gathered outside the hut my father gave us his last instructions. They were simple and to the point. 'Don't fire blind,' he warned. 'Wait till you can see. Remember, we've used more tin in the bullets than normal so don't shoot at distance. Let them press close and one bullet will count for two and even three.' We went to our places.

Ngwadi's warriors were already waiting, crouched down in the shadows next to the wall, their bodies hidden from the outside by the heavy thorn branches. They kept their assegais behind them so the points would not show.

At first I was worried at the thinness of the line of defenders. The stockade walls were so long that even Ngwadi's army could not stand shoulder to shoulder and there seemed ominous gaps between the men. Tanga led me to my place near the main gate, whispering: 'Do you hear them?' Above the subdued snuffling and breathing of our own warriors and the muffled thud of my heart I could faintly discern other voices in the night: shufflings and scrapings and low voices. 'They are near now.'

The moon was down and the darkness was intense, as it often is just before first light. I pressed my face to a chink in the stockade but all I could see was a tangled mass of branches. I held the rifle more tightly, feeling the slipperiness of my sweating palms and I rubbed my hands on my clothing to dry them. God, I thought, they'll rush us and have the fence down before we even see them!

'There,' Tanga said. 'And there! And there!'

I strained my eyes and for a moment seemed to see dark shapes rising from the ground, but when I blinked and tried again they were gone. Then suddenly a whole line of dark bodies came into view just on the far side of the thorns. My breath was coming faster now and I shifted the rifle to a larger slit in the walls. Immediately Tanga's hand gripped my arm. 'No!' he hissed. 'Let them come on!' Abruptly I realised what was happening. Instead of attacking part of the walls with a powerful wedge of men and trying to force a breach, Mbopa had decided that we were all fast asleep in our huts and had encircled the entire kraal, which meant that his men were as thinly spread as ours. He was going to try and scale the stockade quietly and then converge on the huts from all sides, killing us where we lay. I thanked God the army was not being led by Chaka or even one of the regimental commanders. With Mbopa in charge we stood a good chance.

At that moment Mbopa's warriors reached the barricades of thorn. Quietly they began to move them. To do so they had to come within feet and sometimes inches of the stockade wall. We could hear their breathing in our ears and smell the sweat on their bodies. I carefully rested the rifle barrel in a natural loophole. I was aware of a rustle next to me as the warriors performed similar movements with their assegais. Somewhere away to my right the silence was suddenly split by a great cry of: '*Si-gi-di!*' and as one every warrior plunged his assegai at arm's length through the stockade wall.

Mbopa's forces were taken completely by surprise. I don't know how many died in that one bristling thrust for I was firing through the loophole, trying to line up at least two targets for every shot, but by the screaming and yelling which suddenly rose up the numbers of wounded and dying must have been substantial. It was a total surprise and the attackers panicked, many of them turning on their heels and fleeing into the dark, leaving the thorn bushes covered in writhing bodies.

It had been a beautifully executed move and Ngwadi's forces were elated, smiling and laughing, many seeming to feel that the victory was already theirs. 'They will be careful next time,' Tanga said.

Our sudden over-confidence was almost our undoing. There was so much chattering and self-congratulation in our ranks that

201

we did not hear them come again. I don't know how Mbopa managed to rally them, but he did and his cunning mind must have seen that what we had done could be almost as perfectly executed against us.

The first thing I knew of the second attack was a sudden shriek next to me as a Zulu staggered backwards with an assegai in his stomach. Then there were further shouts and our men, crouching against the fence, reeled back with the combined thrust of assegais. Abruptly we had begun to fight in earnest. The walls began to shake and tremble as the attackers tried to pull themselves up, but the stakes were about eight feet high and it had to be done by the strength of their arms.

'Strike!' I heard myself yelling. 'Strike at them now!' Their climbing bodies made easy targets, but our men were confused and did not make the effort soon enough. First one, then another, landed among us and the battle raged hand to hand. It was useless trying to reload in the mêlée and I used the rifle as a club, swinging it in a murderous arc whenever I got close enough.

The walls had been breached in parts and we would have been overwhelmed right then if it had not been for Ngwadi. He, with a cohort of picked men, was running from one end of the kraal to the other, wherever danger threatened most. The din was enormous. Both sides were shouting war-cries, there were screams as spears found their targets, some were swearing, others howling with blood lust. The dust from a thousand feet was rising from the ground, choking throat and nostrils. I was unable to distinguish friend or foe and stood now, with my back to the fence, trying to catch my breath.

Slowly the attackers were forced back through the holes they had made and they drew off to regroup. The ground was slippery with blood and frequently I stumbled over dead, but still warm, flesh. At that moment Ngwadi ran past with his platoon and shouted something to Tanga, pointing over his shoulder towards the inner part of the kraal.

'Come!' Tanga said, grabbing my arm. We ran together and came to the great stone-walled cattle-pen in the centre of the kraal. We clambered up over the walls and dropped down onto the carpet of hard dung.

The first angry red streaks of dawn were lighting the sky and I could see more easily. The pen, huge as it was, was almost filled with women, children and warriors. I could make out my mother and Nerissa and Donald with the big fowling-piece, and my father and Stone-Axe, but not Cupido; now my mother held a rifle in her hands and I realised he must have been killed.

We had hardly taken up our positions when Mbopa attacked again. But this time he had six-foot stone walls to contend with. There was no possibility of breaching them and as his warriors climbed the rough stone-work their shields could easily be hooked aside. Many died at the top of the walls, falling backwards on to others behind them, others tried to vault the barrier only to come plunging down onto our raised spear points. In five minutes the attack was beaten off.

My lungs were heaving with the exertion and blood was dripping down from my brow where a spear had grazed it. I leant on the rifle thankful for the respite. Then I heard my father's voice. 'Robbie! Here! Over here!' I pushed my way towards him and found the others of our group assembled in one corner of the pen. 'We're going over the walls,' he said. 'It's our only chance.'

'But we can't leave—'

'Don't argue, boy! We're in a damned trap and we're going to get out! Now listen. I'm going first, then your mother and Nerissa. Then Stone-Axe and Donald, and you last. We'll keep the women in the centre.' And with that he was over the wall and calling for my mother to make haste.

I helped my mother up and then Nerissa and watched Donald and Stone-Axe scramble after them. I found the footholds and scrambled to the top myself. It seemed that what we were doing was wrong. These people had taken us in and now we were deserting them. Our guns had wreaked a terrible havoc in the close-packed ranks of the attackers and now they were to be withdrawn. I looked back for an instant and saw Tanga's face turned in my direction. He appeared confused, almost stricken, as though trying not to believe what he was seeing. I felt a hot wave of shame sweep over me and then I dropped out of sight on the far side. We ran through the kraal like a phalanx; our guns forming the defensive perimeter of our own fortress. We sprinted from hut to hut searching for a break in the outer stockade. 'There!' Stone-Axe said, pointing to a gap.

'Ready?' my father asked. We had to cross open ground to reach it. 'All right, then!' He led off and we followed closely. I heard a shout to our left and a flying wedge of Zulus raced across the kraal trying to cut us off. 'Stop!' my father yelled, and we dropped to our knees, trying to aim as well as our trembling limbs allowed. The hail of lead, mostly, I feel from the fowling-pieces which were loaded with a type of canister, ripped the Zulus apart, sending them sprawling in heaps on the ground. We loaded and began to run again.

We were almost out of breath by the time we reached the fence. Bodies were piled here from the first encounter and we had to step over and sometimes onto them to reach the exit. 'Wait!' my father ordered. 'Let me go first.' He ducked his head and passed through the torn fence and stood just outside it looking left and right. I noticed something that made my heart stop. He was almost straddling a dead Zulu, only the man wasn't dead. I saw a black arm rise from the ground clutching a broken assegai. I opened my mouth to yell a warning. I saw Stone-Axe fling the fowling-piece to his shoulder and heard the roar of the explosion, but we were both too late. The dying Zulu had used the last of his strength to thrust upwards and the blade of the assegai had buried itself in my father's groin. He gave a terrible frightened cry and fell backwards onto the grass, clutching at the wooden shaft that stuck down between his legs. I heard my mother scream and we all dashed forward, fighting our way through the narrow aperture to get to him.

My mother reached him first and threw herself across his chest, trying to cradle his head in her arms. He was making a horrible groaning noise and pulling himself backwards along the ground on his elbows. I don't think he knew what he was doing, the agony was so intense. For a short time we were totally confused, standing over him like frightened children to whom a great calamity has occurred and if the Zulus had attacked us in those moments we would have had no answer. The only one among us who kept his head was Stone-Axe. He shouted and pointed and hurriedly Donald and I fired at the loose group of about eight warriors who were running headlong towards us. I saw two of them drop to our guns and two more to the spraying canister which Stone-Axe unleashed. The other four ducked behind a hut for cover and at that moment we heard the war-cries roll around the hills as Mbopa launched another attack on the cattle-pen. But we had had our warning and now Donald and I knelt near my father's body but faced outwards, ready for them.

If it had not been for Stone-Axe we would never have left that place. He spoke sharply to my mother but she did not seem to hear him and finally Nerissa came forward to help him. They took her under the arms and lifted her away from my father. Stone-Axe slit open my father's trousers and I, half-watching for any attack, saw for the first time how grievous the wound really was. The blade had entered between the scrotum and the inside top of his thigh and had buried itself so completely that only wood showed. The blood was dripping steadily on to the ground.

Stone-Axe delved quickly into the skin bag that hung from his wrist and brought out a length of leather *riempie* with which he lashed the broken shaft of the assegai to my father's left leg. Then he performed a feat that, looking back on it now, was one of the most prodigious I think I ever saw. He took my father under the armpits and hoisted him over his shoulder. It seemed almost impossible that so frail and gnarled a little man could even raise my father from the ground but he did so without help. He stood there for a second, letting his sinews take the strain, and he said: 'Claw is ready.'

I blinked at him. I saw everyone was looking at me. I half turned as though awaiting the word from my father and then I realised they were all now on *my* shoulders.

'The cave,' I said. 'Let's get him to the cave. We can decide then.' Donald led out and I held the rear but from the sound of the screaming and shrieking in the kraal it seemed likely that our escape would pass unnoticed.

There was no question of scaling any cliffs. We approached the river openly and the only thing that watched us was the brooding ruins of Morile. None of us cared then.

Stone-Axe carried him as he might have carried a child but even so the journey was rough. Luckily, for most of it my father was unconscious. Every few moments a groan issued from his open mouth and my mother echoed it, running to his head and wiping the sweat from his brow with a kerchief. At other times she was with Nerissa who took her arm and helped her across the uneven ground. It was only when we reached the cave and Stone-Axe gently lowered him to the sandy floor that I realised how much blood he had lost; the whole of the Bushman's right side was stained a coppery colour.

The first thing I did was to send Donald up the cliff-face to keep watch and then I waited for my mother to come forward and attend to the wound. But whatever it was that had kept her going had now finally drained away. She was hunched against the wall sobbing hysterically. Nerissa was with her and had taken her in her arms to try and soothe her. I realised that from now on whatever was to be done I had to do it.

I turned to Stone-Axe and he must have seen the despair and confusion in my eyes for he took my hand in the wonderfully gentle and unselfconscious way I remember from my childhood and said: 'We must move the spear.' First we went down to the stream and collected moss from the damp rocks and brought it back to the cave, then I asked Nerissa to tear up her vest for bandages. Finally we worked the blade of the assegai gently out of the mutilated flesh. It left a gaping cavity from which the black blood pumped and I found my hands trembling as I helped Stone-Axe fill the hole with moss. As soon as it was packed the green veins ran red. We bandaged him as best we could but even before we'd finished a red stain had already appeared.

My father's eyes flickered open and I think the pain must have left him, for he was able to turn round and take us all in. I saw him glance at my mother and his eyes filled with pity.

'Oh, Jamie! Jamie!' Her face was wet and blotched with weeping and she knelt by him, putting her head on his chest and holding him.

'Here,' he said, trying to smile—and I shall never forget the ghastly whiteness of his face. 'Now then, now then. You'll not get rid of me this easily, you know.'

I told him briefly what had happened. 'You did well, son, but we can't stay here. They'll pick up the tracks. There must be a drop of blood every foot of the way.'

'I know, but where else is there?'

'We've got to move. Put distance between us.' It was pitiful hearing the weak voice make statements of this kind. 'I don't know how long Ngwadi will hold but as soon as he breaks Mbopa will send after us.'

'But we can't move you,' I said desperately.

He lay back staring at me and I could see his eyes dart from side to side as thoughts wheeled through his mind. At last he said: 'There is a way. Just one.'

'A litter.'

'Aye, a litter.'

'But we'll travel too slowly.' It was a cruel thing to say but it was a fact.

'It'll not be far,' he said.

I didn't understand him. There was only one place to make for and that was the Port and it was well over a hundred miles away. But there was no question of leaving him. I called Stone-Axe and ordered him to cut branches.

It was mid-morning before we finished the litter and left the cave. Stone-Axe and I carried front and rear and once again Donald led out. The streaks of dawn had given way to purple rain clouds and a high wind blew dust in our faces. I was thankful my father had made the women change their clothes for the bush along the stream was heavy and they would already have begun to suffer from thorns.

'Strike south-east,' my father had said just before we left. 'There's broken ground across the Tugela and if we can make that, we've a chance.'

He had spoken with authority and I had left it at that. The Tugela River was a long way off and our passage to it would be marked by his blood and not even my father had enough in his veins to last the trek. His leather trousers were already soft and slimy with the ooze from the bandage.

I can remember little more of that day. If the journey my father and I had made from Dukusa to Morile a few days before had stretched us to the limit of our endurance, this went far beyond. Even now, to think about it, makes me feel physically ill. We had to rest frequently and after a time gave up all pretence that we could defend ourselves. Four of us carried him, three permanently and the women taking it in turns. Our rifles were slung on our backs unnoticed and almost forgotten. There was only one pervading feeling, the dreadful ache in our arms. Had it not been for the steady drip, drip of my father's blood which turned this into a race between our tortured muscles and his very life, we would long since have given up. Towards dusk Donald began to sob with exhaustion and I decided to call a halt for the night.

My father, who had mercifully slipped into oblivion during the bucking and wrenching of the journey, now came to consciousness.

'Why have we stopped?' he said weakly. 'We must get on! We must get to the Tugela!'

I was too tired even to move my head and was huddled in the grass where I'd sat. 'We can't, father,' I mumbled. 'We can't go further without rest.'

'Can't!' He struggled up on his elbows. 'You damn coward!' His face was almost phosphorescent in the gloom and his eyes were wild. 'Well, leave me here! Leave me to die! For that's what will happen to us all!'

Something seemed to give inside me. 'You!' I shouted. 'If it wasn't for you we wouldn't be here now!'

'What's wrong? What's happening?' My mother had crawled towards us and was trying to take my father in her arms.

'Let me loose, woman!' He flung her off. 'D'you *want* me to die? D'you *want* it to happen? I haven't come this far to be let down by cowards. Stone-Axe! Donald! Here! You, Donald, in front. Stone-Axe at the back. All right now, lift.'

And so we plunged on. All that night I hoped he would die. At intervals I touched his forehead and once he said: 'Leave off, I haven't gone yet!' About midnight it began to rain, a steady, soaking downpour. 'Hurry!' he called as the heavy drops spattered down on his face. 'If the Tugela rises we'll be trapped!'

By daylight the rain stopped and the sun came out but there were heavy clouds further inland and I knew it was still raining there. I was past caring if the river came down or not, there was only one thought left and that was to reach it. After that, nothing.

We came in sight of it in the misty, rain-washed morning. We had been staggering through a narrow defile in the hills and suddenly there it was, gleaming dully like old silver below us.

'So,' my father said, and his voice was no more than a whisper. 'Thank God.'

We lowered the litter and dropped down in the wet grass, too far gone to appreciate the magnitude and triumph of our efforts.

'Robbie!' The very sound of my name filled me with loathing for him, but like an animal that has been well-trained, I crawled across. He put out a thin, etiolated hand and gripped my shoulder. 'I'm sorry, son,' he said, 'but it had to be done, and there was only the one way to do it.'

I nodded dully, not understanding nor caring. Then he pointed to a smooth ledge of turf on one side of the defile. 'Help me up there.' I staggered automatically to my feet and grasped one end of the litter. The others were already asleep on their arms and what I could have done I do not know but in my present state orders were the only things I understood. 'No, no! Not like that!' He put his arms around my neck and I half-pulled, half-carried him up the slope. By the time I got there my own legs were covered in blood. 'Now fetch the rifle.' When I returned with the gun he had laid out a powder horn and all the ammunition in his belt and had moved himself so that his head and shoulders were hidden by two boulders. In this position he could look down into the defile. Slowly the truth of what he was doing dawned on me. He could see it come into my face. 'Don't argue, son,' he said. 'There's little enough left in me as it is without wasting it on that.'

I realised what our race had been for. Like a miser he had been hoarding his blood against this moment. 'Take them down now,' he said.

I shook my head. 'I can't. I can't leave you here.'

'Here or on the other bank, what difference is there? I haven't more than a few hours, you know that and I know that, what sense is there in pretence.' He lay for a moment in silence, then said: 'Don't let your mother know. Keep it from her as long as you can. She'll only hold you up. And, Robbie . . .' His hand came out again and I gripped it. 'Explain it to her one day.'

But what was there to explain? Was everything not self-evident?

'I'll try,' I said, dropping my voice to his own level, and in that moment I sacrificed him. To plead any different now would be hypocrisy. I could say that in my mental and physical state I hardly knew what was happening. I could say that he was dying and there was nothing any of us could do finally to save him. In fact, I have; I have tried to tell myself there was no other way and each time I have become nauseated by my own excuses. It is quite plain what happened: I agreed to leave him.

Sensing what must have been in my mind he began to speak again. 'All my life has been built on one factor,' he said, trying to smile, but only contorting his face a little. 'And that is when you decide to act, then act—no regrets. I could say now to please you, to give you something for your mother, that I had changed, learnt my lesson, benefited from experience and I would be lying.

I haven't changed. I feel the same. But regret? Yes, there is always regret in dying. But I'll not fool you. Things would have gone on as before, we'd have been at each other's throats over the girl. So I've learnt to know at least one thing : myself.'

It was then that I felt the tears streaming down my cheeks and yet there was nothing I could say to comfort him. Nor would he have wanted idle phrases.

'But there is one thing that haunts me. The woman. The Ndwandwe woman I shot after the battle.'

I remembered it as clearly as if it had been yesterday. It had stayed in my mind as a festering sore.

'I did it for you, Robbie,' he said. 'She was your target.'

'I don't understand,' I said, a cold feeling stirring in my stomach.

'It was Chaka's way. A test of loyalty.'

'And you . . .'

'You would have done the same in my place. Any father would. Now go. Take them down quickly. Make for the Port. Drive them! Remember that, drive them!'

I left him there with his gun and his ammunition and his clear field of fire when the Zulus came and went down to the others. 'Hurry,' I said roughly, trying not to think too clearly about what I was doing. 'Get moving! We're going to cross the river now.'

My mother looked around wildly for him. 'We'll get you across first,' I said. 'Then we come back for him.'

'But why is he off the litter? Why is he up there?'

'Can't you see?' I shouted.

'I must go to him!'

I caught her by the arm and forced her onto the slope. 'Nerissa! Take her! Donald, the other arm!' They led her down to the bank of the river and took her gently into the water. The current was already running fiercely as I stepped onto the shining black stones. 'Hurry!' I shouted above the noise of the flood. 'Hurry or we'll be too late!'

I looked around and saw Stone-Axe standing on the bank. 'Come!' I yelled, beckoning him with my arm. He shook his head and said something. Against the roar of the water I cannot be sure what it was, but it would not be hard to guess. He raised a hand in one final gesture of farewell, then he turned and trotted up the hill to my father.

210

I tried to turn after him but my feet slipped out from under me and I fell heavily into the rapids. It took me a moment or two to fight my way upright and by that time I saw my mother, Donald and Nerissa pulling their way up the far bank. I floundered after them. The roar became louder. It seemed to split my head. I fell forward, grasped a branch and hauled myself up on the bank beside them. A solid wave of water about two feet high came racing into view. Its yellow, foaming crest rushed past us. I saw bodies of cattle and great branches whirling by and then the river was one wide roaring avalanche of water. The rain on the far mountains had reached us and there was no way across.

'You've got to go back!' my mother was screaming. 'You've got to fetch him!'

'Yes,' I said. 'Of course. But first let's get away from the river, it may come up even further.'

We staggered up the broken side of the gorge, leaving the terrifying noise behind us. And as we reached the top I heard a different sound; the dull thud of guns.

'You've got to fetch him! You've got to go back!'

'Yes! Yes! In a moment! Just a little further.'

'Now! You must go now!' She was struggling to free herself from my hand.

'Of course! Yes! Naturally!'

But there was no way back for any of us. The gunfire stopped. There was only the sound of the river. I drove them forward into the broken hills, moving south-east to the coast, as my father had ordered.

EPILOGUE

Murray, Tate & Black,
Solicitors,
No. 21, Strand Street,
Cape of Good Hope
12th April, 1838.

Donald Fraser Black, Esq.,
College of Physicians,
Edinburgh

My dear Donald,

I make haste to reply to your letter which reached me yesterday in the hope that mine will take tomorrow's tide with the Indiaman *Beaufort* (Capt. Lindsay). By the time you read this you may have already received my letter of 2nd February in which I mentioned the funeral, but we have had news of a great storm at St Helena with the loss of several vessels and it may be that all the letters went down. Bear with me then if I repeat parts.

I can well imagine the shock our mother's death must have caused you. It did not come so unexpectedly for us though our sadness was in no way diminished thereby. In the three years you have been away there was a marked decline in her spirits, or rather an unevenness, with weeks in which she seemed as of old, and other periods when she was lost to us all. Nerissa spent much time with her towards the end and I think gave her comfort. Because my own presence might have distressed her I remained at our house here in town, visiting her from time to time as Nerissa thought fit.

For a year past our relationship was uneasy. She began to live more and more among her memories and our father's death on the banks of the Tugela was much in her thoughts. It is proper that she blamed me for this since I have always blamed myself. The passing of ten years cannot alter facts.

I did not write to you about these matters wishing not to distress you unduly nor take your mind from your studies—for above all she would have wanted you to continue them, just as

213

our father would. In any case, there was nothing to be done. She was seen by the best physicians available and it was their opinion that the melancholy which struck her down from time to time had no possibility of amelioration.

In spite of this there were long periods during these last years when I am sure she was, if not happy, then at least not unhappy. There were her childhood memories of Paradise to comfort her, and her grandchildren, to whom she gave much affection.

I have never been quite sure whether it was our father's death or the frightful journey from the river to the boarding of the vessel at Port Natal which affected her so. I had been fearful for Nerissa because of what had happened before. I am probably again to blame in that I did not observe how desperate was our mother's anxiety. I can only state, and you will remember this yourself, that all of us were close to death.

Nerissa has told me that in the last months she spoke more frequently of our father. In the end she recalled only his virtues —and these became heroic. Both of us were pleased that she should remember him so, and I know you will be as well.

We buried her above Paradise, on the shoulder of the Mountain. She loved nothing better than to climb to a vantage point midway up the slope and sit there for hours looking across the isthmus. Once she remarked to Nerissa that she would like to stay there forever. Her wish has been granted.

Talk of money at this moment may strike you as ill-timed but nevertheless it is of importance that you are apprised of such facts as I am in possession of. The executors are still at work on the will but I may state that the bequests are substantial. I knew our mother was not poor—how else could she have educated us as she did?—but her estate, which she inherited from her parents as well as her guardian, Dr Goodsir, is apparently greater than anyone had thought. I tell you this only to ease your mind against the future.

As for the rest, our lives continue evenly and unexcitingly, for which both Nerissa and I are continuingly thankful. To look ahead now into a future in which the most lively event is likely to be a dinner party with friends or an infrequent journey upon Circuit is strangely beguiling. For myself, I have only to close my eyes to be transported back into the wildness and violence of the past. One day perhaps I may try to set down the events as they occurred and so come to understand them.

214

In the meantime our greatest wish, as I have written more than once, is for your return when you have completed your studies and for us all to be together once more.

Until that time Nerissa and your two nephews join me in sending our love.

Affectionately,
Robert